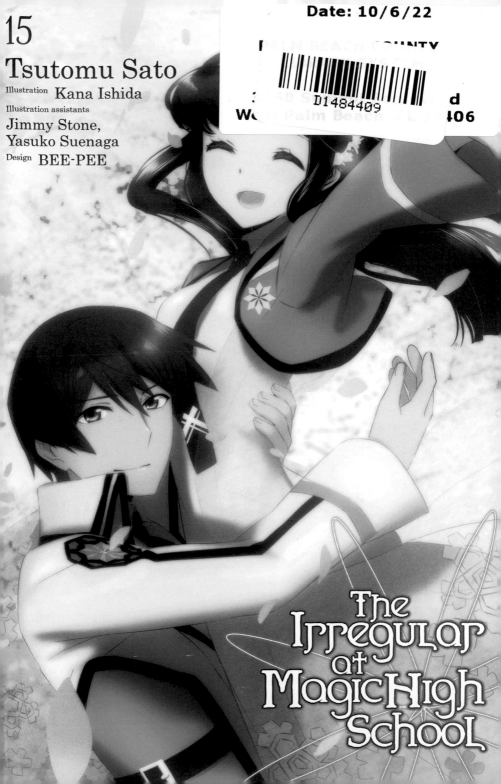

"Are these guys ninjas or somethin'?"

**Leonhard Saijou**

Nicknamed Leo.
Class 2-F. Course 2 student.
Tatsuya's friend. Father is
half-Japanese and mother
is quarter. Specializes in
hardening magic.

"Yes,
Big Sister
Miyuki."

**Minami Sakurai**

A new student who enrolled
at Magic High School this year.
Presents herself as Tatsuya and
Miyuki's cousin. A Guardian
candidate for Miyuki.

"Leo, keep your spirit hot, but your mind cool!"

"I'll back you up."

## Mikihiko Yoshida

Class 2-B. This year, he became a Course 1 student. From a famous family that uses ancient magic. Has known Erika since they were children.

## Erika Chiba

Class 2-F. Tatsuya's friend. Course 2 student. A charming troublemaker with a bright personality that gets everyone caught up in her mess. Family is famous for *kenjutsu*, which combines sword skills and magical combat.

"It's delicious."

## Miyuki Shiba

Class 2-A. Tatsuya's younger sister. Honors student who was the class representative last year. Cooling magic is her specialty. Adores her brother. A severe case of brother complex.

# The Irregular at Magic High School

SILVERHORN TRIDENT

"I know that!"

## Masaki Ichijou

A junior at Third High.
Participated in the Nine School
Competition two years in a row.
Next head of the Ichijou family,
one of the Ten Master Clans.
Interested in Miyuki.

"I'm sure making things blow up isn't the only thing you're good at, Ichijou."

**Tatsuya Shiba**

The older brother of the Shiba siblings. In Class 2-E of the National Magic University Affiliated First High School. Detached from life, other than in his commitment to serve as his sister Miyuki's Guardian.

"But none of you are capable of capturing me."

**Gongjin Zhou**

Handsome young man who guided Lu and Chen from the GAA to Yokohama during the Yokohama Incident. Secretly joined forces with Makoto Kudou during the Parasidoll incident.

"Begin the operation!"

**Fumiya Kuroba**

A boy who is a candidate for next head of the Yotsuba family. Tatsuya and Miyuki's second cousin...but during missions, his older sister Ayako makes him cross-dress.

**Minoru Kudou**

Grandson of Retsu Kudou, the Sage who was once the world's strongest magician. Though he is extremely gifted in magic, he's prone to bouts of illness. Kyouko Fujibayashi's stepbrother.

"Are you saying my deductions are wrong?"

"You won't get away."

"You sure made a fool out of me back then."

Map of Kyoto Prefecture

Mt. Kurama

Sanzen-in,
Oohara

Sakyou Ward

Kita Ward

Takaraga-ike

Kyoto New
International
Conference Hall
(Thesis Competition Venue)

Kinkaku-ji

Kamigyou Ward

Tenryuu-ji

Ukyou Ward

K.K. Hotel

C.R. Hotel

Arashiyama
Park

Kiyomizu-
dera

Kyoto
Station

Yamashina Ward

Higashiyama Ward

Minami Ward

Fushimi Ward

Kyoto

Uji

Uji
River

Japan Ground
Defense Force Uji
Resupply Base
Number Two

Uji Bridge

The Irregular at
Magic High School

# The Irregular at MagicHigh School

## ANCIENT CITY INSURRECTION ARC II

# 15

### Tsutomu Sato
Illustration Kana Ishida

YEN ON

NEW YORK

THE IRREGULAR AT MAGIC HIGH SCHOOL
TSUTOMU SATO

Translation by Andrew Prowse
Cover art by Kana Ishida

MAHOUKA KOUKOU NO RETTOUSEI Vol. 15
©Tsutomu Sato 2015
Edited by Dengeki Bunko
First published in Japan in 2015 by KADOKAWA CORPORATION, Tokyo.
English translation rights arranged with KADOKAWA CORPORATION, Tokyo, through Tuttle-Mori Agency, Inc., Tokyo.

Yen On
150 West 30th Street, 19th Floor
New York, NY 10001

Visit us at yenpress.com
facebook.com/yenpress
twitter.com/yenpress
yenpress.tumblr.com
instagram.com/yenpress

First Yen On Edition: April 2020

Yen On is an imprint of Yen Press, LLC.
The Yen On name and logo are trademarks of Yen Press, LLC.

Library of Congress Cataloging-in-Publication Data
Names: Sato, Tsutomu. | Ishida, Kana, illustrator.
Title: The irregular at Magic High School / Tsutomu Sato ; Illustrations by Kana Ishida.
Other titles: Mahōka kōkō no rettosei. English
Description: First Yen On edition. | New York, NY : Yen On, 2016–
Identifiers: LCCN 2015042401 | ISBN 9780316348805 (v. 1 : pbk.) | ISBN 9780316390293 (v. 2 : pbk.) |
    ISBN 9780316390309 (v. 3 : pbk.) | ISBN 9780316390316 (v. 4 : pbk.) |
    ISBN 9780316390323 (v. 5 : pbk.) | ISBN 9780316390330 (v. 6 : pbk.) |
    ISBN 9781975300074 (v. 7 : pbk.) | ISBN 9781975327125 (v. 8 : pbk.) |
    ISBN 9781975327149 (v. 9 : pbk.) | ISBN 9781975327163 (v. 10 : pbk.) |
    ISBN 9781975327187 (v. 11 : pbk.) | ISBN 9781975327200 (v. 12 : pbk.) |
    ISBN 9781975332327 (v. 13 : pbk.) | ISBN 9781975332471 (v. 14 : pbk.) |
    ISBN 9781975332495 (v. 15 : pbk.)
Subjects: CYAC: Brothers and sisters—Fiction. | Magic—Fiction. | High schools—Fiction. |
    Schools—Fiction. | Japan—Fiction. | Science fiction.
Classification: LCC PZ7.1.S265 Ir 2016 | DDC [Fic]—dc23
LC record available at http://lccn.loc.gov/2015042401

ISBNs: 978-1-9753-3249-5 (paperback)
          978-1-9753-3250-1 (ebook)

10 9 8 7 6 5 4 3 2 1

LSC-C

Printed in the United States of America

# The Irregular at Magic High School

## ANCIENT CITY INSURRECTION ARC Ⅱ

*An irregular older brother with a certain flaw.*
*An honor roll younger sister who is perfectly flawless.*

*When the two siblings enrolled in Magic High School,*
*a dramatic life unfolded—*

# Character

## Tatsuya Shiba

Class 2-E. Advanced to the newly established magic engineering course. Approaches everything in a detached manner. His sister Miyuki's Guardian.

## Mikihiko Yoshida

Class 2-B. This year he became a Course 1 student. From a famous family that uses ancient magic. Has known Erika since they were children.

## Miyuki Shiba

Class 2-A. Tatsuya's younger sister; enrolled as the top student last year. Specializes in freezing magic. Dotes on her older brother.

## Leonhard Saijou

Class 2-F. Tatsuya's friend. Course 2 student. Specializes in hardening magic. Has a bright personality.

## Honoka Mitsui

Class 2-A. Miyuki's classmate. Specializes in light-wave vibration magic. Impulsive when emotional.

## Erika Chiba

Class 2-F. Tatsuya's friend. Course 2 student. A charming troublemaker.

## Shizuku Kitayama

Class 2-A. Miyuki's classmate. Specializes in vibration and acceleration magic. Doesn't show emotional ups and downs very much.

## Mizuki Shibata

Class 2-E. In Tatsuya's class again this year. Has pushion radiation sensitivity. Serious and a bit of an airhead.

## Subaru Satomi

Class 2-D. Frequently mistaken for a pretty boy. Cheerful and easy to get along with.

## Eimi Akechi

Class 2-B. A quarter-blood. Full name is Amelia Eimi Akechi Goldie. Daughter of the notable Goldie family.

## Akaha Sakurakouji

Class 2-B. Friends with Subaru and Amy. Wears gothic lolita clothes and loves theme parks.

## Shun Morisaki

Class 2-A. Miyuki's classmate. Specializes in CAD quick-draw. Takes great pride in being a Course 1 student.

## Hagane Tomitsuka

Class 2-E. A magic martial arts user with the nickname "Range Zero." Uses magic martial arts.

## Mayumi Saegusa

An alum. College student at the Magic University. Has a devilish personality but weak when on the defensive.

## Azusa Nakajou

A senior. Former student council president. Shy and has trouble expressing herself.

## Suzune Ichihara

An alum. College student at the Magic University. Calm, collected, and book smart.

## Hanzou Gyoubu-Shoujou Hattori

A senior. Former head of the club committee. Gifted but can be too serious at times.

## Mari Watanabe

An alum. Mayumi's good friend. Well rounded and likes a sporting fight.

## Katsuto Juumonji

An alum and former head of the club committee. Has advanced to Magic University. "A boulder-like person," according to Tatsuya.

## Midori Sawaki

A senior. Member of the disciplinary committee. Has a complex about his girlish name.

### Kei Isori

A senior. Former student council treasurer. Excels in magical theory. Engaged to Kanon.

### Kanon Chiyoda

A senior. Former chairwoman of the disciplinary committee. As confrontational as her predecessor, Mari.

## Kasumi Saegusa

A new student who enrolled at Magic High School this year. Mayumi Saegusa's younger sister. Izumi's older twin sister. Energetic and lighthearted personality.

## Izumi Saegusa

A new student who enrolled at Magic High School this year. Mayumi Saegusa's younger sister. Kasumi's younger twin sister. Meek and gentle personality.

## Minami Sakurai

A new student who enrolled at Magic High School this year. Presents herself as Tatsuya and Miyuki's cousin. A Guardian candidate for Miyuki.

## Koutarou Tatsumi

An alum and former member of the disciplinary committee. Has a heroic and dynamic personality.

### Isao Sekimoto

An alum and former member of the disciplinary committee. Lost the school election. Committed acts of spying.

### Takeaki Kirihara

A senior. Member of the *kenjutsu* club. Junior High Kanto Kenjutsu Tournament champion.

### Sayaka Mibu

A senior. Member of the kendo club. Placed second in the nation at the girl's junior high kendo tournament.

### Takuma Shippou

The head of this year's new students. Course 1. Eldest son of the Shippou, one of the Eighteen, families with excellent magicians.

### Kento Sumisu

Class 1-G. A Caucasian boy whose parents are naturalized Japanese citizens from the USNA.

## Koharu Hirakawa

An alum and engineer during the Nine School Competition last year. Withdrew from the Thesis Competition.

## Chiaki Hirakawa

Class 2-E. Holds enmity toward Tatsuya.

## Tomoko Chikura

A senior. Competitor in the women's solo Shields Down, a Nine School Competition event.

## Tsugumi Igarashi

An alum.
Former biathlon club president.

## Yousuke Igarashi

A junior. Tsugumi's younger brother. Has a somewhat reserved personality.

## Kerry Minakami

A senior. Male representative for the main Monolith Code event at the Nine School Competition.

## Satomi Asuka

First High nurse. Gentle, calm, and warm. Smile popular among male students.

## Kazuo Tsuzura

First High teacher. Main field is magic geometry. Manager of the Thesis Competition team.

## Masaki Ichijou

A junior at Third High. Participating in the Nine School Competition this year as well. Direct heir to the Ichijou family, one of the Ten Master Clans.

## Shinkurou Kichijouji

A junior at Third High. Participating in the Nine School Competition this year as well. Also known as Cardinal George.

## Gouki Ichijou

Masaki's father. Current head of the Ichijou, one of the Ten Master Clans.

## Midori Ichijou

Masaki's mother. Warm and good at cooking.

## Akane Ichijou

Eldest daughter of the Ichijou. Masaki's younger sister. Enrolled in an elite private middle school this year. Likes Shinkurou.

## Ruri Ichijou

Second daughter of the Ichijou. Masaki's younger sister. Stable and does things her own way.

## Jennifer Smith

A Caucasian naturalized as a Japanese citizen. Instructor for Tatsuya's class and for magic engineering classes.

## Harumi Naruse

Shizuku's older cousin. Student at National Magic University Fourth Affiliated High School.

## Haruka Ono

A general counselor of First High. Tends to get bullied but has another side to her personality.

## Yakumo Kokonoe

A user of an ancient magic called *ninjutsu*. Tatsuya's martial arts master.

## Gongjin Zhou

A handsome young man who brought Lu and Chen to Yokohama. A mysterious figure who hangs out in Chinatown.

## Retsu Kudou

Renowned as the strongest magician in the world. Given the honorary title of Sage.

## Makoto Kudou

Son of Retsu Kudou, elder of Japan's magic world, and current head of the Kudou family.

## Xiangshan Chen

Leader of the Great Asian Alliance Army's Special Covert Forces. Has a heartless personality.

## Minoru Kudou

Makoto's son. Freshman at National Magic University Second Affiliated High School, but hardly attends due to frequent illness. Also Kyouko Fujibayashi's younger brother by a different father.

## Ganghu Lu

The ace magician of the Great Asian Alliance Army's Special Covert Forces. Also known as the "Man-Eating Tiger."

## Rin

A girl Morisaki saved. Her full name is Meiling Sun. The new leader of the Hong Kong–based international crime syndicate No-Head Dragon.

## Mamoru Kuki

One of the Eighteen Support Clans. Follows the Kudou family. Calls Retsu Kudou "Sensei" out of respect.

## Maki Sawamura

A female actress who has been nominated for best leading female actress by distinguished movie awards. Acknowledged not only for her beauty but also her acting skills.

## Toshikazu Chiba

Erika Chiba's oldest brother. Has a career in the Ministry of Police. A playboy at first glance.

## Naotsugu Chiba

Erika Chiba's second-oldest brother. Mari's lover. Possesses full mastery of the Chiba (thousand blades) style of *kenjutsu*. Nicknamed "Kirin Child of the Chiba."

## Inagaki

An inspector with the Ministry of Police. Toshikazu Chiba's subordinate.

## Anna Rosen Katori

Erika's mother. Half Japanese and half German, was the mistress of Erika's father, the current leader of the Chiba.

## Ushio Kitayama

Shizuku's father. Big-shot in the business world. His business name is Ushio Kitagata.

## Benio Kitayama

Shizuku's mother. An A-rank magician who was once renowned for her vibration magic.

## Wataru Kitayama

Shizuku's younger brother. Sixth grade. Dearly loves his older sister. Aims to be a magic engineer.

## Kouichi Saegusa

Mayumi's father and the current leader of the Saegusa. Also a top-top-class magician.

## Harunobu Kazama

Commanding officer of the 101st Brigade's Independent Magic Battalion. Ranked major.

## Shigeru Sanada

Executive officer of the 101st Brigade's Independent Magic Battalion. Ranked captain.

## Kyouko Fujibayashi

Female officer serving as Kazama's aide. Ranked second lieutenant.

## Hiromi Saeki

Brigadier general of the Japan Ground Defense Force's 101st Brigade. Ranked major general. Superior officer to Harunobu Kazama, commanding officer of the Independent Magic Battalion. Due to her appearance, she is also known as the Silver Fox.

## Muraji Yanagi

Executive officer of the 101st Brigade's Independent Magic Battalion. Ranked captain.

## Kousuke Yamanaka

Executive officer of the 101st Brigade's Independent Magic Battalion. Physician ranked major. First-rate healing magician.

## Sakai

Belongs to the Japan Ground Defense Force's general headquarters. Ranked colonel. Seen as staunchly anti–Great Asian Alliance.

## Saburou Nakura

A powerful magician employed by the Saegusa family. Mainly serves as Mayumi's personal bodyguard.

## Miya Shiba

Tatsuya and Miyuki's actual mother. Deceased. The only magician skilled in mental construction interference magic.

## Honami Sakurai

Miya's Guardian. Deceased. Part of the first generation of the Sakura series, engineered magicians with strengthened magical capacity through genetic modification.

## Sayuri Shiba

Tatsuya and Miyuki's stepmother. Dislikes them.

## Ushiyama

Manager of Four Leaves Technology's CAD R & D Section 3. A person in whom Tatsuya places his trust.

## Ernst Rosen

A prominent CAD manufacturer. President of Rosen Magicraft's Japanese branch.

## Pixie

A home helper robot belonging to Magic High School. Official name 3H (Humanoid Home Helper: a human-shaped chore-assisting robot) Type P94.

## Maya Yotsuba

Tatsuya and Miyuki's aunt. Miya's younger twin sister. The current head of the Yotsuba.

## Hayama

An elderly butler employed to Maya.

## Mitsugu Kuroba

Miya Shiba and Maya Yotsuba's cousin. Father of Ayako and Fumiya.

## Ayako Kuroba

Tatsuya and Miyuki's second cousin. Has a younger twin brother named Fumiya. Student at Fourth High.

## Fumiya Kuroba

A candidate for next head of the Yotsuba. Tatsuya and Miyuki's second cousin. Has an older twin sister named Ayako. Student at Fourth High.

## Angelina Kudou Shields

Commander of the USNA's magician unit, the Stars. Rank is major. Nickname is Lina. Also one of the Thirteen Apostles, strategic magicians.

## Virginia Balance

The USNA Joint Chiefs of Staff Information Bureau Internal Inspection Office's first deputy commissioner. Ranked colonel. Came to Japan in order to support Lina.

## Silvia Mercury First

A planet-class magician in the USNA's magician unit, the Stars. Rank is warrant officer. Her nickname is Silvia, and Mercury First is her codename. During their mission in Japan, she serves as Major Sirius's aide.

## Benjamin Canopus

Number two in the USNA's magician unit, the Stars. Rank is major. Takes command when Major Sirius is absent.

## Mikaela Hongou

An agent sent into Japan by the USNA (although her real job is magic scientist for the Department of Defense). Nicknamed Mia.

## Claire

Hunter Q—a female soldier in the magician unit Stardust for those who couldn't be Stars. Q refers to the 17th of the pursuit unit.

## Alfred Fomalhaut

A first degree star magician in the USNA's magician unit, the Stars. Rank is first lieutenant. Nicknamed Freddie. Currently AWOL.

## Rachel

Hunter R—a female soldier in the magician unit Stardust for those who couldn't be Stars. R refers to the 18th of the pursuit unit.

## Charles Sullivan

A satellite-class magician in the USNA's magician unit, the Stars. Called by the codename Deimos Second. Currently AWOL.

## Raymond S. Clark

A student at the high school in Berkeley, USNA, that Shizuku studies abroad at. A Caucasian boy who wastes no time making advances on Shizuku. Is secretly one of the Seven Sages.

## Gu Jie

One of the Seven Sages. Also known as Gide Hague. A survivor of a Dahanese military's mage unit.

# Glossary

**Course 1 student emblem**

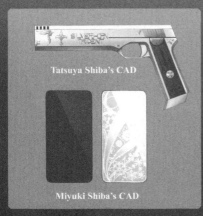

**Tatsuya Shiba's CAD**

**Miyuki Shiba's CAD**

### Magic High School

Nickname for high schools affiliated with the National Magic University. There are nine schools throughout the nation. Of them, First High through Third High each adopt a system of Course 1 and Course 2 students to split up its two hundred incoming freshmen.

### Blooms, Weeds

Slang terms used at First High to display the gap between Course 1 and Course 2 students. Course 1 student uniforms feature an eight-petaled emblem embroidered on the left breast, but Course 2 student uniforms do not.

### CAD (Casting Assistant Device)

A device that simplifies magic casting. Magical programming is recorded within. There are many types and forms, some specialized and others multipurpose.

### Four Leaves Technology (FLT)

A domestic CAD manufacturer. Originally more famous for magical-product engineering than for developing finished products, the development of the Silver model has made them much more widely known as a maker of CADs.

### Taurus Silver

A genius engineer said to have advanced specialized CAD software by a decade in just a single year.

### Eidos (individual information bodies)

Originally a term from Greek philosophy. In modern magic, *eidos* refers to the information bodies that accompany events. They form a so-called record of those events existing in the world, and can be considered the footprints of an object's state of being in the universe, be that active or passive. The definition of *magic* in its modern form is that of a technology that alters events by altering the information bodies composing them.

### Idea (information body dimension)

Originally a term from Greek philosophy; pronounced "ee-dee-ah." In modern magic, *Idea* refers to the *platform* upon which information bodies are recorded—a spell, object, or energy's *dimension*. Magic is primarily a technology that outputs a magic program (a spell sequence) to affect the Idea (the dimension), which then rewrites the eidos (the individual bodies) recorded there.

### Activation Sequence

The blueprints of magic, and the programming that constructs it. Activation sequences are stored in a compressed format in CADs. The magician sends a psionic wave into the CAD, which then expands the data and uses it to convert the activation sequence into a signal. This signal returns to the magician with the unpacked magic program.

### Psions (thought particles)

Massless particles belonging to the dimension of spirit phenomena. These information particles record awareness and thought results. Eidos are considered the theoretical basis for modern magic, while activation sequences and magic programs are the technology forming its practical basis. All of these are bodies of information made up of psions.

### Pushions (spirit particles)

Massless particles belonging to the dimension of spirit phenomena. Their existence has been confirmed, but their true form and function have yet to be elucidated. In general, magicians are only able to sense energized pushions. The technical term for them is *psycheons*.

### Magician

An abbreviation of *magic technician*. *Magic technician* is the term for those with the skills to use magic at a practical level.

### Magic program

An information body used to temporarily alter information attached to events. Constructed from psions possessed by the magician. Sometimes shortened to *magigram*.

## Magic-calculation region

A mental region that constructs magic programs. The essential core of the talent of magic. Exists within the magician's unconscious regions, and though he or she can normally consciously use the magic-calculation region, they cannot perceive the processing happening within. The magic-calculation region may be called a black box, even for the magician performing the task.

## Magic program output process

❶Transmit an activation sequence to a CAD. This is called "reading in an activation sequence."

❷Add variables to the activation sequence and send them to the magic-calculation region.

❸Construct a magic program from the activation sequence and its variables.

❹Send the constructed magic program along the "route"—between the lowest part of the conscious mind and highest part of the unconscious mind—then send it out the "gate" between conscious and unconscious, to output it onto the Idea.

❺The magic program outputted onto the Idea interferes with the eidos at designated coordinates and overwrites them.

With a single-type, single-process spell, this five-stage process can be completed in under half a second. This is the bar for practical-level use with magicians.

## Magic evaluation standards

The speed with which one constructs psionic information bodies is one's magical throughput, or processing speed. The scale and scope of the information bodies one can construct is one's magical capacity. The strength with which one can overwrite eidos with magic programs is one's influence. These three together are referred to as a person's magical power.

## Cardinal Code hypothesis

A school of thought claiming that within the four families and eight types of magic, there exist foundational plus and minus magic programs, for sixteen in all, and that by combining these sixteen, one can construct every possible typed spell.

## Typed magic

Any magic belonging to the four families and eight types.

## Exotyped magic

A term for spells that control mental phenomena rather than physical ones. Encompasses many fields, from divine magic and spirit magic—which employs spiritual presences—to mind reading, astral form separation, and consciousness control.

## Ten Master Clans

The most powerful magician organization in Japan. The ten families are chosen every four years from among twenty-eight: Ichijou, Ichinokura, Isshiki, Futatsugi, Nikaidou, Nihei, Mitsuya, Mikazuki, Yotsuba, Itsuwa, Gotou, Itsumi, Mutsuzuka, Rokkaku, Rokugou, Roppongi, Saegusa, Shippou, Tanabata, Nanase, Yatsushiro, Hassaku, Hachiman, Kudou, Kuki, Kuzumi, Juumonji, and Tooyama.

## Numbers

Just like the Ten Master Clans contain a number from one to ten in their surname, well-known families in the Hundred Families use numbers eleven or greater, such as Chiyoda (thousand), Isori (fifty), and Chiba (thousand). The value isn't an indicator of strength, but the fact that it is present in the surname is one measure to broadly judge the capacity of a magic family by their bloodline.

## Non-numbers

Also called Extra Numbers, or simply Extras. Magician families who have been stripped of their number. Once, when magicians were weapons and experimental samples, this was a stigma between the success cases, who were given numbers, and the failure cases, who didn't display good enough results.

## Various Spells

### • Cocytus
Outer magic that freezes the mind. A frozen mind cannot order the flesh to die, so anyone subject to this magic enters a state of mental stasis, causing their body to stop. Partial crystallization of the flesh is sometimes observed because of the interaction between mind and body.

### • Rumbling
An old spell that vibrates the ground as a medium for a spirit, an independent information body.

### • Program Dispersion
A spell that dismantles a magic program, the main component of a spell, into a group of psionic particles with no meaningful structure. Since magic programs affect the information bodies associated with events, it is necessary for the information structure to be exposed, leaving no way to prevent interference against the magic program itself.

### • Program Demolition
A typeless spell that rams a mass of compressed psionic particles directly into an object without going through the Idea, causing it to explode and blow away the psion information bodies recorded in magic, such as activation sequences and magic programs. It may be called magic, but because it is a psionic bullet without any structure as a magic program for altering events, it isn't affected by Information Boost or Area Interference. The pressure of the bullet itself will also repel any Cast Jamming effects. Because it has zero physical effect, no obstacle can block it.

### • Mine Origin
A magic that imparts strong vibrations to anything with a connotation of "ground"—such as dirt, crag, sand, or concrete—regardless of material.

### • Fissure
A spell that uses spirits, independent information bodies, as a medium to push a line into the ground, creating the appearance of a fissure opening in the earth.

### • Dry Blizzard
A spell that gathers carbon dioxide from the air, creates dry-ice particles, then converts the extra heat energy from the freezing process to kinetic energy to launch the dry-ice particles at a high speed.

### • Slithering Thunders
In addition to condensing the water vapor from Dry Blizzard's dry-ice evaporation and creating a highly conductive mist with the evaporated carbon dioxide in it, this spell creates static electricity with vibration-type magic and emission-type magic. A combination spell, it also fires an electric attack at an enemy using the carbon gas-filled mist and water droplets as a conductor.

### • Niflheim
A vibration- and deceleration-type area-of-effect spell. It chills a large volume of air, then moves it to freeze a wide range. In blunt terms, it creates a super-large refrigerator. The white mist that appears upon activation is the particles of frozen ice and dry ice, but at higher levels, a mist of frozen liquid nitrogen occurs.

### • Burst
A dispersion-type spell that vaporizes the liquid inside a target object. When used on a creature, the spell will vaporize bodily fluids and cause the body to rupture. When used on a machine powered by internal combustion, the spell vaporizes the fuel and makes it explode. Fuel cells see the same result, and even if no burnable fuel is on board, there is no machine that does not contain some liquid, such as battery fluid, hydraulic fluid, coolant, or lubricant; once Burst activates, virtually any machine will be destroyed.

### • Disheveled Hair
An old spell that, instead of specifying a direction and changing the wind's direction to that, uses air current control to bring about the vague result of "tangling" it, causing currents along the ground that entangle an opponent's feet in the grass. Only usable on plains with grass of a certain height.

# Magic Swords

Aside from fighting techniques that use magic itself as a weapon, another method of magical combat involves techniques for using magic to strengthen and control weapons. The majority of these spells combine magic with projectile weapons such as guns and bows, but the art of the sword, known as *kenjutsu*, has developed in Japan as well as a way to link magic with sword techniques. This has led to magic technicians formulating personal-use magic techniques known as magic swords, which can be said to be both modern magic and old magic.

## 1. High-Frequency Blade

A spell that locally liquefies a solid body and cleaves it by causing a blade to vibrate at a high speed, then propagate the vibration that exceeds the molecular cohesive force of matter it comes in contact with. Used as a set with a spell to prevent the blade from breaking.

## 2. Pressure Cut

A spell that generates left-right perpendicular repulsive force relative to the angle of a slashing blade edge, causing the blade to force apart any object it touches and thereby cleave it. The size of the repulsive field is less than a millimeter, but it has the strength to interfere with light, so when seen from the front, the blade edge becomes a black line.

## 3. Douji-Giri (Simultaneous Cut)

An old-magic spell passed down as a secret sword art of the Genji. It is a magic sword technique wherein the user remotely manipulates two blades through a third in their hands in order to have the swords surround an opponent and slash simultaneously. *Douji* is the Japanese pronunciation for both "simultaneous" and "child," so this ambiguity was used to keep the inherited nature of the technique a secret.

## 4. Zantetsu (Iron Cleaver)

A secret sword art of the Chiba clan. Rather than defining a katana as a hulk of steel and iron, this movement spell defines it as a single concept, then the spell moves the katana along a slashing path set by the magic program. The result is that the katana is defined as a mono-molecular blade, never breaking, bending, or chipping as it slices through any objects in its path.

## 5. Jinrai Zantetsu (Lightning Iron Cleaver)

An expanded version of Zantetsu that makes use of the Ikazuchi-Maru, a personal-armament device. By defining the katana and its wielder as one collective concept, the spell executes the entire series of actions, from enemy contact to slash, incredibly quickly and with faultless precision.

## 6. Mountain Tsunami

A secret sword art of the Chiba clan that makes use of the Orochi-Maru, a giant personal weapon six feet long. The user minimizes their own inertia and that of their katana while approaching an enemy at a high speed and, at the moment of impact, adds the neutralized inertia to the blade's inertia and slams the target with it. The longer the approach run, the greater the false inertial mass, reaching a maximum of ten tons.

## 7. *Usuba Kagerou* (Antlion)

A spell that uses hardening magic to anchor a five-nanometer-thick sheet of woven carbon nanotube to a perfect surface and make it a blade. The blade that *Usuba Kagerou* creates is sharper than any sword or razor, but the spell contains no functions to support moving the blade, demanding technical sword skill and ability from the user.

## Strategic Magicians: The Thirteen Apostles

Because modern magic was born into a highly technological world, only a few nations were able to develop strong magic for military purposes. As a result, only a handful were able to develop "strategic magic," which rivaled weapons of mass destruction.

However, these nations shared the magic they developed with their allies, and certain magicians of allied nations with high aptitudes for strategic magic came to be known as strategic magicians.

As of April 2095, there are thirteen magicians publicly recognized as strategic magicians by their nations. They are called the Thirteen Apostles and are seen as important factors in the world's military balance. The Thirteen Apostles' nations, names, and strategic spell names are listed below.

### USNA

Angie Sirius: Heavy Metal Burst
Elliott Miller: Leviathan
Laurent Barthes: Leviathan
* The only one belonging to the Stars is Angie Sirius. Elliott Miller is stationed at Alaska Base, and Laurent Barthes outside the country at Gibraltar Base, and for the most part, they don't move.

### New Soviet Union

Igor Andreivich Bezobrazov: Tuman Bomba
Leonid Kondratenko: Zemlja Armija
* As Kondratenko is of advanced age, he generally stays at the Black Sea Base.

### Great Asian Alliance

Yunde Liu: Pilita (Thunderclap Tower)
* Yunde Liu died in the October 31, 2095, battle against Japan.

### Indo-Persian Federation

Barat Chandra Khan: Agni Downburst

### Japan

Mio Itsuwa: Abyss

### Brazil

Miguel Diez: Synchroliner Fusion
* This magic program was named by the USNA.

### England

William MacLeod: Ozone Circle

### Germany

Karla Schmidt: Ozone Circle
* Ozone Circle is based on a spell codeveloped by nations in the EU before its split as a means to fix the hole in the ozone layer. The magic program was perfected by England and then publicized to the old EU through a convention.

### Turkey

Ali Sahin: Bahamut
* This magic program was developed in cooperation with the USNA and Japan, then provided to Turkey by Japan.

### Thailand

Somchai Bunnag: Agni Downburst
* This magic program was provided by Indo-Persia.

# The International Situation
## State of the World in 2096

West EU and East EU are allied states, but nations are independent

New Soviet Union

Japan, Mongolia, and Kazakhstan are in an alliance

Japan

USNA (United States of North America)

Indo-Persian Federation

Great Asian Alliance

Arab Alliance

Taiwan is an independent nation

African Continent (southwestern portions are mostly lawless)

Southeast Asian Alliance (includes Taiwan, the Philippines, and New Guinea)

Brazil

Other nations have broken into regional local governments

World War III, also called the Twenty Years' Global War Outbreak, was directly triggered by global cooling, and it fundamentally redrew the world map.

The USA annexed Canada and the countries from Mexico to Panama to form the United States of North America, or the USNA.

Russia reabsorbed Ukraine and Belarus to form the New Soviet Union.

China conquered northern Burma, northern Vietnam, northern Laos, and the Korean Peninsula to form the Great Asian Alliance, or GAA.

India and Iran absorbed several central Asian countries (Turkmenistan, Uzbekistan, Tajikistan, and Afghanistan) and South Asian countries (Pakistan, Nepal, Bhutan, Bangladesh, and Sri Lanka) to form the Indo-Persian Federation.

The other Asian and Arab countries formed regional military alliances to resist the three superpowers: the New Soviet Union, GAA, and the Indo-Persian Federation.

Australia chose national isolation.

The EU failed to unify and split into an eastern and a western section bordered by Germany and France. These east-west groupings also failed to form unions and now are actually weaker than they were before unification.

Africa saw half its nations destroyed altogether, with the surviving ones barely managing to retain urban control.

South America, excluding Brazil, fell into small, isolated states administered on a local government level.

The Irregular at Magic High School

# [Summary of Part I]

One Sunday in late September, with the 2096 All-High Magic Thesis Competition close at hand: The Kuroba siblings visit Tatsuya with a message from Maya Yotsuba, current head of the Yotsuba family. The message is a request that he assist them in capturing Gongjin Zhou, who has escaped Yokohama. Even though he's suspicious that it's a request rather than the usual order, Tatsuya still visits the Kudou family, whose headquarters is in Nara, to follow Zhou's tracks; the man escaped into the Nara region of Kyoto. There, Tatsuya and the others meet a young man and magician named Minoru Kudou, who possesses equal beauty to Miyuki.

With Minoru's guidance, Tatsuya and the others search for a base of operations belonging to the Traditionalists (a group of ancient magicians harboring Gongjin Zhou), but the Traditionalists and Chinese Taoists stand in their way. Meanwhile, Kouichi Saegusa, head of the Saegusa family, has been secretly communicating with Zhou but now wants to hide his own involvement and orders his confidant, Nakura, to assassinate the revolutionary. Zhou and Nakura meet in a deathmatch on the bank of the Katsura River in Kyoto. The one killed, however, is Nakura.

At the sudden notice of the death of her bodyguard, Mayumi begins to act in order to learn the truth.

# [6]

October 15, 2096, after school. With the Thesis Competition two weeks away, a hushed stir filled the First High school building, though it was a different kind than the clamor of their competition preparations.

The topic on everyone's lips was a sudden visitor: a famous alum, a familiar face for the juniors and seniors, and known to all but a few freshmen as well.

The person in question, Mayumi Saegusa, had been led to the guest reception room. The school apparently decided to receive her not as the former student council president, but as the daughter of the Saegusa, one of the Ten Master Clans. The only one talking to her right at the moment was Tatsuya. This was because she'd called on him.

"I'm sorry, Tatsuya. I figured it would be safest to come here, so…" Mayumi offered, head lowered, because she'd noticed the commotion outside.

Her innate skill dealt with sight rather than sound, so she obviously hadn't heard the students gossiping or anything like that. Still, it wouldn't have been hard for anyone to guess, based on all the people furtively glancing at her on the way to the room, that the two of them were currently objects of much curiosity.

"Please, don't worry about it."

Tatsuya, too, had realized they were the subject of groundless conjecture. But his reply to Mayumi wasn't to comfort her, sincerely or otherwise. Certainly, he would have to steel himself for about three months' worth of bothersome rumors now that she'd come to visit the school, but it was still better than her barging into his house. There was plenty in his home he wouldn't want other Clans to see; he hadn't carelessly left sensitive items lying around, of course, but with *Mayumi's eyes*, he couldn't ignore the risk of her randomly catching a glimpse of something.

As for the young woman herself, if she'd really needed to contact him, it would have been more convenient to intrude on his home than come here to school, since it would've been easy for her to find out where he lived. Additionally, in terms of reputation and gossip, this school visit would definitely bother Mayumi longer. And yet, she'd still decided to meet him in such a visible place. In the end, the public setting was chosen entirely for his benefit; even Tatsuya understood at least that much.

"Well, um… How has it been going?"

She seemed uncharacteristically nervous, Tatsuya reflected after hearing her cut straight to the chase without any greeting or preface. Maybe a difficult matter had brought her here.

Still, Tatsuya was concerned that time would only be idled away at this rate, so he decided to kick the main event off himself: "My main job for the Thesis Competition this year is to help with venue security on the day of, so I'm not very busy."

"Is…is that so? I'm a little surprised you're not part of the presentation team…"

"Yes, so depending on what you need to talk about, I may be able to help."

Tatsuya knew from the start that Mayumi hadn't just come to visit him. Their relationship was not so intimate that it made sense that she was simply dying to see him again. Tatsuya wasn't exactly *just* her underclassman, either, but that was also exactly why she must have had a clear goal when she decided to meet him.

"…You're right. I suppose there's no sense wasting time."

Mayumi's eyes wavered with hesitation again. Nevertheless, as she herself pointed out, they would spend all their time fruitlessly the way things were going. And free time was limited for the both of them. There was obviously a pressing issue, and she couldn't allow herself to leave First High in disappointment without having told him what it was.

"Would you happen to remember Nakura?"

"Yes. And I'm terribly sorry for your loss."

"Thank you… So you knew about it, huh?"

"I saw it in the local news."

"Oh… Gathering info on the area for Thesis Competition security?"

"Yes, something like that."

"Then…" Mayumi's short silence was enough for her to throw away the last of her hesitation. "Do you know about how he died?"

"They said it was a homicide."

"So that's all the information that was made public, then?" She gave a bitter smile with unexpected ease. "Yes. Nakura was killed. And I myself don't know who the culprit is."

Tatsuya gave a look of minor confusion at how she phrased that. "You yourself?"

"My father…" Mayumi paused for a moment. But she'd already cast away her indecision. "My father knows who is responsible."

Tatsuya didn't hide his surprise. "Did your father say that?"

"No. But it's certain he knows—or, at least, has an idea. He was the one who ordered Nakura to go to Kyoto on a secret job."

"A covert mission in Kyoto…?" Tatsuya was more familiar with it being called *dirty work*—an illicit task, or something close to it.

"I didn't hear that verbatim, either. All my father said was that it was a job. And that I didn't need to know."

"I see."

That was the same as saying her father made Nakura do some wet work. By Tatsuya's interpretation, Kouichi Saegusa probably hadn't meant to hide it at all.

"What are you thinking of doing, then?"

It wasn't as though the question took Mayumi by surprise. Still, she visibly flinched when he brought it up so directly and bore into her with his piercing eyes.

Nevertheless, she didn't look down and fall silent, or anything of the sort. Driven by something like a sense of duty, or perhaps personal responsibility, she met his gaze.

"I want to know the truth."

"You want to find the culprit?"

"…Yes, I do."

There was a subtle pause before her answer came. This wasn't a reflection of her hesitation, but rather a moment she needed to tamp down her impatience.

"I'll be honest," Mayumi confessed. "Nakura and I were never close."

Tatsuya raised his eyebrows in surprise but held his tongue. With a nod, he prompted her to continue.

"To Nakura, I was nothing more than a job to him. And I'd never thought of him as anything more than a chaperone-slash-bodyguard."

"But you still want to find his killer?" Tatsuya prompted. "That seems like it could be rather risky."

His provocative words elicited a look of suppressed rage. "Don't get me wrong. I'm not saying this because I'm naive or something."

"Then why?"

"My bodyguard lost his life because of an order from the Saegusa family. I know he wasn't commanded to die, but if his mission carried a high chance of death, it's ultimately the same thing. I don't want to turn a blind eye to that. As a member of the Saegusa, I at least want to figure out the truth."

"That is a noble reason," Tatsuya noted with a sigh. Mayumi raised her eyebrows. "However," he interrupted sternly before she could say anything, "you need to understand that you're only doing this to satisfy yourself in the end."

"I know that. Is there something wrong with that?"

Rather than lapsing into self-deprecation, she used a willful, defiant tone with him. Even Tatsuya couldn't immediately think of how to argue with her.

"I'm not convinced," she went on. "I'm not satisfied. I can't be proud of being the eldest daughter of the Saegusa if I leave things like this."

"...Then you're doing this as the daughter of the Saegusa?"

"That's right. For better or worse, that's my position. I can't run away from it. If this is how I have to live, then I want to be proud of the title. Is that a strange way to think?"

"No, I don't think it's strange at all," Tatsuya insisted.

Tatsuya was hit with envy and irritation all at once. His sister, Miyuki, *still* couldn't call herself a direct descendant of the Yotsuba. She was being forced to lie about her true identity. Tatsuya didn't think that being a part of the Yotsuba family was particularly wonderful, or that it was something to be proud of, but he imagined that it was a sad thing to have to hide who you really were.

Compared with his sister, the fact that Mayumi could talk about wanting to be proud of her birthright at all seemed like something covetable, something enviable.

"I see. What did you want to ask me, then? I can't exactly find the culprit for you—I don't have any detective skills, or the connections to get people to help me search. Unfortunately, I don't think I'd be much help."

However, apart from those *natural* sentiments, he also truly felt he couldn't help her. He already had no idea where to start his search for Gongjin Zhou despite having plenty of clues. It didn't seem possible for him to help find a criminal whom he didn't know and who had left no leads.

"Wait!" Despite his clear refusal, Mayumi called out to him just as he was about to get up from his seat. "The criminal is probably related to Yokohama!"

"Yokohama?"

Tatsuya didn't think he was showing any signs of surprise, but Mayumi, for some reason, had donned a slightly smug face.

"Someone involved with the Yokohama Incident last year. It looks like Nakura was nosing around in Chinatown recently."

She probably thought her ploy to pique his interest had worked. And it had, though not for the reason she thought it would.

"I'm surprised you know that much."

"He often got me souvenirs whenever he had to go away for other tasks. He'd brought me a lot from Chinatown recently. I'd thought maybe he was mistaking me for some child, but... Now I feel like he was trying to leave me hints about what he was doing."

"I get it."

Mayumi might not have been aware of it, but that remark was rife with implication.

Nakura's employer was Kouichi Saegusa, and while Mayumi was part of his job, she was not directly involved with his employment or business dealings—she was a third party, an outsider.

That would mean a subordinate, who was both the eldest daughter's bodyguard and someone entrusted with covert operations—or, at least, trusted enough to be involved with work his employer didn't want getting out—was leaving hints about his tasks to an outsider.

Which meant, in turn, that Kouichi Saegusa didn't have full control over his people.

Perhaps the Saegusa family currently had *no one* in their employ whom they could truly call a confidant.

And maybe, just maybe, that would mean something important much later down the road...

However, Tatsuya forced himself to stop thinking about the Saegusa family's internal affairs then and there. "You may be correct that Nakura was involved with jobs related to Yokohama Chinatown. But

I don't see how that proves the criminal is related to the Yokohama Incident."

At this point in time, Tatsuya had been thinking about asking Mayumi to help *him*. Physically, the young woman was unremarkable or even a little below average, but she had proven her combat ability on the Yokohama battlefield. And as a university student, she had a more flexible schedule than Miyuki or Minami, who were in high school.

His argument was only to cool her down a little. He wanted to splash her excited mind with some cold water so she would consider the possibility that she might be mistaken. If she still requested his assistance after that, Tatsuya would take it as an acceptance of the fact.

"Well…no," said Mayumi, letting her indecision show for a moment—she seemed to have at least considered what he'd just pointed out. "Wait, you think I'm just assuming the killer is related to the Yokohama Incident?!"

But that only lasted a second or two before she turned a strong, possibly terse, attitude on him.

"I'm not saying that," he offered back, flashing a polite smile. "Just that you might lose sight of the facts if your preconceptions are too strong."

Mayumi almost seemed like she was on the brink of pouting—though now that she was in university, she seemed to be restraining herself from actually doing it.

"Assumptions, preconceptions—what's the difference?" she muttered.

Her words had reached Tatsuya's ears just fine, but he decided to treat it as though she were talking to herself. In other words, he let it slide—until she looked at him straight and gave him a clear answer, forcing his hand. "I know that much, at least," she snapped.

"And do you understand this is dangerous, too?" Tatsuya asked. He'd been waiting for a chance to say it.

"Yes. But I have to do *something*." She clearly felt like she'd come too far to turn back now. "So please, Tatsuya—will you help me?"

But Tatsuya didn't mind at all, personally. Responding to an urgent request from an upperclassman would be good for him.

"…All right," he stated.

The energy drained from Mayumi's face as she relaxed. Though it didn't show in his expression, Tatsuya was just as relieved. "What exactly should I do?" he went on.

"You're going to Kyoto to scope the place out for security, right?"

"Yes, this Saturday."

"I want you to come with me for a bit. I want to investigate the place where Nakura was killed."

And to his final question, Mayumi shrewdly *gave him the answer he wanted*.

"Is that really all?" Tatsuya, depending on the situation on-site, had already planned to be with her for more than just "a bit."

But that question was one he shouldn't have asked. "…Look, I get it," she grumbled.

Tatsuya was a brute, but it wasn't like he ignored others except when it was beneficial for him. Seeing someone he was rather close with becoming depressed due to something he'd said didn't make him feel very good.

"I know I'm still just a daughter of the Saegusa, and that I don't personally have any influence or power. My skills and talent as a magician aren't almighty. They won't help me make the police act or search for the criminal in their place."

Her murmured complaints were all the truth, and Tatsuya didn't have the words to console her like he should have. He'd only gotten his revenge on No-Head Dragon and dealt with the recent invasion because he had backup from the Independent Magic Battalion. Even being able to interfere in the Parasidoll project was largely thanks to Yakumo's help and having received a MOVAL suit from the Battalion.

He wouldn't have been able to deal with any of those matters nearly as capably if he'd only been relying on his personal strength. Tatsuya had never forgotten that. His power was limited on his own, and his keen awareness of this fact prevented him from offering any hollow words of consolation.

"You were right about what you said at first. I'm really only doing this to satisfy myself. Maybe I'm an idiot for risking danger for that, but—"

"All right," he interrupted, using the same words as before. "Sunday the twenty-first. You can pick a time and place at your convenience."

"…Thank you, Tatsuya." Mayumi bowed deeply from her seat on the sofa. "I'll send you a text tomorrow, with a time and place."

"May I ask one more thing?" Tatsuya wondered, stopping Mayumi as she got out of her seat. "Nakura's remains have already been cremated, correct?"

"Y-yes."

"Do you still have what he was wearing when he passed? The clothes he had on at the time, for example?"

"The police said they wanted to keep it all as evidence, so I had them do that. Nakura didn't have any family, so I figured if it would help them catch who did it…"

"Would it be possible to examine them?"

"…I'll try asking the detective who contacted the house."

Tatsuya lowered his head slightly in thanks. Mayumi seemed like she had something she wanted to say, so he urged her on with his eyes.

"I'm sorry," she stated. "I didn't think you'd be so receptive to this…"

"I'll do everything in my power to help you," Tatsuya explained, getting up before Mayumi could say *thank you* again.

In this short time, he'd rethought things—the chance that Nakura had been killed by Zhou wasn't low. The theory that Kouichi Saegusa had been using Saburou Nakura to independently investigate Gongjin Zhou was certainly not far-fetched. And if there was any chance of that, then there was even a possibility that the Saegusa's current head had secretly been in communication with Zhou.

Tatsuya wanted to see Nakura's effects because they might contain a clue connecting him to Gongjin Zhou. Which was certainly nothing Mayumi should have been thanking him for.

After seeing Mayumi to the school's front entrance, Tatsuya headed to the student council room.

For some reason, the student council members and current disciplinary committee chairman weren't the only ones there—the former club committee chairman was present as well.

"Welcome back, Brother."

"Sorry I'm late."

Miyuki stood up and smiled. Tatsuya waved for her to sit back down and went to his desk. He noticed several people furtively looking at him, too, but decided not to react.

"Shiba?"

The one who ended up calling out to him was Izumi Saegusa, who had been struggling with her terminal since he'd entered the room, not sparing him a glance until that very moment.

"Are you having trouble with something?" he asked politely, full well knowing where this was going.

"No, that's not it!"

And of course, his prediction was spot-on.

"Did Big Si—er, my sister go home yet?"

"She did. Why? Did you need her for something?"

"No, not particularly… I was just wondering what sort of matter she might have had that required your attention."

It was clear Izumi's remark was probing. She wanted to know what her sister and Tatsuya had talked about.

"Sorry, did I make you worry? There's no need for concern, Izumi."

But using that type of inquiry against Tatsuya would only lead to him taking advantage of it to change the topic.

"I was not worried about *you!*" Izumi shot back. And then, as per usual, her upperclassmen looked at her with heartwarming gazes, making her face glow red.

Miyuki took over the questioning for the blushing, downcast Izumi. She hadn't been stealing glances at her brother or anything, but she was obviously still interested in how and why he'd met with Mayumi *alone*. In fact, she was probably the *most* interested.

"So, Brother, what were you talking to Saegusa about? If you have no objection, I would like to know."

Right after Miyuki asked that, Tatsuya sensed everyone's ears perking up at once. After looking around the room, he found that, though some people looked away and others looked right at him, everybody was waiting for his answer.

"She told me she also has some business in Kyoto in the near future."

As he said that, Izumi gave a start. He couldn't see her expression, since she was still looking down, but it was easy to guess she'd thought of what had happened to Nakura. Still, he decided being reserved with her or trying to comfort her would backfire. He continued, pretending not to have noticed.

"She wanted to go with me during our scouting next week. She wouldn't tell me what she needed to do there, so I declined, but she gave me a fairly grave look."

Hattori exhaled a bit at this adaptation of the events. He clearly had the same sort of *concerns*.

But then, as if to divert attention from his true feelings, he dug into Tatsuya with an especially harsh tone: "Shiba, why did you refuse if you knew it was a serious matter? Our 'scouting' is just going to be us looking around the city. We're not under any time constraints, so you wouldn't be making anything difficult just by going with her."

*It must be hard to be such a good, serious young man when, in reality, you* want to be the one to accompany her, Tatsuya ribbed inwardly. He nearly loosened his lips, and he had to concentrate to keep them tight.

But that wasn't the end of the criticism laid at his feet.

"Tatsuya, I agree with him," Honoka said. Hattori's reprimand was within expectations, but Tatsuya hadn't foreseen Honoka reacting like this. "Ichihara and Juumonji are already at the Magic University, too, but she came all the way here. I think maybe she was really hoping she could rely on you."

Not understanding what Honoka was after, Tatsuya couldn't immediately answer. He struggled to think of any benefit she might gain if Tatsuya met with Mayumi in Kyoto. If Miyuki had been a complete stranger to him, Honoka might have had the idea of using Mayumi to reveal his true feelings. But in reality, Miyuki was his blood sister. And it was pretty clear from Minami's normal attitude that she'd distanced herself a bit from Tatsuya.

Could her remark have been—and this idea might be rude to Honoka—purely out of sympathy toward Mayumi?

"Tatsuya, if it'll only take up a little bit of time, does it really matter?"

"...I guess not."

When even Mikihiko said something to him, he had to admit his outlook was grim. Mikihiko didn't know his true goal—to capture Gongjin Zhou—but he was a conspirator in their plan to provoke the Traditionalists secretly during their Kyoto scouting trip. If he continued to stubbornly refuse even when *Mikihiko* urged him to help Mayumi, it would probably invite more suspicion than necessary.

And besides, this was all how Tatsuya wanted things to unfold. As long as he had a reason to be with Mayumi, he wouldn't have to pass off meeting her as a coincidence.

At the end of the day, he didn't have high hopes that she would be incredibly helpful. But it was best to have as many people as he could. Tatsuya was under the impression that his role wasn't to search for Zhou, per se, but to deal with things after he'd been found. Still, since Maya's request had been to assist in his capture, and that capture was impossible without finding him, he needed to at least pretend to be looking for him to smooth things over. The more people Tatsuya rounded up, the better it would look.

"Then I'll contact her about it and apologize, too. Izumi, is it all right if I give her a call?"

"Why are you asking me?" Izumi asked back, a little irritated. She'd rightly sensed from his question that he was treating her as though she had a sister complex.

But an annoyed underclassman wasn't enough to make Tatsuya flinch. "Because you're her family?"

"There's no need for my permission. You can do whatever you want."

Tatsuya's tasteless response was met adorably with Izumi's cold shoulder.

A nameless village in a narrow basin surrounded by mountains in old Yamanashi Prefecture, near the border with old Nagano Prefecture. This small mountain village, which didn't even show up on any maps, was the home base of the Yotsuba family, infamous around the globe to anyone involved with the magic world.

Located at the village's center was the main Yotsuba residence, a remarkably large, single-story mansion with several detached buildings covering a wide swath of land. In one of its rooms, the proprietress of the mansion, Maya Yotsuba, was listening to a report from her butler and confidant, Hayama.

"…And that concludes the situation in Nara."

"The JDF Information Bureau…" A scornful smile appeared on Maya's rosy lips. It was by no means crude; in fact, it actually engendered a noble air.

"We are currently investigating which department has interfered. Should you consider that an offense—"

"No, not at all. The JDF has their own honor to uphold. It's only a bit of meddling—we shall overlook it," boasted his master.

The old butler gave a respectful bow. He had no doubt that Maya considered the JDF below her.

"More importantly, about Tatsuya…"

Maya's interest quickly shifted away from the JDF. To be fair, they'd been speaking about Tatsuya to begin with, so she was just getting back to the topic at hand.

"I expect he's working diligently?"

"Yes, madam. He hasn't particularly been hiding the new spell he's developing, and we haven't seen any other rebelliousness."

"That new spell… I heard that it's a close-range, physical attack spell. Do you have any guesses as to what kind?"

"Yes, though it is only a guess."

"That's fine. I'd like to hear what you think about it, Hayama," asked Maya without hiding her interest.

Maya, who never took part in real combat and very rarely in negotiations, was generally cooped up in the mansion. Still, that didn't mean she had an abundance of free time. Of course, that wasn't because of an addiction to sensual pleasures nor because of an obsession with online games. The Yotsuba family placed utmost importance on raising one's capabilities as a magician, and as one of their number, she mainly spent her time on magical research.

To her, the news about Tatsuya developing a new spell was purely a topic that whet her curiosity.

"Judging by his note that it's based on Angie Sirius's Brionac and its name, 'Baryon Lance,' I would assume it is a sort of particle cannon that dismantles matter into protons and neutrons, then fires it."

"An electrically-charged particle cannon, then?"

"If it was, I believe Mr. Tatsuya would have called it a recreation of Brionac rather than a new spell. In my humble opinion, it is more likely to be a neutron cannon."

"A neutron cannon… Neutron barrier magic has already entered the realm of completion, but this is Tatsuya—I'm sure he's considered that."

As Maya happily laid down another deduction, she paused, her expression seeming like something had suddenly occurred to her.

"...Baryon Lance. Not *Launcher*, or *Cannon*, or *Gun*—but *Lance*. I wonder why."

Hayama had been wondering about that, too, but he'd already decided how he'd answer the question. "I cannot fathom. He did say, however, that he would unveil it at the New Year Reception, so perhaps it would be best to see it in person."

He didn't have to use the expression *A picture is worth a thousand words*; Maya was perfectly aware that it was both faster and wiser to observe something rather than pile up speculations. She couldn't help feeling like he was trying to delay, though, so a mean-spirited question made its way out of her mouth.

"Why didn't you ask for details? It might have been a good way to find out whether he really is obedient or not."

"I merely thought that learning any more would be unnecessary for the madam's ends."

But it may have come back to bite her. At Hayama's admonishing tone, she gave an almost invisible shrug. "You talk about my 'ends' as though they're so important," she said, Hayama's stare making her feel like she needed to excuse herself. "It isn't because he's my nephew. Driving him out wouldn't do the Yotsuba any good."

"I would think his being your nephew would be enough of a reason in its own right."

"Hayama..."

"Please excuse me."

Upon hearing Maya say his name in a reprimanding tone, Hayama bowed respectfully. Still, it wasn't the appropriate apology for this sort of situation. Normally, one would use a phrase like *I went too far* or *Please forgive my unnecessary meddling* or something along those lines.

And the reason he hadn't called his own remark "unnecessary meddling" was not wholly unrelated to why Maya's cheeks had slightly reddened.

* * *

"Mr. Hayama."

After leaving Maya's room, and while he was on his way back through the yard to the detached building lent to him as living quarters, somebody addressed him from behind.

His inability to sense their presence caused him no distress. Plenty of people in this village had the ability to blend in with the wind or the dark.

And more importantly, the voice was one Hayama was familiar with.

"Lord Kuroba. I apologize deeply for not noticing you were watching."

If nothing else, they knew each other well enough that he could offer a snide remark like that.

On the other end, Mitsugu Kuroba frowned in distaste, but he similarly kept himself from showing affront at something of this degree. "Not at all—please excuse my rudeness. I hadn't realized I was still hiding my presence."

Hayama couldn't determine whether Mitsugu's comment was true or false. It seemed perfectly reasonable that Mitsugu's sticking to the shadows on a daily basis had become a habit, but it also seemed suspect that the man could properly do intelligence work without being aware of whether he was currently well-hidden, blending in, or exposed.

"No, you needn't be concerned."

But it didn't matter. If Mitsugu Kuroba had seriously been concealing himself, he could have been standing right in front of Hayama without being noticed. It wouldn't do Hayama any good to get annoyed over something so trivial with someone who could decide his fate at any time. Besides—and this was the more important part—the Kuroba family was a powerful branch of the Yotsuba, and Mitsugu, its leader, was one of the people Hayama was meant to serve. He'd be a failure as a butler if he was offended by every one of his master's whims.

"In any case, Lord Kuroba, was there something you needed of me?"

"Something I needed… Yes, I suppose I wanted to talk to you for a few moments."

Hayama's eyebrow twitched. An expression of unhappiness—but one he'd made a point of showing. A moment later, he put on a courteous smile.

"You have something you wish to…discuss, then?"

Mitsugu realized what Hayama was thinking and quickly waved his hands in refusal. "No, no—I meant what I said. There was something I wanted to ask you, and something I wanted your opinion on. It will only take a moment."

"Oh—then I must apologize." Hayama bowed respectfully in the darkness, giving away no hint of his true thoughts. "Come right this way."

He turned his feet back to the main house he'd just left. As head of the butlers employed to the Yotsuba, he was given a degree of discretion to freely use the reception room in the main building. Even if he didn't, nobody would criticize him for using a room to discuss something with the head of the Kuroba family. In fact, continuing the conversation while standing would be the most likely thing to land him in hot water.

But Mitsugu didn't go along with his sensible response. "Actually, if it's all the same to you, here would be fine."

Hayama stopped, turned around, and gave Mitsugu a dubious look.

Mitsugu ignored his suspicions and pushed on. "When you were talking to the head of the family, were you discussing that man—Gongjin Zhou?"

Hayama nodded in understanding. "I suppose it's only natural for you to be curious if others are going to become involved in your work, yes?"

When the reply made his question seem almost foolish, Mitsugu quickly tried to deny it. "No, I—"

"But you need not worry." Hayama, however, didn't give him the chance. "As I'm sure you're aware, Lord Kuroba, Lady Miyuki's Guardian has been given a test."

Mitsugu frowned for real this time. "…Yes, I've heard."

The so-called *test* had begun not in the latter part of September, when his children had visited Tatsuya, but on one particular day in August. Because of it, Tatsuya had seen him in nearly the most disgraceful state possible. Mitsugu was grateful he still had two arms, but the deep gouge in his pride was another matter entirely.

"I've been reporting on its progress. After all, Lady Miyuki is a strong candidate to be the next head of the family. Discerning if there is the possibility that her Guardian would rebel against the Yotsuba will be of utmost importance to the family in the future."

Mitsugu was letting more and more of his displeasure show, but Hayama didn't pay it any mind.

"It is an extremely vital matter, and we believe we have done you a disservice, but we have used the incident as a means of judgment."

"There is no way that man would *ever* be loyal to the Yotsuba family," Mitsugu spat. This was what he truly believed, and also something he'd never show in front of the Shiba siblings themselves.

"I fail to understand what basis you have for determining that, Lord Kuroba…" With his eyes, Hayama asked for him to explain.

But Mitsugu only stared back at him silently.

Without seeming bothered at all, Hayama offered an answer himself, his tone a lofty one—and his words more scathing than anything anyone else would be able to say.

"*Mr. Tatsuya* is unaware *he* was nearly killed by his relatives soon after he was born. Any concern in that vein would be naught more than paranoia, don't you think?"

"Hayama!" Mitsugu snapped.

That was something Mitsugu's generation had always kept quiet about. The only one who knew of it, other than the seven families with Yotsuba blood—the Shiiba, the Mashiba, the Shibata, the Kuroba, the Mugura, the Tsukuba, and the Shizuka—was Hayama. It was so secret that even those under twenty years old who *did* have the right lineage had never been told. Suddenly bringing it up had been a surprise attack, understandably causing Mitsugu Kuroba to lose his cool.

Hayama accepted the death in the air with a courteous smile. "Even I understand *that man* doesn't have loyalty toward the Yotsuba, and that this will remain the same in the future. And the mistress, of course, is obviously concerned about this. And yet, she trusts him with Lady Miyuki's safety even still."

Mitsugu ground his teeth. He was the one who had started this conversation, but suddenly, he found himself being roundly criticized.

"Lord Kuroba, loyalty is unneeded. Actions are all that matter. Even if he is traitorous and only pretends to obey, as long as he doesn't betray his position, our expectations, or the results we need, he's better to have than a loyalist who produces no results. Tools require no loyalty. Weapons need no mind of their own."

"Are you calling magicians 'weapons,' you…?!"

"Perhaps you've forgotten, but I, too, am a magician," said Hayama, before smiling in a lighthearted way and adding, "Though nearly powerless, compared with everyone else."

Mitsugu found himself trapped in heavy silence.

"Weapons do not know fear. Weapons do not know anxiety. But can we really say someone who would kill an innocent person out of fear of the mere *possibility* of what they might become is truly any better than a mindless weapon?"

After driving that wedge deeply into Mitsugu's heart, Hayama bowed and left.

Friday, October 10. Ten full days, including today, until the year's Thesis Competition. The preparation for the presentation had at last entered its final stages.

Unlike the previous year, nothing suspicious had occurred at the school. It may have been more accurate to consider the previous year an exception, and to think of the present year as a return to normalcy—but either way, thanks to that uneventfulness, the work had been proceeding apace ahead of the competition, without needing to get any extra hands on board.

Even Tatsuya and the others had managed to obtain about ten days' peace. In addition to the effort that Yakumo's disciples put in, the mercenaries that Hayama had hired through Hanabishi, the butler, seemed to be doing well. Hanabishi was second in the Yotsuba servant hierarchy, the butler in charge of various responsibilities related to the rougher jobs the family undertook—including personnel procurement—and he never cut corners in his work.

In terms of raw numbers, the Yotsuba family didn't actually have many magicians. Even those who had no direct blood ties but were still employed by the family and could freely use magic at any time were few in number compared with the Saegusa, and the difference only grew when looking at the Ichijou and Itsuwa.

All the Yotsuba magicians were powerful enough to make up for the numerical disadvantage, but some situations still called for quantity. For such cases, the Yotsuba had organized collaborators who, in the outside world, were *disposable*.

Magicians who had engaged in grave acts of rebellion against the state or had attempted to. Magicians who, though they had not taken any direct hostile action toward the state per se, had tried to leak militarily applicable magical technology to foreign powers. Magicians who had betrayed the state in such ways were often targets of purges that were supposed to be carried out by the Yotsuba.

These jobs were a vital source of family income. Not only did the Yotsuba gain financially, they also procured combat personnel through them. They brainwashed captured rebellious magicians and made them into pawns.

They never stole a person's mind like No-Head Dragon had with their Generators. The Yotsuba were well aware of how directly will-power and emotion were related to the strength of magic.

Their brainwashing was more typical. Little by little, they'd imprint a fear of the Yotsuba in the magicians and make them believe only death awaited those who disobeyed. They'd overwrite their ide-ologies with the fear of death. They never approached those extremists who, in a true sense, didn't fear death to begin with. They would only bring their deals to those who *did* fear it—by telling them they'd be set free, *alive*, if they worked hard enough.

In that way, the Yotsuba used magical mercenaries, who risked their lives in the hope of keeping them as payment, for several different types of work. Quantity was everything in this guard mission where any magician who acted even slightly suspiciously in the area was kid-napped. The Yotsuba family had used so many people for security that it seemed like they'd blow through their entire stock of brainwashed soldiers. However, thanks to them, not only Tatsuya's friends but all of First High was in a state of near-perfect tranquility.

Even with the pretext of Thesis Competition prep work, female students weren't allowed to stay at school late into the night. Whether it was gender discrimination or sexism didn't matter; the night hours permitted to male students was simply disallowed for female students.

It was nearing closing time again today. Cleanup had already started in the student council room. Still, everything was paperless in this day and age, so it was different from the kind of "packing up" that was commonplace a century ago, when papers would be returned to cabinets or stuffed into bags. With almost no need to bustle about, they quickly finished getting ready to go home.

"Sorry Miyuki, I'll be heading out first," Izumi called.

The Shiba sister wouldn't be coming to school the next day—Saturday—and instead was going to Kyoto. She'd requested a time extension at school to finish the handover report. That was why Izumi was leaving before her.

"I'll be counting on you tomorrow and the day after, Izumi."

"It's an honor! I could never do as well as you, but I will do what little I can!"

Izumi had been idling reluctantly near the door, but once Miyuki said that to her, she pivoted and went on her way home in a good mood.

"It seems like you've gotten used to how to interact with Izumi, huh?" Honoka quipped with a dry smile after shutting down her terminal and standing up.

"You have the makings of a bad woman," piped in Shizuku, who had come to the student council room to go home with Honoka.

Objectively, the remark was impossible to ignore, but Miyuki knew she didn't mean anything by it, so she simply smiled and said, "There are no bad or good women when it comes to dealing with another girl, is there?"

"...You're heartless, Miyuki."

Shizuku sighed earnestly, but Miyuki only smiled back.

Shizuku's main duty in the Thesis Competition was to guard the main presenter, Azusa, but she'd been going home with Honoka every day lately. They were frequently with many others, including Azusa, until they reached the station, but from there, it was just the two of them. And while there were professional bodyguards watching over them from the shadows, they were taking care to not be spotted. This meant that in cabinets and commuters, at least, she was alone with Honoka.

"Hey, Shizuku?"

In the line of people waiting for cabinets, Honoka spoke up apprehensively.

"Hmm?"

But Shizuku had no idea what she was worrying about. Just as she tilted her head in confusion, a two-seater car arrived in front of them.

After giving a light bow to the three-person party waiting for a four-seater, they boarded, then held their passes up to the card reader, which specified a destination. Shizuku looked at Honoka again, a question in her eyes.

"Oh… Well, I was just wondering if this was all right."

"What?"

"Umm, I'm talking about protecting Nakajou…"

"Oh, that?" Shizuku relaxed her shoulders; her face seemed to say *Is that all?* "Nakajou was the one who told me to."

"Told you Chikura was enough of a bodyguard for going home?"

As might be expected from good friends, Honoka filled in the part that Shizuku left out.

"I guess maybe it's easier, since they're both seniors," Shizuku hedged.

"Yep… I think I can understand it," Honoka agreed. "Even when it's a younger student, there's times you'd end up unsure on how to talk to them."

"Kasumi and Izumi seem like exceptions."

"Ah, ah-ha-ha-ha… But even Minami is…like, she has this wall around her."

"Yeah." Shizuku agreed in a word to Honoka's claim. She was the one who had brought up that it was easier to get along with students in the same grade, so this was natural.

"And she'll be okay with Chikura there."

"Huh? Oh. Now that you mention it, Chikura's magic is good for protection, right?"

"Yep."

Honoka couldn't immediately fill in this time when Shizuku said Azusa would be fine, but a moment of thought clued her in to what Shizuku wanted to say—the power of friendship, perhaps.

Tomoko Chikura specialized in a spell that reflected vectors. If she knew beforehand that someone would shoot her, she could even bounce back anti-material rifle rounds, given how much event influence she possessed. She couldn't do much if someone sniped her without warning—and that was something that applied to most magicians, not just Tomoko—but she was extraordinarily strong in situations where it was obvious that someone was pointing a gun at her.

And her magic didn't only work against projectile weapons. If a person charged at her, she could reflect their kinetic energy. So long as the target didn't weigh more than a passenger car and wasn't going at something like two hundred kilometers per hour, she could deal with it.

Like Honoka said, Tomoko Chikura was the most well-endowed of all of First High's security detail when it came to magic that was well suited for protection.

"Anyway, what about you, Honoka?"

"Huh… What about me?"

Shizuku gave a hard stare in response to Honoka's cluelessness.

A message popped up in the cabinet's window, stating that their ride was about to reach its arrival station.

"I'll ask later," said Shizuku, turning to face forward.

Shizuku brought the topic up again after they'd finished eating, while they were in the bath.

"Are you doing okay, Honoka?"

"Huh? Did you say something? One sec."

Honoka had been washing her hair; she turned the water off and looked at Shizuku, who was soaking in the tub.

"No, you can finish your hair first."

"Okay. It'll only take a second."

After scrubbing her hair with shampoo one more time, Honoka took a towel from the storage rack, which was covered with a water-proof sheet. She ran it through her hair to dry it off, then put the damp towel into a mesh laundry bag before finally picking up the bottle of conditioner.

"Do you want me to do it for you?"

"No, that's okay. Whenever I ask you, you take a lot of time because you try to be perfect."

"That's fine, isn't it? Let me do it."

Shizuku got out of the bathtub. While dripping hot water onto the floor, she took the bottle away from Honoka with just a tiny bit of force.

"Your hair is so straight and pretty. I'm jealous," sighed Shizuku as she ran her hand through Honoka's wet hair.

"No, I... Well, compared with Miyuki..." murmured Honoka, looking down a little at the frank, straightforward praise.

"There's no point comparing yourself with her," objected Shizuku in all seriousness.

"Yeah, I guess not." Honoka laughed a little, too.

Shizuku gently applied the conditioner to Honoka's thinly bunched hair. "And I like your hair better anyway."

"What?! That's nepotism—or, at least, favoritism."

"You're my friend. Of course I'd be biased."

Honoka was at a loss for words when she heard how seriously Shizuku had spoken.

"And if you ask me, Miyuki's hair is too dark."

In contrast, Shizuku was unusually talkative.

"I like your brighter hair better."

"R-really? ...Thanks."

Did that final, softly spoken word reach Shizuku's ears?

For a while, Shizuku worked through Honoka's hair in silence, and Honoka let her do so.

Shizuku picked up the showerhead.

Honoka squeezed her eyes shut.

Careful to not miss a single spot, Shizuku used the water pressure to get the lather out.

Shizuku only brought up what she had wanted to say after Honoka was done washing her hair, as promised.

Honoka sat down in the bathtub facing her. The bath in Shizuku's house was large, and despite this being the second bathroom, it was twice as spacious as a normal home's. The tub itself was large, providing plenty of free space even with both of them in it together.

"Honoka?"

"Yeah?"

"Are you doing okay?"

"Wait, what do you mean? You asked that before, too…"

Shizuku gazed at Honoka's face again. Deciding she didn't seem to be feigning ignorance, Shizuku filled in the gap in her question. "Are you really okay with staying here in Tokyo? Didn't you want to go to Kyoto, too?"

Honoka sucked in her breath and froze.

The temperature of the water lapping up against her skin hadn't changed. But when Honoka's body and face stiffened, it almost made Shizuku feel a chill.

"Well, I…"

"Sorry, I guess that was insensitive, huh?"

Shizuku looked away; Honoka had gone pale all the way to her lips.

"…It's okay. You've always been rooting for me, so of course you'd want to know."

Saying "Hold on a second," Honoka took a few deep breaths. As she calmed herself, the color returned to her face. "Phew… It's fine now, Shizuku. You can look this way."

Shizuku obeyed and turned back. Once again, they were facing each other.

"To tell you the truth, obviously, I wanted to go to Kyoto with Tatsuya. I wouldn't ask to be alone with him—that would be too much. I wouldn't mind if Miyuki was there, too. I would've been okay as long as I could be with him."

"…Then why?"

"Because I didn't want to slow him down."

Shizuku looked at Honoka's face in surprise. Honoka gave a

feeble, lonely smile in response. "I'm sure you've noticed it, too. The Thesis Competition wasn't why Tatsuya told me to stay at your house."

The light of comprehension flickered in Shizuku's eyes.

"He's really, truly worried about *us*. He's not worried about lowly thieves going after competition data. I think there's a strong enemy lurking around, like last year."

"You think Tatsuya is on a *mission*, right?"

Shizuku hugged herself, shivering.

Honoka waded through the water and moved next to her.

When they sat next to each other like this, even the made-to-order tub was a little tight.

Nestled up against each other, Honoka put an arm around Shizuku's shoulders.

Shizuku let down her own arms.

"Yeah... I think he's on a mission for the JDF right now. And that maybe he's up against a pretty big organization. So big he couldn't ignore the possibility that one of us might be held hostage."

"And that's why he assigned a bodyguard to you?"

"It's not just me. Assigning me a bodyguard means you'll be protected, too, since you're with me. I think that's why Yoshida is sticking with Mizuki, too. Yoshida's so good that he can make even pros look bad."

"He's definitely at home there."

"Yeah."

The two girls giggled, sharing a moment of skinship together.

But Honoka's laughing soon faded.

"Even this first trip to Kyoto—I think their security preparation is nothing but a side thing. They're making the trip for something else. Depending on how things go, it might turn violent. Everyone who Tatsuya picked to go with him tomorrow is good in real combat. Even Minami will probably be a big help if she needs to, what with that barrier magic."

"I think you're pretty good yourself, Honoka."

"No, I wouldn't work out. If I was just supporting from a distance, that would be one thing. But if I got attacked directly, I'd only slow Tatsuya down…"

Speaking from the perspective of a regular magician, Honoka's combat skills certainly weren't low. It wouldn't be an exaggeration to call her first-rate for a high school student, at least. But compared with Miyuki, who was above first-rate even among regular magicians; and Tatsuya, who ranked further above that as a military magician even when rated solely on his combat abilities, even her best friend Shizuku couldn't deny that she fell one or two levels below the others in terms of direct fighting strength. She had no more words of comfort to offer anymore.

"That's why it's okay."

After her friend fell awkwardly silent, Honoka held Shizuku's head in her arms.

She buried Shizuku's face into her chest, leaving it barely more than half exposed over the water.

"Hnnka, thaph hrtts!"

"Hyaa?!"

Honoka let out a tickled-sounding cry and let go of her friend's head.

Her mouth and nose free, Shizuku took a deep breath. She stared at Honoka bitterly—not at her face, but at her chest.

"Sorry, sorry!"

Apologizing, Honoka pushed herself against the side of the bathtub, covering her chest with her hands.

They both laughed out loud at the same time.

The awkward mood dissipated in an instant.

"I'm sorry, Shizuku."

"No, I'm sorry."

"No, you brought it up because you were thinking about me. Like I said, there's no need for you to apologize," said Honoka, smiling, free from worry. "I really do want to go to Kyoto with them. But I also don't want to slow them down. That's why I'm being considerate and waiting in Tokyo this time. If Tatsuya doesn't want me to notice, I'll pretend not to notice. I'll let myself be deceived, just like he wants."

Shizuku offered a warm smile to those words. "You're such a good woman, Honoka."

Honoka broke her relaxed attitude in the blink of an eye.

"What…what do you mean by that?!"

"If I were a boy, I wouldn't ever leave you alone."

"Umm… Shizuku? That's a scary look…"

"You have a great figure, too… And you look so cute, like you're easy to get along with…"

Shizuku traced her slender finger up Honoka's chin.

"Sh-Shizuku?! You're acting kind of like Amy right now!"

"Hrm. I'm bigger than she is."

"That's not the problem here!"

"Are you trying to say there's no real difference compared with you?"

"I was not saying that!"

"Let's see here."

"Kyaa!"

"…I knew it already, but this really is unfair."

"Wait—Shizuku, please, sto—"

…What happened at this time in this place was not recorded here. But suffice it to say, being in the hot water for too long ended up making them very dizzy.

[7]

Saturday morning, October 20.

Five-day weeks were still used in some liberal arts schools, but six-day weeks were standard for most high schools. Magic high schools were no exception, with their classes filling every day from Monday to Saturday.

Normally, a student would be focusing on their terminal in their classroom, practicing magic, or in a lab, but at the moment, Tatsuya was on his way to Kyoto with Miyuki and Minami.

They weren't skipping out on classes, of course. This trip was being treated like a paid holiday, the pretext of which was to prepare in advance for the Thesis Competition. They were moving via trailer this time, rather than a linear express train.

A trailer, in simple terms, was a two-story, linked train, with a cabinet on the first floor and a passenger amenity area on the second. It didn't levitate, but it still used a linear motor, so its speed wasn't much slower than that of a linear express.

Its wheels were metallic, and it ran over a metallic track—a system that, compared with linear expresses and cabinets, loyally retained the sense of a railroad.

In order to board, a parking pallet would first slide out of the trailer, slipping between the cabinet and the track. The trailer was faster than the cabinet, so it would approach the cabinet from the rear. Then, the parking pallet would scoop up the cabinet's wheels from behind. After that, the pallet would once again slide back into the trailer. Through this method, passengers would board the trailer while inside the cabinet. This was possible because a cabinet's wheels were only there to hold it up—they weren't hooked up to the power mechanism.

As soon as they were in the trailer, Tatsuya and the others exited the cabinet and went up to the second-floor amenity area. Though the cabinet might have guaranteed more privacy, he'd decided it would be a waste to shut themselves up in its narrow confines when there was a place they could stretch their legs available to them.

Thankfully, the lounge chairs were empty. Tatsuya and Miyuki took seats next to each other, while Minami went to the one in front of Miyuki and turned it around to face them before sitting.

"Want something to drink?" Tatsuya asked, taking an order terminal out of his armrest and showing it to Miyuki.

"…I'm sorry to trouble you, Brother. I'll have this."

Apologetic, Miyuki pressed the terminal herself. Tatsuya tried to show it to Minami, too, but she'd already taken hers out of her own seat. And, in fact, she was now trying to show hers to him—but Tatsuya smiled at her and put in the order on his. She didn't look too happy about it, but she did make a point of ordering her own.

Within less than a minute, their drinks arrived. The robotic arms running along the ceiling lowered a tray in front of each of the three. They worked under essentially the same principles as the HARs (Home Automation Robots) used in most homes.

Tatsuya, Miyuki, and Minami each took their plastic cups, designed to be reused, and the arms holding the trays retracted back into the ceiling. After taking one or two sips, they placed their cups on a side table.

Right after that, someone called out to Tatsuya from behind.

"Wait—Tatsuya?"

He'd set his cup down partly because he'd noticed her approach.

"Good morning, Erika," Miyuki replied.

"You ended up in this trailer too, huh?" Tatsuya asked as Erika took the seat in front of him.

"Yeah. What a crazy coincidence."

His classmate nodded, honestly surprised. Trailers ran at even intervals on intracity rails, and cabinets moving long distances would board whatever trailer was closest. It was all controlled by the public transit system, and passengers couldn't choose which trailer to board.

However, it wasn't actually that shocking. If the destination and estimated time of arrival were identical, cabinets would end up running at the same time in the same area, ramping up the chances of sharing a trailer.

Erika followed their lead and ordered her own drink, then took a big stretch in her lounge chair.

"Wow, it sure is nice to be able to stretch your legs, huh?"

"Erika, are you the type who thinks cabinets are too cramped?"

Cabinet interiors were made to be spacious compared to cars, but a certain segment of people felt that they were uncomfortable.

"Huh? No, not really. Not compared with the hours of sitting on my knees I do in small rooms for training."

"I didn't know *kenjutsu* involved such a thing," Miyuki said, surprised.

Erika scowled bitterly. "My shitty dad *says* it's for *kenjutsu* anyway..."

Tatsuya and Miyuki exchanged looks. Erika only seemed crude at a glance; oftentimes, she'd give off an impression of being raised to have good manners. Calling her older brother stupid was one thing, but using swear words was probably not something she enjoyed doing.

"So it doesn't have anything to do with training?"

It made Miyuki curious, but the brief eye contact led her to the conclusion that she shouldn't ask a personal question like that. Neither she nor her brother wanted to be interrogated about family affairs.

Instead, Miyuki asked something else. From the way Erika put it, perhaps sitting formally atop her knees was training for something else? That didn't seem to suit Erika, and yet, at the same time, it did.

"Tea stuff. You know, ceremonies."

Her guess happened to be right on the mark—which only surprised her even more.

"It wasn't that uncommon in the olden days to combine tea ceremony with martial arts."

Tatsuya immediately followed up, though, so Erika didn't realize Miyuki was so surprised that she didn't know how to react.

"I guess not. Dad's probably trying to imitate that... But don't you think he should make his son and heir do that first?"

"Well, maybe."

"I think that's a little severe, though, Erika," chimed in a rebooted Miyuki with a smile. "Students in tea ceremony classrooms are almost all female. Wouldn't that hurdle be a little high for your older brothers?"

"And unlike them, it's not strange that you'd be learning it," added Tatsuya.

Erika looked away. "Huh. Really. You don't think I'm not suited for that kinda stuff?"

"Not at all. I've been invited twice to a class Miyuki attends, and I think the atmosphere suits you."

"...But I bet you think it doesn't suit *me* as much as her," muttered Erika, shying away.

Tatsuya let out a grin. It was pretty obvious she was pretending to sulk to hide her embarrassment.

When they emerged from the ticket gates at Kyoto Station, Leo and Mikihiko were waiting for them. The pair hadn't coincidentally been on the same trailer, but that was only natural. Tatsuya, Miyuki, and Minami also split up with Erika in the trailer and returned to their original cabinets, arriving separately.

After the six of them grouped up in the station, they decided to head straight for the hotel they were planning to stay at. But Tatsuya, who was heading for the commuter boarding platform, noticed a familiar presence approaching from behind. He stopped walking and turned around.

"Tatsuya, Miyuki, Minami."

"Oh, is that you, Minoru?"

The one who trotted up to them was, as Miyuki had named, the youngest son of the Kudou family they'd met two weeks ago: Minoru Kudou.

He must have also noticed that they'd noticed him. There was no hesitation in his voice when he'd called out; a smile was gracing his almost radiant features.

Tatsuya suddenly sensed someone to his right was visibly shocked. He glanced over and saw Erika's eyes had gone wide. Her mouth was even open a little—she must have been quite taken aback.

"Wow."

And as he was thinking that, the girl herself admitted that very thing.

"He's like a male version of Miyuki... I can't believe there's anyone besides her with such attractive features."

Tatsuya agreed on that point, but he also didn't think it was the sort of thing to say about someone who was standing right there. "Minoru, did you come to pick us up? The plan was to meet up at the hotel, wasn't it?"

"Yes, it was, but I was on the lookout, since I figured you'd be arriving about now..."

Commenting on how Minoru was clearly happy they hadn't missed each other might have been interpreted as being insensitive so Tatsuya decided to keep to himself.

What he said instead was a few words of introduction to acquaint those who had never met. "This is your first time meeting everyone, right?"

When he said "everyone," he meant his friends to his right side. Miyuki was to his left, and Minami was waiting behind her.

"This is Minoru Kudou, son of the Kudou family."

"Good to meet you. My name is Minoru Kudou, and I'm currently a freshman at Second High."

After Tatsuya spoke, Minoru introduced himself, focusing on his school instead of his family out of a hope that they'd treat him not as part of the influential Ten Master Clans, but as a fellow student like themselves.

"I'm Erika Chiba, a junior at First High."

Erika, quick to recover even after her initial shock, was the first one to introduce herself.

"And I'm Leonhard Saijou. I'm a junior at First High, like her."

"Mikihiko Yoshida. I'm also in my junior year at First High. It's nice to meet you, Kudou."

"The pleasure is all mine."

Minoru's eyebrow moved a little upon hearing Erika's and Mikihiko's names; based on name alone, he'd probably realized she was a swordswoman of the Chiba family and he was a mage of the Yoshida family. It seemed he wasn't as skilled at hiding his thoughts as he was with his magical abilities.

Of course, unlike his magical abilities, that inexperience was a *little* more appropriate for his age.

"Minoru. We're going to drop off our things at the hotel for now—do you want to come?"

"Yes, if you'll allow me. That will be a more efficient use of our time."

"Yeah."

Tatsuya started off toward the commuter platform again. Miyuki was next to him, while his friends trailed behind him. Minoru walked next to Minami, also following in Tatsuya's wake.

It still wasn't check-in time at the hotel yet, but they were able to keep their luggage behind the desk regardless. This type of service remained unchanged from the olden days.

The group of seven, including Minoru, first headed to the Kyoto New International Conference Hall, the venue for the Thesis Competition. Before the war, it had been called the Kyoto International Conference Center, but its name had been changed upon its rebuilding after the Twenty Years' Global War Outbreak from "conference center" to "new conference hall."

The location had always been bursting with nature, surrounded by a pond and hills as it was, and that remained the same even after its rebuilding. The construction of large, industrial facilities had been virtually forbidden, and the small stadium a short distance away had been demolished after it got too old to use; in its place was a woody park.

There were no dilapidated buildings—like the ones the foreign saboteurs had set up as their headquarters during the string of events that had occurred preceding the Yokohama Incident last year—anywhere near the New Conference Hall. Aside from the hotel right next door, there weren't even any buildings close by at all. Only residential housing, two stories at most, making the place seem too difficult for a large group to infiltrate.

"…On the other hand, it's perfect for a small group to spread out and hide," mused Mikihiko.

Erika remained doubtful: "Think so? I doubt the mountains around here are deep enough to set up camp while staying hidden."

"They don't need to sleep out in the mountains, do they?" argued Leo. "They just have to hide on the day of, right? Seems like there's plenty of places for that."

Erika blinked several times. Then, she realized she'd been assuming *hiding* meant *infiltrating*.

"And they don't need to set up a camp in the mountains, either," pointed out Mikihiko again, though probably not to back up Erika, who had fallen sullenly silent. "They could hide in the houses, too, in groups of two or three. Ancient magicians have plenty of ways to prevent others from catching on, like hypnotizing the residents or putting up perception-blocking fields."

"Yeah, that's true. Given the area, there's probably a ton of ancient magicians," murmured Erika with nonchalance to fill the air, perhaps concerned that her silence signaled defeat.

Then, Tatsuya, who had been silent until now, proposed something to Mikihiko. He didn't expect it to fly, but he wanted Erika to feel a little better about the process, at least. "Would you like to split up and walk around? Hypnotism aside, bounded fields should be easy enough to detect."

"No, that wouldn't be efficient." There was no particular script, but Mikihiko gave him the answer he wanted. "If small groups wanted to hide in houses, they'd be keeping their bounded fields to an absolute minimum so nobody outside would detect them. Not that I'm doubting your abilities or Miyuki's, but without some amazing luck, we won't get anywhere walking around blindly trying to feel them out. I don't think we have time to spend relying on coincidences."

Tatsuya nodded easily. "Makes sense. What should we do, then?"

"I'll try using a search *shiki*," he answered, before looking to Erika and Leo. "Could you two help me out?"

"What's the plan?" responded Leo, though from his expression, it was clear he would do whatever it was.

"I can't help it, but while I have a *shikigami* out, I can't pay as much attention to my surroundings. I want you two to be on the lookout for things nearby."

"Right. Leave it to me!" Leo nodded with a grin.

"If it's the only way, I guess I'll protect you." Erika was pretending not to be interested in this, but her voice and face betrayed the eagerness quietly leaking out.

"Thank you." Mikihiko nodded to Erika and Leo—who frowned a little, either feeling like their friend was being too formal or too standoffish—before turning back to Tatsuya. "As for Tatsuya and the others… Could you, Miyuki, and Sakurai take a look around the city, like we decided last week? And, uh…"

As Mikihiko looked at Minoru, who was standing next to Minami, his expression faltered.

"I can show them around. Second High would be just as troubled if something like last year happened again."

"Minoru is Ms. Fujibayashi's cousin," mentioned Tatsuya.

Mikihiko, Erika, and Leo were all there when *it* happened on October 30 last year: They'd learned Tatsuya was a special officer in the JDF and been firmly asked to keep that secret. All three of them also remembered the beautiful female officer who had gone with them to the station in Sakuragi Town, including her name.

"R-right…"

"Huh… So the two of you are family."

"Oh, you're related?"

They understood they weren't supposed to look too deeply into the connection between Tatsuya and Minoru, and each gave a different stumbling reaction toward that end.

"Her family's house is in the area. When we talked about looking around the city of Kyoto, she introduced Minoru to be our guide."

Tatsuya knew the three would interpret "talking to Fujibayashi" as "talking about something related to a military mission" and gave the explanation anyway so as to amplify the misunderstanding.

"I see," said Mikihiko, very nearly stammering but stopping himself. "Thanks for doing this, Tatsuya."

"Yeah, you too."

"Yoshida, Saijou, Erika—we'll see you later," Miyuki called to them.

"Right, see you at the hotel!" Erika answered before the seven split into two groups.

The first place Tatsuya's group headed to was Oohara, known for its famous temple, Sanzen-in. He had no plans to visit the temple grounds and sightsee, of course; this was the last region in which Gongjin Zhou had been sighted.

Tatsuya had gotten Minoru to bring them here first, since it was in the same direction as the New Conference Hall from the heart of the city. Unfortunately, it was farther away than he'd expected. He'd had a mental image of Kyoto being compact and organized.

According to the information he'd received from Hayama, the skirmish between Gongjin Zhou and the Kuroba search team had occurred near the imperial tombs of Emperor Go-toba Oohara and the Emperor Juntoku Oohara. It looked like even they hadn't gone so far as to step into a cordoned-off memorial site. Word was that Zhou had gone along a small river flowing between the imperial tombs and Sanzen-in before escaping downstream.

Having heard only that, Tatsuya figured the pursuers must have lost track of their prey somewhere deep into the mountains. Surprisingly, though, the direction in which Gongjin Zhou had fled had its fair share of house-lined roads, with not only sightseers but plenty of locals out and about. When he compared the scenery to his map, he felt like it would have been better to flee upstream instead, toward the Otonashi Waterfall, but remembering the search team's assault on the man, he shook his head.

Qimen Dunjia scattered the victim's sense of direction. Putting together all the information acquired so far pointed to the technique being a type of illusion that forcibly confused a caster's sense of direction. On the surface, it seemed like a spell that truly shined in overgrown mountain forests with dense oceans of trees, but maybe its true value came out when used in crowds of people.

In unpopulated places, sensing Zhou's presence was an option.

But in crowds, losing track of him because of a spell that ruined his enemy's sense of direction—if it wasn't possible to follow him visually—there'd be no other way of finding him.

Before coming here, Tatsuya had assumed Zhou would sneak off to some hideaway in the mountains that nobody ever went near. But he changed his mind after surveying the area. If Gongjin Zhou fled downstream, not toward the mountains but toward a village, he could still be hiding in an urban district with plenty of people in it instead of somewhere relatively empty.

"The closest Traditionalist base in the direction he escaped is in Mount Kurama. Should we go there, Tatsuya?" asked Minoru when they were on the short bridge spanning the Ritsu River.

With Miyuki and Minami looking on, Tatsuya shook his head. "No, let's go back into the city."

"The city?" repeated Minoru, sounding a little surprised.

"Do you believe Zhou is hiding somewhere crowded, Brother?"

After hearing Miyuki's question, Tatsuya nodded. "Yeah."

"I see. Trees are best hidden within forests, after all."

Minoru's comment was slightly different from Tatsuya's, but not enough for him to correct him.

"A place, populated to a certain degree, with a Traditionalist headquarters… That narrows it down to the street leading to Kiyomizu-dera, the neighborhood around Kinkaku-ji, and the area behind Tenryuu-ji."

"That's not as many as I expected."

He'd heard from Minoru that the Traditionalist bases were scattered throughout Nara and Kyoto, but Mikihiko had said Kyoto was their main base. With that and several other pieces of information, Tatsuya had been under the preconception that the Traditionalists were crowded all over the city of Kyoto.

"In Kyoto, the religious faction dedicated to preserving true traditions is stronger than those in Nara. Groups that are New Age religions in name only have been forced into the nearby mountains."

"And yet, they call themselves the Traditionalists—do they have some kind of complex about tradition?" Tatsuya jibed.

Minami rolled her eyes at the rhetorical question—but she restrained herself to make sure Miyuki couldn't see, of course. She doubted it would have angered her master, but she decided she should avoid any unnecessary friction.

——Although, in reality, both Miyuki and Tatsuya did notice it.

Meanwhile, unlike her, Minoru seemed to take his muttering literally. "I'm not sure. As you know, the Traditionalists formed around a core of ancient magicians who had participated in Lab Nine's operations. Their objective must be to take revenge on Lab Nine and the families of the Nine."

Maybe it was revenge, but the resentment the Traditionalists felt was nothing if not misguided. They were under the assumption that when they took part in Lab Nine's research, in exchange for providing their own secret arts, they would in turn be provided with newly developed and expanded magic.

Lab Nine had billed itself as a fusion of modern and ancient magic, but it wasn't exactly a secret that, in reality, it was for developing modern magic that integrated ancient magic techniques and methods. It had been written in the establishment objective in the documents explaining Lab Nine's purpose given to them when the lab had requested help from ancient magicians. As a reward, they promised only money, facilities, and social status—there was no rule saying they'd provide them with new magic.

The idea that they would receive secret arts in return for offering secret arts was no more than a fiction of their narrow sensibilities, and it could even be said that it was childish to assume it was a matter of course.

"But if all that's true, then why are they scattered around Kyoto and away from Nara, which is both their birthplace and destination? I don't have any idea."

"Really?" Tatsuya asked smoothly. "Their motives for calling themselves Traditionalists aside, the reason they left Nara is fairly clear."

"Huh?" Minoru widened his eyes.

"The Traditionalists aren't a monolithic group—you're the one who taught me that."

"Well, yes. I did say that…"

"Then wouldn't there be a pretty massive variation in how they feel toward the old Lab Nine? The ones with stronger, vengeful feelings toward the families of the Nine stayed in Nara. And they've been waiting for their chance for over thirty years."

"How foolish…" Miyuki muttered, in a tone of clear loathing. "If they'd only use that passion for more constructive things, they could contribute to the country and academia."

"Now, don't say that," Tatsuya chided, comfortingly combing his fingers through her hair. "Most people can't keep looking forward all the time through every situation, can they? At least, not as far as we've seen."

Forefront in Tatsuya's mind were his own father and the man's current wife.

"…I suppose not."

Miyuki's smile sunk a bit as she nodded, doubtless because she'd envisioned the same faces he had.

His hand movements stroking her hair became a little rougher.

Miyuki puffed out her cheeks slightly and looked up at him. Her eyes, though, were smiling.

Tatsuya, also smiling, removed his hand from her hair.

"But for the ones who stayed in Nara, even though their goals are backward, you could say they're still trying to move forward with their actions."

Miyuki gave him a mystified look. And of course, Tatsuya wasn't planning on ending the conversation on such a high-and-mighty note.

"The ones who moved their bases to Kyoto may pretend to be resisting the old Lab Nine, but I think they're probably just scared of it and the associated families."

"They were scared? I don't recall the Kudou, the Kumo, or the Kuzumi ever making threats or actually attacking any ancient magicians who helped in the research…" Minoru objected, although he sounded slightly uncertain. All this history happened before he was born, and he hesitated to ask questions about it directly. His knowledge was based on hearsay, which was why his attitude was indecisive.

"I don't think they did, either. The magicians of the Nine were among those experimented on, to boot. They see themselves as the victims when it comes to the ancient magicians, not the victimizers. Since they were all test subjects at Lab Nine together, there wouldn't have been any enmity."

Calm returned to Minoru's uneasy, wavering eyes. Tatsuya's own viewpoint was also only speculation, but Minoru must have been relieved he'd gotten an agreement to his own remark.

"I think the Traditionalist ancient magicians were scared of their own shadows, to an extent. The government controlled Lab Nine, so if they were resentful about being taken advantage of, it would make sense to turn it on the government. But they decided the families of the Nine, who were test dummies like them, are the enemy. They probably know they're taking it out on the wrong people just as much as anyone else."

Tatsuya paused and reflected on his thoughts for a moment. "Either they didn't want to don the shameful label of *rebels* or they simply didn't have the guts to oppose the government... Either way, since they knew, in truth, that their grudge against the families of the Nine was unfounded, they may have been afraid they'd be exposed to irrational violence themselves. They would have personally seen the true power of the magicians that Lab Nine created. And those magicians don't have a responsibility to oblige them and wait obediently like cannon fodder. If the ancient magicians attack, it's only natural to expect retaliation—with the magic they helped create, of course."

Perhaps thinking something was funny, Tatsuya gave a wicked grin. "Or maybe they took the saber-rattling too far and found themselves unable to back down. Maybe, at first, the leaders of each group reined in the extreme discontent of younger mages by blaming the families of the Nine. It could be that one group discovered they couldn't put their flag back down after raising it and stayed close to Lab Nine, while the other groups left for Kyoto. And *maybe* the idea that separate denominations have separate bases is just a façade, and they simply changed their signboards based on their differences in viewpoint. The Traditionalists aren't loyal to *true* traditions, are they?"

The last question was directed at Minoru.

"Yes..." he agreed, nodding at the assessment. "I've heard some of the ancient magicians who participated in Lab Nine's experiments actually belonged to several different denominations."

"But is a silly reason like that reason enough to keep this petty harassment up for decades?" asked Miyuki, not with a face of disbelief but with one that didn't want to acknowledge the sheer ridiculousness.

"They've probably only been doing it for such a long time *because* they've kept to petty harassment," Tatsuya replied, implying that if they'd taken more decisively hostile behavior, these groups would have been stamped out long ago.

His sister seemed convinced by this. In the end, the one who tilted her head at Tatsuya's answer was Minami.

"However, Big Brother Tatsuya..." There may have been no reason to hide the fact in front of Minoru, but Minami used her outdoor nickname for him just in case. "I agree that what you're saying seems plausible, but..."

Hesitating at that point was only natural given her position. However, driven by a sort of sense of duty, she didn't fumble her next words.

"If that's true, would the Traditionalists in Kyoto really be harboring a foreign magician who caused several disasters in Japan?"

*That was sharp of her to notice*, thought Minoru.

But Tatsuya's answer came with virtually no delay. "This is merely an idea, but I wonder if they actually wanted to decline to help. I think they were maybe in too deeply involved with Gongjin Zhou and couldn't pull out of the agreement."

"Was there some reason they couldn't sever ties?"

"I think Minoru would know that better than me, but the Traditionalists were taking in a stream of defected immortalists from Gongjin Zhou. On the surface, it looks like the Traditionalists helped him, but in reality, Zhou was the one helping them bolster their combat forces."

Tatsuya looked to Minoru, who nodded.

"Some of the attackers the other day in Nara Park were immortalists from China, too. We can assume the defected immortalists wield a certain degree of influence within the Traditionalists. Enough that the organization wouldn't be able to withstand infighting or splintering."

Minami silently thanked Tatsuya, a sign her doubts were resolved.

He returned it with a slight nod, then looked at Minoru. "We got pretty far off track, but anyway, that's why I want to look for the bases in the city. Our suspects are Kiyomizu-dera, Kinkaku-ji, and Tenryuu-ji, right?"

"Yes, that's right."

Tatsuya opened up a map—not by taking out an information terminal, but in his mind.

"Kinkaku-ji and Tenryuu-ji are in the same direction, but Kiyomizu-dera is on a different route…"

"Either way, we should probably meet up with Yoshida and the others for now," Miyuki proposed, looking at her own information terminal.

She was right—whether they decided to go on the route that had two temples or the other route that only had one, they would end up passing by the New Conference Hall.

But Tatsuya shook his head. "We don't really have time to join up with them. Thanks to Minoru, we've narrowed down the search area, but there's still only four of us. And it's also possible I'm reading this wrong and they're not hiding in the city at all."

The undeniable fact was that four people was too few to conduct a search like this in the first place. Detectives in stories could solve crimes all by themselves because the criminal conveniently appeared for them; weeding out a hidden suspect in reality required the manpower of an entire police force, or the equipment to match.

Unfortunately, none of the magic Tatsuya or Miyuki had learned could serve as wide-area surveillance cameras. Besides, if cameras were all it would take to find Zhou, Tatsuya wouldn't have been brought onboard at all.

"I understand. Where shall we go first, then?"

He must have had an answer in mind already. Tatsuya immediately responded to Miyuki's question.

"To Kiyomizu-dera. After that, we'll check Kinkaku-ji and Tenryuu-ji."

After splitting up with Tatsuya, Mikihiko had been walking around the New Conference Hall neighborhood, making a show of using a search spell, as they'd decided on last week. Since the conference hall was made for foreigners to use, hotels had been established nearby, as had a forested park. They looked out on a large pond, though it did not match the size of Takaragaike at the hall; a verdant, hilly copse unmarred by urban development wrapped around the water.

Erika and Leo followed right behind Mikihiko, engaged in idle banter but never neglecting to be attentive of their surroundings while serving as bodyguards.

The situation changed at about the time Tatsuya decided on Kiyomizu-dera as their group's next destination. Mikihiko had just been observing the competition venue from the opposite bank of Takaragaike.

Mikihiko was the first to notice the stifled presence drifting to them from the slightly elevated mountains behind them, with Erika and Leo sensing it not more than a moment later.

Erika dashed to Mikihiko's left side, tilting her parasol to look at him from underneath it—it was probably for camouflage, but the action almost seemed like someone about to grab a lover out of affection—and whispered, "Looks like we have company."

Leo stuck his head in to get between Erika and Mikihiko, then also whispered in a low voice, "From the mountains?" Whether he was quick on the uptake or just had a good relationship with them, the acting was pretty realistic.

Unfortunately, Mikihiko wasn't as versatile an actor as the two of them, but he still frowned in unease, turned around to Leo, and warned, "I only sense them from the mountains, but that doesn't mean the enemy won't come from elsewhere. And it might not only be humans who attack us. Be careful."

"Look at those kids, all grown-up with their love triangle."

"They just look like flirting-obsessed students. Do we really need to risk taking them out?"

This sort of conversation was being had among nine men who were hidden behind a grove and looking down at Mikihiko and the others.

They were speaking out loud, normally. Their whispers were faint, just barely audible, but they weren't using any spell to talk without sound, or a communicator that would pick up lip movements with a camera and convert it into a voice to be sent through an osteophonic speaker; doing that would have increased the danger of eavesdropping, as well as someone detecting the waves—magic or electromagnetic—even if they couldn't intercept the conversation itself.

They were having such a silly conversation despite all their caution because Erika's and Leo's presences—and acting, of course—were peaceful, no different from the boys and girls walking down a busy street.

Some, of course, were still tense.

"You've been watching the boy—he's not trying to hide the fact he's using a *shiki*. He may be a child, but he's a direct descendant of the Yoshida. We can't afford to let him go."

A remark to admonish the others of their slipup.

"But I heard the second son of the Yoshida had lost his power."

At the raised question, a middle-aged man, probably the leader of the bunch, scolded him in a significantly more severe tone. "Old intel. Mikihiko Yoshida has regained his power—power said to be higher than that of the first son and heir. Brace yourselves and get them. Make sure you put them to sleep. You can wound them somewhat, as long as you don't kill them."

The man who was scolded certainly didn't look convinced, but he didn't say any more. Instead, he took out a scroll, small enough to fit in his palm, from his inside pocket.

The other *seven*, including the leader, followed suit. The white-haired *Taoist* waiting at the rear took no action, watching without a word.

"Hah!"

Erika was the one to react to the enemy's initial attack. She vigorously swung the parasol in her hand toward the presence approaching from behind. A piece of it slipped out, ramming into a pale blue will-o'-the-wisp in midair, bursting into flames. Several more rained down on the three of them, piercing the umbrella, which she knocked out of the air with a weapon hidden inside the umbrella's handle.

For a second and third successive wave of will-o'-the-wisps, too, she used an armament device—a slender, silver-colored staff; perhaps it could be called a rod—to intercept.

It was an integrated armament CAD that Tatsuya had, in great haste, asked FLT R & D Section 3 create and then lend to Erika for this Kyoto reconnaissance. The activation sequences recorded in it were momentum-control and acceleration spells that focused on speed rather than weight. It was a fiendish thing—because the weapon was accelerated along with the body, it meant that if too much strength was applied, the user's arm wouldn't be able to keep up with the silver rod's movements, leading to injury for bones or tendons. However, Erika had easily mastered it on day one.

The wispy rain stopped. But that wouldn't mean, of course, that the assault had ended.

Wind blades came for them this time, whipping up the colored red and yellow leaves. Erika had brought down substance-less demonic flames, but could she intercept blades of wind without any color or form?

An intrepid smile worked its way onto her face, but after hearing a voice filled with confidence saying "Leave this to me," she returned to a one-handed, centered stance.

Mikihiko would challenge the wind-razors in her place.

He chose magic from his spell assistance tool, which was composed of several metallic amulets gathered together in the shape of a fan. His choice of spell was blades of wind, just like the enemy.

Several tiny sparks broke out in midair. Despite having cast the spell after, Mikihiko's wind deflected all of the enemy's blades.

Erika and Mikihiko were both intently waiting for the next attack to come down from the air.

Then the shadow of a tree on the ground behind them took human form.

A black shade abruptly stood up.

Without a sound, without adjusting its presence or even the air around it, it closed in on Mikihiko from behind.

"Uryaahhh!"

Leo roared at the shadow. His fist howled, punching into the man in the black sweater.

The man, while being punched by Leo, jumped back himself to neutralize the impact, then somersaulted backward and out of range.

"Are these guys ninjas or somethin'?"

When he looked more closely, the sweater he'd perceived as black was actually dark green. The slim pants the man wore were the same color. The outfit was completely different from traditional ninja garb—it was more modern, more sensible. But he didn't need to see the kunai ready in his right hand and the scroll in his left to know the person was a trained ninja.

The number of attackers multiplied—three, then five. Leo couldn't see where they'd come from.

"Heh. Interesting."

But that wasn't enough to crush his spirit. Leo didn't have the problematic habit of purposely seeking out strong opponents, but he did have a tendency to get more fired up the stronger his enemies were rather than grow timid.

And perhaps it was the genes of his grandfather, who had been *created* as a biological weapon, that made him do that. Leo occasionally thought so himself.

But every time he did, he asked himself,

*So what?*

It was a lot better than giving up before the fight even started. If his spirit broke, he wouldn't even be able to run away. That was his creed.

Letting his spirit break was the same as surrendering his life. Escaping was something you did because you believed you could. Because you hadn't given up on escaping. When faced with a tiger baring its fangs, could a person say to themselves *run*, then be able to get away? Wouldn't they either flee blindly without thinking or stand there dumbly having given up survival?

*That's the* worst *kind of death—and the one I can't tolerate. I will fight, and I will live.*

The sweater-wearing ninjas inched back, widening the distance between them and Leo. Whether consciously or not, they'd withdrawn from him.

At *his side*, a scream went up.

A ninja who had blocked Erika's silver rod with his arm was hunched over, grasping at it. His position being so far away from her was the result of two factors: He'd jumped away to get out of her range, and she hadn't followed up on her attack out of caution.

"Leo, keep your spirit hot, but your mind cool. You're not fighting alone."

Erika's comment made Leo realize he was about to get ambushed from the side.

"Sorry—thanks."

The sound of wind blades spraying sparks as they rammed into things reached Leo's ears.

"You too, Mikihiko. Thanks—I was supposed to be the one doing the guarding."

"You protected me from their shadow-melding surprise attack, didn't you? The feeling's mutual."

"Okay then. Let's leave it at that."

Leo took his knuckle-dusters out of his pocket and put them on. They only looked like plastic toys, so even if a police officer saw them, he could pass them off as a fashion statement.

If that was all they were, anyway.

An activation sequence coiled up his left wrist before being absorbed.

This wasn't his usual voice-input CAD.

It was the activation sequence output of a fully thought-controlled, specialized CAD, the latest product of Rosen Magicraft, a German CAD manufacturer. Leo had obtained it through a certain connection—well, received it as a sign of certain *apology*—and lately, he'd just been getting the hang of it.

Their current inspection trip demanded they not stand out too much.

That was also why Erika had hidden an armament device in her parasol.

His usual CAD basically gave off the impression to anyone who saw that he was ready for combat, so he'd brought this one along on the trip instead.

The expansion speed of an activation sequence depended on the hardware, while the construction efficiency of a magic program depended on the software. The latest CADs showed exceeding processing speed that made up for the time lag, and since Tatsuya had personally optimized the activation sequences, they could build magic programs so quickly that their effects would manifest at nearly the exact moment he intended them to.

His plastic knuckle-dusters gained the hardness of solid metal.

Then another activation sequence came.

This time, his completely unremarkable long-sleeved shirt and jeans quickly changed into the highest-efficiency bulletproof, stab-proof clothing.

"All right, I'm ready this time." Leo clapped his left and right fists together with a *clank*.

"Leave your flanks to me." Erika waggled her silver-colored armament device and assumed a stance.

"I'll back you up." Mikihiko fanned open his spell tool.

"Let's go! Orahhh!" Leo let out a roar, then charged.

Of course, the enemy *ninjutsu* users didn't just sit idly by. The leaves sprang up on Leo's path, blocking his view—wind magic splashing up the fallen leaves.

By itself, it wasn't lethal. But instead of stopping, Leo raised his arms and covered his face.

He felt light impacts on his arms, chest, and thighs. Kunai, thrown by the enemy.

They'd possessed speed unthinkable for physically thrown objects, but they didn't pierce Leo's hardening magic.

From behind him, another gust blew through.

Thanks to Mikihiko's magic, his view cleared.

The *ninjutsu* user standing in front of him put his scroll in his mouth, then used his other hand, now free after throwing the kunai, to undo its seal.

The enemy before him was nothing like the historical ninja, but a magician of the ancient style that possessed real power. Leo

understood that, but when the man struck such a clichéd pose, it actually threw him off.

It didn't dull Leo's charge, but his attention was elsewhere for a moment.

The *ninjutsu* user's chest swelled, then immediately deflated.

A sharp noise came from him, and dizziness assailed Leo.

The man hadn't actually been holding a scroll in his mouth—it was a flute made to look like a scroll. And not just any flute—it was probably one that activated a spell that interfered with an opponent's sensory organs via sound.

The ninja pulled out a large knife. Not a katana, but a knife—it seemed even magical ninjas couldn't fight the flow of time.

Furthermore, the man must have been confident in his technique, as he didn't hesitate a moment in launching his attack.

His miscalculation came, instead, from how the specs of Leo's physical body were far above those of a normal person. Leo's magical talent was low when graded on the general evaluation scale, but on the other hand, he was easily top-class when it came to physical abilities. Even with his sense of balance thrown off, he used his other senses to make up for it, maintaining control over his body.

He punched the enemy's thrust-out knife with his right hand. His knuckle-dusters met the knife's tip, and the impact knocked it right out of the man's hand.

A left hook, slightly downward.

Leo's fist crushed the man's jaw.

"Ah, shit!"

That unintended swear was an expression of regret at having put too much force into the attack. It showed his inexperience and was a weakness that one could take advantage of—but Leo was also fast enough at shifting gears to make up for it.

The next enemy appeared from behind his fallen comrade. This one had his mouth aimed at Leo.

On the spur of the moment, Leo ducked.

Flames exploded from the man's mouth.

The band of fire passed over Leo's head, then wheeled around in midair to attack the caster. It scorched the assailant's face, and he fell down after being thrown into a somersault.

The flames had done a U-turn because of a spell Mikihiko had cast.

Behind Leo, Mikihiko frowned at the wretched sight he'd helped create. But he still didn't hesitate with his next attack. He wove his next spell.

Erika, like she'd said herself, had been intercepting one side of the *ninjutsu* users who were trying to catch Leo in a pincer attack. Her slender weapon lacked the power of her usual katana, but it won out in speed. After a sharp strike made an enemy combatant drop his knife, his body split into two a moment later.

"Afterimages?!" she cried out as the twin ninjas readied their kunai in an identical manner, smirks and all.

But each look soon changed to shock.

One of the afterimages faded, and the man returned to a single person. Not on purpose, as one could tell from his expression. Mikihiko's spirit magic had broken the *ninjutsu* technique.

And Erika would never let go of an opening like that.

Four times, a silver arc trailed through air.

The *ninjutsu* user, a bone in each of his limbs cleanly broken, fell to the ground before a weak lightning attack flew at him.

The electric light coiled over all the assailants.

The eight *ninjutsu* users, already having lost the power to fight, then lost their consciousnesses, too, to Mikihiko's lightning magic.

Mikihiko let out a long breath.

"Is this all of them?" Leo asked, looking around.

Erika, who had remained cautious even after the fighting, lowered her weapon. "Doesn't seem like there's any reinforcements at the moment."

Leo breathed a sigh of relief. "Still. Ninjas? Really?" he asked, letting out a chuckle. He knew they existed, but he'd never thought he'd end up brawling with one.

Erika, though, didn't empathize with his laughter, instead replying shortly, "More specifically, *ninjutsu* users. It's not that strange. This place is crawling with ancient magicians."

"Yeah," Mikihiko agreed, "not too far from here are the birthplaces of Iga and Kouga *ninjutsu*. There's supposedly an ancient magician base in Mount Kurama, too, structured around *ninjutsu* users. Maybe that's where these people were from."

"Hmm. You think so? That's interesting. You know, I'm never bored when I'm around you two."

But Leo didn't take offense to it. In fact, his smile had grown even more entertained.

"Wait a minute—would you stop pinning things on me? We have Tatsuya to thank for getting tangled up in *this* incident."

Not to *blame*, but to *thank*. Erika was pretending to complain, but she was obviously of the same mind as Leo.

"You're not wrong," nodded Leo with a wry grin. He looked to the side and saw Mikihiko giving one of his own.

"Anyway, what do we do with them? Hand them over to the police?"

Erika had no qualms calling the police. Not just because she had connections there, but because she had zero doubts about her actions being justified this time around.

"The police? Hmm…"

Leo, in contrast, appeared to feel the opposite. But it wasn't enough for him to oppose her viewpoint.

"Would that be appropriate…?" Mikihiko asked, taking out an information terminal with his free hand. He seemed to be willing to handle the call to emergency services himself.

But his finger stopped right before he booted up his voice call function.

Then he shoved the terminal into his pocket, probably an unconscious move.

With his fan device at the ready, he glared into the woods. A lump of psions leaped from his hands. He'd released a search *shikigami*.

"Bad guys?!"

Mikihiko didn't have time to answer Leo's question.

"Look!" Erika called out at the same time as Mikihiko felt the spell trigger.

Her eyes were focused on the pond.

Leo and Mikihiko looked that way, too.

—Just as four small, watery monsters jumped out of it.

"Compound forms?!" shouted Leo.

"No! Puppet *shiki* demons made from water—like golems! They have solid form!" Mikihiko cried in response, staring at the monsters without even blinking. "A *lingling*? A *heyu*? A *changyou*? And even a *fuzhu*?" he muttered, voice rife with surprise.

A cow-like beast with a tiger-stripe pattern on its body—the *lingling*.

A boar with the face of a man—the *heyu*.

A long-armed ape with four arms—the *changyou*.

A deer with four horns—the *fuzhu*.

All of them were Chinese monsters said to cause flooding—and these were miniaturized versions of them. This was clearly a spell from a Chinese mainland ancient magician.

"The hell are these?!" yelled Leo.

"Enemy spell! The rest doesn't matter!" Erika shouted back, swinging her silver rod at the *changyou* puppet, the one that landed closest to her.

It wasn't a range in which her weapon would reach.

What did reach, though, was a razor-sharp blade of psions.

Erika's typeless magic carved through the spell holding the golem together. The imitation monster, formed of water, turned back into water and scattered.

But there was no time to be relieved.

The monsters numbered more than just those four.

More *lingling*, *heyu*, *changyou*, and *fuzhu* continued bounding out of the pond and onto land. Their visual creepiness aside, the monsters, the size of household dogs, weren't large enough to be threatening. But with this many of them, even small dogs couldn't be ignored. All the more so when they were magical creations. It wasn't clear what sort of abilities they possessed.

"Crap. We should get out of—huh?"

Erika, about to propose a retreat, fell silent before finishing.

The miniature monsters weren't swarming to them, but to the *ninjutsu* users lying on the ground.

"...Are they friendly?"

Erika wasn't the only one seized with such extreme surprise that she'd stopped moving. Leo aside—he didn't have any way to attack from a distance—even Mikihiko had stopped breaking the spells, entranced by the sight.

"...?!"

As they watched for what would happen, all three of them gasped.

The miniature monsters given transient bodies of water had begun devouring the living bodies of the paralyzed *ninjutsu* users.

"Are you kidding me?!"

Erika, snapping out of it, swung her silver rod, bringing the type-less magic blade around.

Her voice broke Mikihiko out of his own trance, and he shot a demon-slaying technique: Garudaflame.

The psionic blade ripped through the puppet demons, and the conceptual flames scorched the spells giving them shape.

The aberrant beasts reverted to water.

With cautious footsteps, Leo drew near the *ninjutsu* users, who were moaning in pain. He'd already triggered a hardening spell, of course, but he couldn't help being a little bit timid since his face and neck were exposed.

"Yuck!"

That was the first thing he said after squatting and taking a close look.

"Those are some nasty bites… Doesn't look like they got to the bone, though."

Leo stood up again, then turned to Erika and Mikihiko.

"And they're all alive."

Even paralyzed, they seemed to have protected their vital points—their throats and eyes, if not much else. Hearing that, Mikihiko made a look of relief.

But Erika's face remained stuck in its severe grimace. "That's weird."

"What?" Mikihiko tensed again at her unusual behavior.

"Why isn't the water seeping into the ground?"

The ground here wasn't paved. The water that had been forming the golems would normally have been absorbed into the earth.

But in actuality, the water, mixed with blood, was flowing into the pond.

"Whoa?!" Leo reflexively jumped back. Over thirteen feet, without any lead-up, preparatory action, or magic—his jumping abilities were staggering, but Erika's and Mikihiko's eyes were glued to something else.

A moment after they'd noticed the water's unnatural movements, the flow toward the pond had suddenly intensified. Leo's reaction had been to the rush of blood and water pressing up near his feet.

"What the…?" Erika murmured.

"Enemy spell!" Mikihiko's answer was a warning at the same time.

But maybe it wasn't necessary. The emergency was clear to Erika's and Leo's eyes, too.

The pond water began to swirl.

Slowly, at first, but quickly picking up speed.

And then, with a thunderous noise, from out of the whirlpool came a big, malformed snake made of muddy water, rearing its head.

*"Xiangliu?!"*

A giant serpent with nine human faces. One of the most prominent Chinese mythical beasts, said to be a minister serving directly under *Gonggong*, evil god of floods. It was said that wherever *Xiangliu* appeared, the water would go rancid, transforming the land into a fruitless swampland...

"Dodge!"

Seeing the nine faces open their mouths, Mikihiko shouted to his friends.

At the same time, a barrier of wind expanded. Streams of muddy water shot out of the nine mouths, one at a time.

The three of them each avoided taking a direct hit from the dirty liquid, but only just barely. The swirling wind barrier around them repelled the water splashing off the ground.

But the *ninjutsu* users, who could no longer move, couldn't escape the aftermath.

The men cried out with screams of agony louder than when the miniature monsters had been gnawing away at them.

Their bodies, awash in the muddy water spat out by the snake, began to bubble and melt.

"Acid?!" Erika shrieked.

"No, it's a corrosion curse!" Mikihiko shouted. "Be careful! Unlike acid, it'll even melt parts it doesn't touch!"

Considering that the melting was still spreading on the ninjas, there was no room to doubt the warning.

"Gah! Where's the caster?!"

Given the large crowd of golems under their control, the caster had to have been somewhere nearby.

Actually, though... The spell Mikihiko had thought he'd felt, coming out of the woods earlier—that must have belonged to the magician controlling these monsters. But he hadn't gotten a response yet from the *shikigami* he'd sent out before. Either their enemy was extremely skilled or had some special equipment—a Qimen Dunjia curse tool, for example, which could throw even a magician's sense of direction.

Even with Erika's and Leo's physical abilities, it was all they could do to dodge the cursed streams flying unceasingly from the nine mouths. Mikihiko had his own hands full avoiding a direct hit and keeping the barrier up—he didn't have time to send out another *shikigami.*

"Erika, Leo, let's pull back!"

"Totally agree with you, buddy, but—!"

"How are we supposed to do that?!"

Mikihiko gritted his teeth at Erika's objection.

There was a way. The puppets modeled after legendary, magical beasts drew power from those legends. Thus, using a spell that borrowed the symbol of something higher than them in those legends would cancel out that boost, and the spell itself that maintained the puppets could break. And even if it didn't, it would end up being a contest of brute force between magicians.

*Xiangliu* was kin to an evil god, but it belonged to water. If Mikihiko could access the highest spirit of water, *Ryuujin,* the dragon god, and bring it out…

*Am I able to do that?*

He felt like he could, now.

But his hesitation lingered.

It was the ritual that had caused him to fall into his slump—a slump so bad that he thought he'd lost his power.

But in the end, Mikihiko never made the decision, because a moment later, the need for it vanished.

A brutal psionic light appeared before their eyes, within the nine heads of *Xiangliu,* right in the center of their faces.

The projection of a magic program via the Idea. Psionic information bodies, not fired in a projectile arc, but defined to suddenly manifest at those coordinates.

The nine-headed, human-faced serpent's giant body exploded.

When the space holding the spell materialized, the spell to create the puppet itself also collapsed.

The resulting spray of water was no longer affected by the curse. It had reverted to simple pond water. The corrosion eating away at the *ninjutsu* users' bodies stopped as well.

"Are you all right?"

The three of them didn't need to worry about what had just happened—the answer to that had just appeared in front of them and asked them a question.

A dark-red blouson, slim black pants, black boots, all reminiscent of the Third High uniform. A boy about their age, holding a red, specialized CAD in the shape of a gun. The three, of course, knew who that gallant figure was.

"Masaki Ichijou..."

Leo muttered his name.

The ace of Third High, eldest son of the Ichijou family, which was second highest among the Ten Master Clans, stood before them.

On guard for anyone lying in wait, Masaki was observing their surroundings while trying to sense any presences—any signs of magic being used. But after a while, he determined there were no more hidden enemies and relaxed.

The eight people in front of him were on the ground, all with severe wounds. Masaki had considered the possibility that they were not the victims but the attackers who had the tables turned on them, but they didn't show any signs of moving, so he directed his attention to Mikihiko and the others, partly to confirm the situation.

"Hm? You're from First High...?"

And he remembered Leo's and Mikihiko's faces from battling them in Monolith Code last year.

"I'm Mikihiko Yoshida. Ichijou—thank you for helping us out."

But he didn't seem to have remembered his name in turn. After Mikihiko refreshed his memory, a look of obvious relief washed over Masaki's face.

"Oh, well, you're welcome. The Ten Master Clans can't have malignant magic like that being used in the city. Don't worry about it."

"Still, thanks. Things were taking a pretty dangerous turn for a minute there."

"Ah, yeah... By the way, what in the world *was* all that?"

Was his sudden change in topic a way to cover his embarrassment? If it was, then Masaki must have been rather shy, much more in line with his youth than Tatsuya—though that particular comparison might not have been appropriate.

"Puppet demons, created with a blood offering, made of water, and modeled after monsters of legend—a kind of golem."

"Ancient magic?"

"This spell is used by magicians from China called immortalists."

Erika impatiently butted into Masaki and Mikihiko's Q&A session. "Hey, can we leave the magic lecture for later? That immortalist could still be hiding somewhere around here."

Masaki suddenly looked alert, quickly glancing around. He seemed to have forgotten to consider that possibility.

But Mikihiko shook his head at Erika's words. "No, no need to worry."

"And how do you know for sure?!"

Mikihiko opened his mouth several times but eventually shook his head again. "...Seeing is believing. Let's go check."

"You saying this immortalist or whatever is down for the count?"

Mikihiko nodded, not answering Leo's question verbally.

"You know where he is?" put in Masaki, sounding like he couldn't stop himself from asking.

"You coming too, Ichijou?"

Receiving a question in response, this time Masaki nodded.

* * *

They climbed the sloped woods, making their way through the sparse underbrush. For the four of them, the route wasn't a difficult one. They found the immortalist they were looking for before anyone broke a sweat.

"I figured it wouldn't be a pretty sight—and it's really not, huh?"

The immortalist was lying upside down on the incline, with his head below, and facedown.

"Is he dead…?" Masaki wondered.

Without any visible fear, Leo squatted down next to the white-haired immortalist and put a hand to his neck.

"No pulse. He's probably gone," he announced flatly, unusually impassive. With a dead man in front of him, he obviously couldn't have stated the truth with a smile on his face; his attitude was the most considerate one he could muster.

But his disquieted behavior crumbled the moment he turned the corpse over.

A muffled shriek came from Erika. Even her usual steadiness couldn't ready her to see the man's face in death, which was extreme and shocking.

"…Recoil from his spell being broken," said Mikihiko. "Ancient magicians who predominantly use puppets maintain a constant mental link between themselves and their spells, even after casting them."

"Really?" chimed in Masaki. "That's fairly different from modern magic—when we cast a spell, we cut off the magic program from the magician so that reversal of information flow won't happen."

Right after that, though, he realized the true meaning behind Mikihiko's words and unconsciously frowned.

"You mean since I destroyed that monster along with its spell, he took so much mental damage that he died…"

"It's not your fault. Those who use this type of magic understand the risks. Especially when using a puppet that huge. It's only natural the recoil would be similarly massive. It may sound cold, but this mage reaped what he sowed."

"I see…"

This wasn't the first time Masaki had ever directly caused someone's death—killed someone. But all the times he'd taken life were in situations where he'd been forced to do so; and he still considered blowing up that water monster with Burst the correct decision.

But witnessing this old man's death was so brutal that even *he* couldn't fully justify it to himself.

"…Sorry, Yoshida. You were concerned for me."

"Don't worry about it. We were the ones who got rescued, after all."

Seeing that Masaki was doing his best to keep a smile on his face, Mikihiko flashed him a smile as well, waving off the other boy's apology.

"We can take care of explaining all this to the police, Ichijou."

Masaki, though, couldn't agree to the words *so you can go now* that Mikihiko had left unspoken. "No, I'll come, too. More importantly, the girl over there—umm…"

"Erika Chiba. No need to walk on eggshells with me. I'm used to this stuff."

Those words made Masaki's eyes widen. He froze. But then, perhaps deciding such a reaction was even ruder, he quickly rebooted himself. "Oh. Are you part of the Chiba family…?"

"Erika Chiba, *junior at First High.*"

Masaki blinked at her brusque reply. Aside from his little sister, he'd almost never been treated so curtly by a girl his age. "My apologies. I'm Masaki Ichijou, a junior at Third High," he said, realizing he hadn't introduced himself yet, and determined to quash the awkwardness.

"That's nice of ya. I'm Leonhard Saijou, a junior at First High." Then, in a bright tone of voice that dispelled the uncomfortable mood—probably purposefully—Leo introduced himself to Masaki.

"Anyway, don't you have friends to get back to? You don't need to hold back or anything. We'll handle things here."

"No, don't mind me. I came to Kyoto alone. I'm here to scope things out before the Thesis Competition so that nothing like last year happens again. My schedule lines up."

"Oh? We're here for the same thing, actually. We're staying at—actually, we should call this in to the police first."

Even as Leo said that—"Oh, hello? I'm Erika Chiba, a junior at the National Magic University First Affiliated High School. I'd like to talk to the Magical Crimes Division... Yes, we just came under magic-based attack... We're at..."

Hearing her voice, though, Leo and Masaki exchanged wry grins.

At just about the same time as their fierce battle was ending thanks to Masaki's intervention, on the opposite shore of the pond across from the Kyoto New International Conference Hall, Tatsuya's party made it to the path leading to Kiyomizu-dera.

Tatsuya hadn't chosen to visit this temple first for any deep reason. He simply figured that out of the three places, this was the mostly likely place for *something* to be.

With the first "barbarian-subjugating" shogun, Sakanoue no Tamuramaro, being involved in its creation, as well as an episode in which the temple apparently contributed to the suppression of eastern Japan with magic, it was a natural place for ascetic training, known for miracle-workings. It was of the North Hosso religious sect, but Tatsuya knew from the Kyoto-related information he'd stuffed into his head that, historically, it had connections to esoteric Buddhism. In addition, the Hosso sect itself shared something in common with modern magic—an emphasis on the employment of the unconscious region of the brain. Still, to put it bluntly, it was just one of three choices, so here they were.

The approach to Kiyomizu-dera of Otowa Mountain was a long, uphill slope. It was made so commuters could go partway up, but Tatsuya and the others decided to walk starting from the foot of the mountain. Minoru actually knew there *was* a Traditionalist base nearby, but not its precise location. And so they'd decided to climb slowly, checking everywhere for suspicious-looking buildings.

The path to the temple was just as lively as it had been a century ago. During the world war, tourism in the area had greatly diminished, but thanks to the catchphrase "Rediscover Japan," a larger number of Japanese tourists visited when they couldn't go on overseas trips, so the local economy hadn't taken much of a blow.

At a glance, the hilly road was mobbed with visitors sightseeing around the temple, some with different skin color, hair color, or eye color.

"Wow, there's a lot of people here…" murmured Tatsuya in spite of himself.

"I thought Tokyo had more people, didn't it?" said Minoru, tilting his head in mild confusion.

That moment, a human pileup occurred. The source was several female tourists entranced by Minoru—and, even more impressive, not only young women, either.

People had thankfully been giving Tatsuya's group a wide berth for some time now, so Miyuki and Minami didn't get wrapped up in the minor commotion. The roundabout, peeping stares were annoying, but fortunately, they had both been keeping an eye on the other, leaving enough distance between them.

Of course, Miyuki was clinging to Tatsuya's side, so even if they *were* being swarmed by people, she wouldn't get caught up by them. He'd resort to brute force before letting that happened.

After checking to make sure Miyuki was okay anyway, Tatsuya answered Minoru. "We technically live in Tokyo, but we're pretty far out. Anyway, I don't remember Kyoto Station being this crowded."

"I wonder about that… Maybe it just looks more crowded since there's less room."

"I guess you could say that." Tatsuya had been referring not to the total number of people but to the density, but it wasn't anything worth arguing about, so he didn't object again. "By the way, Minoru—should we be aiming for the Kiyomizu-dera grounds for now?"

"Yes. This close to a city, being in the mountain forests would be more conspicuous. I expect they'll be disguised as a gift shop or an eatery."

"Then we'll have little need to go inside."

As soon as Tatsuya said that, a heavy pressure settled down over top of him like thick snow clouds. A gaze of unmistakable disapproval.

He turned to his left.

"Is something the matter, Brother?"

And there he saw Miyuki smiling modestly.

Any other boy might have chalked it up to an overactive imagination, but Tatsuya wasn't fooled. He'd never mistake her gaze, nor that of several others for that matter.

"Do you want to visit?"

Miyuki's eyes wandered, but it only lasted a moment. "We came all the way here, after all…"

No matter how she beat around the bush, she meant one thing.

*I might have to rearrange today's schedule*, thought Tatsuya.

From the world-class cypress stage set in front of the famous Kiyomizu-dera's main building, the quartet looked out on the scenery of Kyoto.

To Tatsuya's eyes, it looked like the streets were covered in a thin haze of psionic light billowing from the people and the land. Any other magician should have been able to see the same, though the haze might have been lighter or darker. But even narrowing his focus to where psions ran thinner and using Elemental Sight, there was no telling how long it would take to find the data they needed. Tatsuya had never met his target, Gongjin Zhou, after all; and a photograph was an insufficient search key.

Stopping his pointless "sightseeing," Tatsuya spoke to Minoru, who was peering down onto the city in the same way. "See anything?"

"No, not with this many people... Have you noticed anything?"

"Nope, I'm in the same boat," Tatsuya said, as he turned to glance over to Miyuki and Minami.

They were leaning slightly over the stage's handrail, reveling in the view below. Neither of them was the type to cry with glee, so from another person's point of view, it may have only looked like they were nervously gauging the height of the stage. But Tatsuya could tell they were both having fun, innocently having forgotten all about the job they were here for.

"I tried checking every set of eyes *on Miyuki*, but none of them were suspicious."

"Wait, all of them?"

"Yeah. I've noticed a heap of indecent looks, but that goes for you too, Minoru. None of them seemed to have anything to do with our job."

"That's... I'm sorry for making you do all that."

Innumerable men gazing with desire at Miyuki.

Innumerable women gazing with desire at Minoru.

Minoru was aware of the attention he drew to himself. That wasn't narcissism speaking—it was objective fact. Because of that, he found it hard to tell when someone was actually hostile. He also understood that the amount of information someone would need to process this was ludicrous.

"No, I'm used to it. Happens all the time."

But for Tatsuya, this really was a daily occurrence. Still, the only thought waves he filtered were the ones focusing on Miyuki. Even in this state, he could discern hostility directed at him, but he wasn't confident at all that he could tell if someone was directing emotions other than kindness and desire toward Minoru.

And worryingly, the one with the highest chance of the Traditionalists seeing as an enemy was Minoru.

"I don't know if we'll get anywhere like this," Tatsuya murmured.

Minoru visibly shrunk in place. He felt, reflexively, that he'd been criticized, but his making a face like a scolded puppy only made the eyes on him more intense.

With emotions this strong coming in, Tatsuya would notice them even if they weren't meant for him. And he'd *certainly* notice the shift in emotions of the younger boy who caused them, too.

"Hey, I wasn't criticizing you. You're really helping us out here. I was just thinking we have fewer clues than I thought we'd get."

Minoru responded with a bright smile.

*Clap-clap* came the sound of staggering footsteps and people grabbing hold of railings and pillars. Tatsuya had a pretty good idea of what was happening without looking, so he didn't bother glancing over, but Miyuki seemed interested in the noise. After moving her gaze from outside the stage to inside, comprehension immediately came across her face.

She went over to Tatsuya and Miyuki, then faced Tatsuya as if to defend Minoru.

"Brother, you mustn't bully Minoru."

Tatsuya probably hadn't meant any harm, but this was like pouring oil on a flame.

Actually, considering what had happened, maybe it was the opposite.

This formation, a girl unequaled in beauty defending a boy unequaled in beauty.

The men looking at Miyuki and the women looking at Minoru all froze at once.

The strange air propagated to the temple visitors who were actually there for *regular sightseeing* as well.

They wondered what was going on, looked this way—and hardened up, all the same.

Time froze on the Kiyomizu-dera stage.

Tatsuya looked around in bewilderment. His honest impression was *Okay, come on, you're all exaggerating*, but it didn't matter how much he tried to reject the reality happening before his eyes.

The female tourists were looking at Minoru. But there were several exceptions.

The male tourists were looking at Miyuki. But there were several exceptions to this, too, and these gazes were more persistent than the female exceptions.

*Perverts*, thought Tatsuya in disgust. He was a man with a warped sense of morality—he didn't feel any aversion to killing others. But his opinion on same-gender sexuality was stereotypical: Platonic relationships were one thing, but physical desire was altogether off-putting.

Not only to ease the situation, but to escape from these unpleasant stares—even the ones directed toward his acquaintances and not him were still unpleasant—he decided to leave the place at once.

After making his decision, he checked the faces of all those who warranted caution. He wouldn't be able to stand getting mixed up with them later, and he wanted to avoid it before it got to that.

As he did so, he spotted a different stare.

Not an unusual one, but a *different* one.

One man was looking at Minoru.

Just like the other people frozen in place.

However.

It was not kindness,

nor desire,

nor admiration in his eyes—

but annoyance and mild shock.

It was written all over the man's face: *They made me keep an eye on a kid like this?*

And what came up in the back of Tatsuya's mind was an out-of-place thought: *Is this what they call a lucky break?*

"Minoru, Miyuki, Minami. Let's get out of here."

Without waiting for an answer from his traveling companions, he proceeded back to the approach that lead to the temple.

Perhaps having deduced his intent from only that, Miyuki silently obeyed.

Minami made a look of confusion for a moment but quickly followed Miyuki.

But Minoru couldn't resist asking a question. Hurrying to follow Minami, he went past her and Miyuki and next to Tatsuya. "What's wrong all of a sudden?"

The person shadowing them hadn't used magic, so of course Minoru hadn't noticed him. And with his looks, you could say it was inevitable he'd be less perceptive when it came to noticing who was watching him.

In all likelihood, the man watching them—or rather, Minoru—wasn't just not using magic; he *couldn't* use it. They'd probably hired a private investigator instead of a magician or something, predicting that Tatsuya and the others would be on their guard against Traditionalist magicians. Tatsuya thought it was a pretty interesting perspective.

Instead of answering Minoru's question, Tatsuya took an information terminal and stylus out of his pocket. After opening the terminal, he wrote on the screen with the stylus. The handwritten characters were converted into digital, one phrase at a time. When Minoru peered at the display, he saw what Tatsuya had written:

*"I think I spotted a tail. I'll lure him in. Pretend you notice but don't know where."*

Minoru cocked his head, probably because he didn't get what the last sentence meant. But a moment later, he understood—he was supposed to pretend he'd noticed something but couldn't spot them—and began his act of looking left and right uneasily and turning in wrong directions.

Frankly speaking, his acting was bad. So bad that Tatsuya, watching out of the corner of his eye, decided he clearly hadn't ever been trained in anything but magic.

Pretending *not* to notice would have been one thing, but even their tail didn't seem to think his target would be pretending *to* notice. Either the man Tatsuya had marked was confident in his abilities or simply second-rate—he was following Minoru at a fixed distance.

As Tatsuya descended the hilly road from the Inner Shrine to the Otowa Waterfall, he stopped at the fork in the road that led to the Tower of Safe Childbirth.

He turned around to Miyuki and the others. Indeed, with the mannerism of discussing which way they should go, while keeping the tail in the corner of his vision.

The man must have thought it would be unnatural to stop with them; he took out a small camera and began taking pictures of the stage at the main temple. That wasn't a particularly unusual thing for a sightseer to do, per se. But it *was* unnatural to keep taking the same picture over and over again. Perhaps not realizing Tatsuya was spying on him, the man made a bitter expression and began to walk toward the Otowa Waterfall.

"Hey, you," Tatsuya called at the man's back, pretending to be annoyed.

A jolt ran up the tail's spine. But then the man moved to leave, pretending not to have heard him.

"Did you not hear me? You, you there!"

Tatsuya quickly walked toward the man from behind. Tatsuya's features were sharp to begin with, so his fake display of anger had a visual impact. The tourists nearby looked over at them, wondering what was happening.

"Did…did you need something?"

The man turned around, a timid look on his face. At a glance, the scene looked like an upstanding citizen getting involved with a delinquent student. The tail's face made him seem like nothing but a regular working-class man; his acting skill was decent. Had Tatsuya been alone, the onlookers might have sided with the tail.

"You were secretly taking pictures of my friends, weren't you?"

But with that, the gallery's hostility immediately turned on the tail. Without a doubt, they now believed that snapping peeping photos of a beautiful girl like Miyuki and a beautiful boy like Minoru was definitely something this sort of unremarkable older man would do.

"That's not true! What proof do you have?!"

The man loudly proclaimed his innocence, but an array of cold, scornful glares began to coil around him. Noticing the onlookers' gazes on the camera he was holding, the tail hastily shoved his small camera into his shoulder bag. The act made the suspicions look even more truthful.

"We'll let the police decide if it's true or not," asserted Tatsuya decisively. The peanut gallery was now completely on his side.

Suddenly, the tail began to run, pushing through the crowd. Exactly what Tatsuya wanted him to do.

Before he'd even escaped more than a few steps, Tatsuya had easily taken him down.

Tatsuya brought the tail into the shadows. A few in the peanut gallery had tried to report it to the police before that, but Tatsuya stopped them by having Minoru tell them that he felt sorry for the man, since he didn't want to ruin his life by unnecessarily involving the police.

The man's timid-looking expression immediately warped into a hateful one as he looked at Tatsuya.

Tatsuya looked back impassively.

The man wavered; looking into the young boy's eyes were like staring into a machine's.

"What do you plan to do with me?"

"With you, personally? Nothing."

Suspicion surfaced in the tail's expression.

"I know this goes against work ethics, but I'm asking anyway. Where is your employer?"

The man's eyes wandered left and right. Probably looking for an escape route out of reflex. Tatsuya and the others didn't exactly have him penned in, but Tatsuya reacted to his scanning gaze—purposely, to make sure he had seen it—which made him give up on flight.

"…What are you talking about?"

The option he chose instead was to play dumb. Which was what Tatsuya expected.

"You know he's a direct descendant of one of the Ten Master Clans—the pinnacle of magicians in Japan, right?"

The man's eyes betrayed nothing. But that was the same as admitting he did know.

"He would have detected magic usage. Having a non-magician detective keep an eye on us was one correct answer."

As he spoke, he reached for his wristwatch.

The man visibly shivered. Tatsuya, still with a total lack of any emotion on his face, smiled with only his lips.

"If you use magic without permission, they'll throw you in a cell instead!"

Miyuki giggled. She probably found the man's outdated expression amusing. But to the man's eyes, it looked like the smile of a cruel witch.

Though CADs were as familiar to a magician as clothing, they were basically OOParts to a non-magician. A normal person with only a cursory knowledge of modern magic only knew that CADs were tools for using magic that magicians often put on their arms. One couldn't decry the man as ignorant, even though he'd mistaken Tatsuya's gesture of going for his wristwatch to be preparing to use magic.

"I'm only asking one more time."

Tatsuya energized his psions. If that's all he did, the sensors might pick it up, but they wouldn't figure out that he'd used magic. But the energized psionic wave was like a strange pressure to those who weren't magicians, something that whittled away at their nerves.

"Where is your employer?"

The man didn't answer. Even if he was just being stubborn, it could be praised as some impressive work ethic.

But even that was reaching its limit. Humans couldn't endure unknown horrors for a very long period of time. They could endure the fear of something with recognizable form, but fear of something completely alien would easily incite panic.

"I see. That's too bad."

Tatsuya moved his fingers, already riding on his wristwatch, and made sure the man saw it. It was a multifunctional watch linked to his information terminal, but it was just an informational device in the end. It had no ability to assist with magic—

"Okay, okay! I'll tell you where!"

—but this man, who was not a magician, had no way of knowing that.

"This the place?"

The man, his nerves shattered, had brought them to a tofu restaurant on the path to the temple.

"Yes. I'm not lying," added the man quickly, directing an imploring gaze on Tatsuya. "This is enough, isn't it? I'm just a humble private investigator, like you figured, and the guy in there told me to report on what you were doing if you got close. I don't know anything else, I swear!"

"You're pretty sure about where your employer lives considering you're just a humble private investigator."

If someone had requested a third party to do this, they would have kept their identity and location secret. At least, that's what Tatsuya would have done.

"I just don't want to cross any dangerous bridges, you know? Detective work isn't all fun and games these days."

"Must be a tough world for a hard-boiled type to live in."

"You're telling me…"

Tatsuya let out a little grin. He couldn't seem to hate this guy. He may not have been reliable for tougher jobs, but maybe he was still suited for gathering information.

"All right. Thanks—you can go."

The man looked at him in disbelief. He was the one who had suggested it—he apparently hadn't thought Tatsuya would listen.

"…Really?"

"Really."

"You're not gonna stab me in the back, or…?"

"You watch too much TV," answered Tatsuya, shaking his head, a dry grin on his face. Neither that mannerism nor his expression belonged to a boy in his teens, but that actually seemed to set the man at ease, almost like they were friendlier now.

"Oh…okay. Bye, then."

But Tatsuya wasn't so kindhearted that he'd let the man go without saying something first.

"I know who you are now. If you try to go somewhere, I'll know right away—so if you have anything to say, now's your chance."

The man's face twisted in fear. "Hey, look, you might be a magician, but you can't…"

"Why do you think I can't do?"

The man shook his head frantically. "I'm not lying! I'm telling the truth—please believe me!"

"If you're not lying, then you have nothing to fear."

The man began to run down the hilly street that led up to the temple, almost getting his own feet tangled up as he did so.

Leaving Minoru to the side, who just watched the whole thing in a stupor, Miyuki addressed Tatsuya in a chiding tone. "Brother, don't you think you went a little far with your joking?"

Tatsuya turned around with a face of surprise. "I wasn't playing around. I can't *actually* use magic to get him to talk, and I don't have an affinity for mental interference-type spells in the first place."

"Is that why you purposely made a big show of threatening him like that?"

"Yeah."

"...Even so, you seemed to be having quite a lot of fun."

"More effective if it looks that way, isn't it? Anyway, let's go in."

Miyuki still looked like she had something to say, but Tatsuya went into the shop without waiting for it.


"Welcome!"

A bright voice greeted Tatsuya. It belonged to a waitress in a kimono, in her late twenties to early thirties. He felt that a slightly calmer tone would have suited the location better, but he decided that was just his own preconception.

"Will it be the four of you?"

Tatsuya almost shook his head and said *no* to the waitress before he realized Miyuki and Minami were gazing passionately at the menu and that it was already lunchtime.

He'd already caught sight of an eidos he believed belonged to the magician in question in the back of the restaurant. For whatever reason, the person didn't seem to have any intention of hiding it. He took that to mean the person wouldn't flee while they were eating.

"Yeah," he said, nodding to the waitress.

"I'll show you to your table," came the voice in return, bright like before.

Tatsuya followed the restaurant employee, who had started walking and only spared a glance at Minoru—not being entranced by him was some amazing professionalism—while Miyuki and the other two trailed behind. The waitress brought them to a low floor table.

"Is this all right?"

Tatsuya would have rather sat on a chair, but a cursory glance revealed those tables were all full. He looked to his companions for an answer, but none of them responded particularly unhappily. Tatsuya gave the green light to the waitress.

"Please call me once you've decided what to order."

Tatsuya nodded, and the waitress left.

"Why don't we have some lunch for now?"

"Um, is that okay?" Minoru asked, expression uneasy.

"Judging from what it looks like, this is a proper business on the surface."

"Yes, but…"

"If there's any poison in the food, I'll be able to tell, no matter what kind it is. And I found who I think is that man's employer. If he tries to run away, I'll know immediately."

Minoru let out a breath of admiration. "You really can do anything, huh…"

Tatsuya couldn't help but give a pained smile at such a frank response. "I can barely do anything. More importantly, is it okay for you to believe everything I say that easily?"

"I don't believe you," he muttered to the *I can barely do anything* part without thinking very deeply, before realizing he'd just answered the actual question instead. Hastily, he added, "No—I believe you, of course!"

Miyuki let out a giggle.

Minoru reddened considerably.

"Big Sister Miyuki…" Minami said in an unusually admonishing tone.

"I'm sorry, Minoru. It's just that I don't really know any boys who react as normally as you—not my brother, nor his friends."

"You make it sound like I'm some kind of weirdo," retorted Tatsuya immediately, his complaint utterly monotone.

Miyuki began giggling even more. "Brother, *you* make it sound like you're supposed to be a normal person."

Tatsuya gave a shrug in Minoru's direction.

His face still red, Minoru burst out laughing.

Tatsuya and Minoru ordered the boiled tofu, while Miyuki and Minami ordered the tofu skin soup.

Speaking of the boiled tofu—Tatsuya, mired in preconceptions about the temple Nanzen-ji, had wondered about it before entering the shop, but after an explanation from Minoru, he realized he just hadn't done enough research. He hadn't come here for sightseeing anyway, so in a sense, it was only natural he hadn't investigated *that* far.

They spent a good amount of time enjoying their lunch in a lively manner. So much that Tatsuya had to mentally revise their entire schedule. The main cause was the soup: The dish consisted of heated soy milk that was eaten with a bamboo skewer, which was used to pick up the film that formed on the surface. The process itself simply took a long time. If Tatsuya had known before they'd ordered, he'd have made them pick something else from the menu, but it was too late now. As a result, he'd only managed to say one thing to the waitress, even over an hour after entering the shop:

"We actually came here on a recommendation from a Mr. Kudou from Ikoma—is there any chance we could see the owner?"

"Kudou from Ikoma? I'll go check the owner's availability. Please wait one moment."

After giving a fake name, he requested that she convey a message to the owner. As though such a thing wasn't unusual, the employee went into the back without seeming particularly dubious.

They weren't made to wait very long.

"The owner has told me to show you there. Would you mind…?"

"Not at all—thank you."

Without letting the waitress finish her formal expression, Tatsuya stood up from his floor cushion.

* * *

They were ushered not to a tatami-floored reception room, but to a semi-Western parlor. Instead of the usual sofa and table, a lacquered table and wooden chairs with intricate openwork backs furnished the room. Everyone, including Tatsuya, could tell these items were far more expensive than the average high-class sofa set.

The owner—the ancient magician Tatsuya had detected—was not sitting in a chair. After making sure the sliding door was closed, he bowed deeply. No hostility was visible in his attitude.

He wore a tea ceremony master's hat and an article of monk's work clothing. Tatsuya couldn't tell if his outfit showed the proper courtesy for receiving guests, so without reading too far into things, he sat down at the man's suggestion.

The table was wide, made for six people, but three on one side would leave one leftover. Tatsuya sat in the middle, with Minoru toward the back, Miyuki at his side, and Minami in the seat sticking out of the table's corner, which was in front when viewed from the door.

Once again, they faced the owner. The man's face had fine wrinkles; he was perhaps in his early fifties. Among magicians, there were some who aged particularly quickly and others whose age never stood out, so his age wasn't a very good trait to go by, but age wasn't a very important factor in the first place. The older magicians stood at the top to keep organizations running smoothly, the same as normal society, but even non-magician organizations would prioritize actual ability. And in reality, neither Tatsuya nor Minoru nor Miyuki showed any signs of caring about the man's age.

"I certainly hadn't thought a member of the Kudou family would come to visit like this."

The Traditionalist magician suddenly began the conversation. None of his words were to pry into the identities of Tatsuya and the others. The attitude was, perhaps, straightforward, but Tatsuya saw in it a lack of give.

"I will not ask the name of your companions, so I would prefer not to introduce myself, either."

Miyuki and Minami widened their eyes at the insensible request.

Tatsuya, on the contrary, narrowed his eyes sharply, as if he was trying to ascertain the truth. "…Does that mean you don't intend to be our enemy?"

"I don't intend to deal with those of the Nine any further."

"This may be rude of me, but you *are* a Traditionalist, yes?"

The hatted magician breathed a sigh. "Yes—I lead a faction of the Traditionalists as a conjurer."

"A conjurer?" asked Minoru, wondering about the meaning of the word.

"A failure who could not become a priest of esoteric Buddhism, nor an onmyouji, nor a *shugendou* practitioner," said the man in a tone of slight self-deprecation. Sensing the shards of a ruined pride in them, Tatsuya hesitated to pry.

"Why would a Traditionalist magician not be hostile toward magicians from the old Lab Nine, especially one of the Kudou? And in the first place, didn't the Traditionalists come together based on their mutual enmity toward the old Lab Nine?" Tatsuya brought the topic back around; it didn't matter to him who this man was specifically.

"Yes, at first, I harbored anger at how Lab Nine did things. I thought one day, I'd really give them what they truly deserved. My fury was especially strong even among my comrades, so I believe that's why they raised me up to act as a bridge that unites mages belonging to no religious faction."

"You almost make it sound like you were a leader in name only."

"That's how I think of it… But that isn't what you're here to talk about."

After the man expressed his intention not to argue, Tatsuya silently waited for his next words.

"At first, I seriously considered vengeance. None of it had any reality behind it. But it was only toward Lab Nine, who had taken advantage of me—I never had any intent to betray my country."

"Are you referring to taking in defected immortalists?"

The middle-aged man calling himself a conjurer nodded to Tatsuya's question. "I can no longer abide by the methods of those in Nara. They took magicians from the mainland in when they knew they would be traitors within the walls… Even though, just as Japanese magicians' loyalty belongs to none other but Japan, their loyalty belonged only to their own nation."

Minoru looked down as he listened to the conjurer's words, doubtless because he knew what his father had done.

"Did they *not* defect because their country's political system didn't fit with their own beliefs?" Tatsuya prompted.

Earnestly, the conjurer shook his head. "It wasn't a matter of loyalty, but of state of mind."

Tatsuya could only nod a little at those words. "I see. And so you've cut ties with the Traditionalists in Nara and stopped opposing the old Lab Nine?"

"Yes. Time is the great panacea. It heals all wounds. Even if you never go back to exactly the way you were before."

"I would think there are wounds even time can't heal."

"Wounds like that simply had new wounds added to them before they had a chance to heal. Like a flame—without a constant source of fuel, it will eventually burn out."

Tatsuya gave a theatric-sounding sigh. "Let's leave the generalities at that," he said, peering straight into the old magician's eyes. "What proof do you have that you're not a threat?"

His words, at least, seemed distrusting, and this time, the middle-aged magician gave a sincere sigh. "You don't even look a day older than twenty. What sort of education would one need to become that unfeeling…?"

Miyuki's and Minami's expressions shifted slightly. Tatsuya was certainly under twenty, so what this magician was saying wasn't wrong. But the phrase *a day older than twenty* wasn't exactly meant to be flattering, was it?

The person in question, however, didn't mind it at all. "You only gave us a meeting with you because you yourself started seeing things realistically, didn't you?"

The restaurant owner hung his head, suddenly looking a lot older. "I was just starting to think my decision wasn't a mistake. The detective was highly rated, but perhaps the rumors and the Kudou family were too heavy a burden for him…"

Tatsuya certainly didn't think the detective could be called *skilled*. But he didn't say anything about it. Instead, he commented on something more practical. "You mentioned earlier that you couldn't accept them taking in the defected immortalists. Would you mind showing us those words weren't empty?"

"…What would you have me tell you?"

"We're looking for an overseas Chinese magician who escaped Yokohama. His name is Gongjin Zhou. He's a dangerous man, one who caused several disasters in this country."

The conjurer looked up, his expression resigned. "All right. I'll give you what information I know."

"Please, tell us."

Tatsuya responded not because he was impatient, but to put pressure on the man.

"The one you're looking for, Gongjin Zhou, is not currently in Kyoto. The last time we confirmed his presence was on Friday, October 12. He'd just left the stronghold of another faction, composed of former esoteric Buddhist priests, close to a promenade called the Bamboo Grove Road, north of the temple, Tenryuu-ji. We believe he headed south, but we haven't found anything to say he gotten as far south as Uji."

But the hints they got from this magician calling himself a conjurer were unexpectedly detailed.

"How do you know he hasn't gone south past Uji?"

"To be more specific, we know he hasn't crossed the Uji River. There is a bounded field set up on the river to protect Kyoto."

For the first time today, Tatsuya was actually surprised.

"Set up along the entire Uji River? How on earth would you use a spell that was continuously applied over such a massive area?" It was Miyuki who asked that question, in place of her dumbfounded older brother.

However, his sister's question prodded him back to reality, and the answer flashed through the back of his mind. "…No, you didn't set up a bounded field along the Uji River—you used it *on* the river, right? Mixing things that can be mediums for spells into the river water and letting them flow would apply a magical effect to the river itself."

"Wonderful! Ninety points."

The middle-aged magician broke into a smile and clapped. The eyes of the conjurer who had been watching Tatsuya as an equal rival, for this moment alone, had turned into the eyes of an adult watching a child, of a veteran teacher watching a good student.

"…As for the last ten points, you're not mixing anything into the water, but changing the properties of the river water itself—sanctifying it, right?"

"Oh! I must say, it is amazing that you're still a high school student. I suppose I should expect nothing less from a direct descendant of the Kudou."

After hearing Minoru's additional input, the old magician let out a bout of admiration.

"The bounded field's origin is at the Amagase Dam. We spiritually purify the river water there. Not all the water in the dam, of course. To do that, we'd need hundreds of mages stationed there at all times."

Tatsuya and Minoru knew without being told that something like that was impossible.

"Still, we can't set up a bounded field strong enough with the tiny bit of water we can continuously purify. At most, we can only give it an alarm function that detects when an enemy has crossed the river. But unlike mechanical alarm devices, we can assign different settings depending on which mage retrieves the data. And we can set it to respond to specific people as well."

"You mean you're one of the people managing the Uji River field?" Tatsuya inquired.

The conjurer nodded slowly. "I only learned of the field's control incantation by coincidence. The other administrators probably don't know I have administrative privileges on the field. I also don't know who the other administrators are. But in this case, that presents no difficulty."

The old magician paused there, probably because he still had enough pretense to. It was, without a doubt, him showing these youngsters unconsciously that he hadn't rotted away just yet.

"Only those with links to this land of Yamashiro and the land of Yamato can work the bounded field. And I've been watching for Gongjin Zhou to cross the field again ever since he appeared in Kyoto."

"Why?"

"Because that man is a danger to this nation," he answered succinctly. "I was up on my high horse earlier, saying time heals all wounds, but if I were to speak plainly, I haven't fully shed my reserves when it comes to the old Lab Nine. If you had barged in here no questions asked, I probably wouldn't have told you anything about this bounded field or where Gongjin Zhou was."

The conjurer shifted his gaze from Minoru, to Tatsuya, then to Miyuki and Minami, before finally settling it on Tatsuya.

"That was why I maintained a modicum of courtesy to all of you. In my eyes, it was a very impetuous way of going about things, but not enough to spill needless blood over."

As he listened to the conjurer, Tatsuya reflected on this fortunate coincidence. The main reason he hadn't forced his way into the back of the restaurant was simply because Miyuki and Minami had wanted to eat lunch. The only reason he didn't spill blood was because there were no mages here who could set up a bounded field like Mikihiko.

Of course, he wasn't about to reveal something like that. That wouldn't be honest—it would be *foolishly* honest.

"We thank you for the valuable information."

"One more thing—be careful of the groups from Kurama and Arashiyama. The Chinese magicians have won them over completely."

Tatsuya stood and bowed. Miyuki followed suit almost without delay.

Minoru and Minami hastily got up and lowered their heads, a sight the middle-aged magician watched warmly.

By the time they left the restaurant, the sun had started to set. It was still a while until dusk, but it would get dark quickly once the sun went down, given the season. On the west side, where they were in the mountains' shadow, that effect would be even more pronounced. They'd gotten results, which meant they wouldn't have worry about wasting their efforts—but still, there wasn't much time left in the day.

"What should we do now?" asked Minoru to Tatsuya as they went down the hilly path. If they were to believe that "conjurer's" words, the only place they'd be heading for now was where Gongjin Zhou was.

"Five people isn't enough to search the entire area north of the Uji River. I want more clues."

"Will we go to Arashiyama, then?"

"Hmm..."

What came to Tatsuya's mind then was the news about the murder of Mayumi Saegusa's bodyguard. The article had said the crime had occurred along the Katsura River.

The following day, he would be looking into that homicide with

Mayumi. He was meeting her in front of the police station that held Nakura's remains for safekeeping, but after asking the police to show them the remains, they'd naturally be going to the scene. If there were any clues, they'd be in Arashiyama, so obviously, a thorough investigation was the better option. Still, their stay only amounted to two days. It seemed too inefficient to visit the same place two days in a row.

"Let's take a thorough look through Arashiyama tomorrow. Today, we'll go to Kinkaku-ji."

"All right. I'll contact Kyouko about the Uji matter."

"Would you? Thanks."

As Tatsuya's party headed for the commuter boarding platform at the bottom of the hill, they garnered attention from the crowds, which were just as big as earlier—and it went without saying the ones getting that attention were Miyuki and Minoru.

After the police questioning was over, Mikihiko, Erika, Leo, and Masaki were released on grounds of justified self-defense. The names Ichijou and Chiba undeniably affected things, too, but the deciding factor in proving their innocence was the recording from the street cameras set up in the area. Ancient magic was said to be harder to pick up on sensors than modern magic, but that only meant it was harder to match spell with caster; the fact that magic had been used was recorded all the same. If the magician showed themselves, it didn't matter if they were modern or ancient—they couldn't escape from psionic radar and the sensors attached to it, all operating in tandem with the cameras.

The questioning had still taken quite a bit of time, but in the end, the four of them returned to the New Conference Hall.

"Now what? I kind of doubt anything else will happen today, so should we look around some more?" asked Leo.

Mikihiko shook his head. "No, let's get back to the hotel for today."

"Well, the moron's right," Erika quipped. "Nothing else is gonna jump out at us today."

"What? Who are you calling a moron?!"

"Who knows? Anyway, why are you so angry?"

"Youuuuu…wiiiiitch…"

Leo glared at Erika; she looked away, expression cool.

Masaki glanced at Mikihiko, wondering if it was okay to leave them be, but Mikihiko shook his head in response—they were best left alone.

"By the way, Ichijou, what hotel are you staying at?"

Still, possibly feeling awkward watching them in silence, Mikihiko turned to Masaki with a conversation about something completely different.

"O-oh. The K.K. Hotel." Masaki seemed taken aback by the sudden question, but he answered honestly.

"Oh? We're staying at the C.R. Hotel."

"Really? That's right next door."

"Yeah, what a coincidence. Is Kichijouji at the hotel?"

If Tatsuya had been the one who was asked this casual question, Mikihiko would have received a sigh in response. And maybe with an added explanation of how even he and Miyuki were in different places sometimes.

But Masaki answered Mikihiko's question more straightforwardly. "No—I think I said this before, but I came here alone. George is Third High's rep. He's focused on the presentation."

"Oh."

Their school's Thesis Competition representative being absorbed with the presentation was an incredibly reasonable thing. Neither Mikihiko nor Erika nor Leo asked about Kichijouji anymore after that.

"We're going to get back to the hotel now. What will you do?"

"Hmm…"

The pause wasn't intentional—he was actually thinking about it. Like Tatsuya, who was elsewhere, Masaki had planned on checking around a few more places. Unlike them, he'd come alone, so he couldn't split up the work. And he didn't have a guide like Tatsuya did. Kyoto wasn't that far from where Masaki lived, so he visited rather frequently. He didn't need a guide just for getting around, but he didn't have anyone to lecture him on what places should be avoided, so he had planned to ride around the venue in a spiral pattern.

The police response had burned up some time, though, and above all, the troublesome investigation had sapped him of all his motivation.

"Guess I'll go back, too."

"Want to come with us, then?" Mikihiko offered, inviting Masaki to ride in their commuter, even though he felt like he might be acting nosy.

"That would make four people even."

Erika, who was focused on teasing Leo and seemingly hadn't been listening to their conversation, interrupted suddenly with an *I-don't-really-care* tone.

Masaki faltered at her inconsistent attitude. Thinking she was someone who threw everyone off their game, he politely offered his refusal. "No, I actually came on my motorcycle."

"Really? You ride one of them, too, huh?"

A lot of girls would be interested in hearing this factoid. Many of them clung to the odd aspiration of riding double, and he had a faint awareness of that. But he didn't understand the reason why.

Even in this age, riding double on a bike was illegal. The two-person robotic scooters had each person standing up next to each other, and those were popular enough, but motorcycles stimulated the hearts of dreaming maidens with a clichéd situation—only with a motorcycle could a girl be satisfied clinging to a boy's back.

"Too?"

But the way Erika showed interest was clearly different from such "dreaming maidens," and even Masaki felt something off about it.

"Tatsuya—er, you know Tatsuya Shiba, right? He's got a motorcycle, too."

"He does?"

An image formed in Masaki's mind. A girl riding in the tandem seat of a motorcycle driven by a boy. Not sitting astride it, but sitting in a more elegant sideways fashion. Her arms looped around the boy's waist, her body pressed tight against his back.

The boy's face hidden behind the full-face helmet was Tatsuya's. And the girl's face, of course, belonged to Miyuki. Masaki almost scowled in spite of himself.

His focus moved to the boy's face again. The smoke shield steadily dissipated. The face hidden behind it was Masaki's—and on his back, the sensation of Miyuki's soft body...

"...What are you thinking about?"

Erika's mystified voice broke Masaki out of his thoughts. "Oh—er, nothing."

He set his jaw again and shook his head. Erika was looking at him with a somewhat...disgusted expression, possibly, but he ignored it and turned to Mikihiko.

"Anyway, I can't ride with you, but I'll follow you guys."

"Yeah, that's fine with me, I guess..."

Mikihiko wondered what the point of that was, but he didn't say anything.

And Erika, noting pretty clearly he'd looked away from her, traded glances with Leo, head tilted slightly.

Leo gave her a little shrug.

Around the temple grounds of Kinkaku-ji, officially called Rokuon-ji, where they visited just to be safe, Tatsuya and the others were unable to turn up anything. Feeling a sense of exhaustion at not even being able to find a Traditionalist stronghold, they returned to the hotel, even though it was a little early.

The hotel they were staying at was a little bit far from the Thesis Competition venue, the Kyoto New International Conference Hall. Though inconvenient, the plan was for First High's representatives and staff to stay here during the event, too, so given their pretext was conducting reconnaissance for the school, they'd needed to spend the night at the same place as well. Though the students coming to cheer for their school would be leaving the day of, every year, many of them would pay out of their own pockets to stay over the previous night for sightseeing.

Furthermore, Minoru was staying here for the night as well. Considering his transit time, it wasn't too necessary, but the decision seemed to be that his proximity to home was all the more reason to have the sickness-prone Minoru stay out overnight.

Private out-of-country vacations were severely restricted for magicians, and they seldom got to experience a trip overseas while they were minors. Inside Japan, though, they had a reasonable amount of experience going on trips with friends. But because of Minoru's poor constitution, it was difficult for him to leave the house for long periods of time, and he didn't have any friends who were close enough for him to go on a trip with. Tatsuya and the others hadn't come to Kyoto for pleasure this time, but it wouldn't be strange if Minoru's family had considered it a good opportunity for him.

As an aside, he'd be sharing a room with Tatsuya's group. Minoru had turned it down at first, but Tatsuya had pressed the issue—since they'd booked a two-to-five-person Japanese-style room for boys and girls, there wasn't much difference between having three or four people.

After checking in, Tatsuya retrieved the luggage he'd left with the hotel staff. He was just about to head for the room when he saw a crowd of familiar faces coming through the entrance—his friends who had been in the other group. They hadn't decided on any particular meeting time, but it was about time to return to the hotel anyway, so while it was a coincidence to see them here, it wasn't strange.

But when he spotted a surprising face among them, even he couldn't help but say something.

"Ichijou?"

"Shiba?"

The same went for the other boy as well, it seemed. Tatsuya wasn't the one Masaki had spoken to, though.

Tatsuya and Miyuki exchanged glances; the former gave a pained grin, and Miyuki responded Masaki with a formal smile. "It has been a long time. I wasn't aware you were in Kyoto as well, Ichijou."

"Yes, it has, hasn't it? I came to do some reconnaissance for the Thesis Competition next week."

As always, when Miyuki was around, Masaki quickly turned into a pure-hearted youth.

"Oh, is that so? That's what we're here for, too."

"Yes, I heard as much from Yoshida and the others."

Still, he was able to have a smooth conversation with her, either because he was somewhat used to it or was trying really hard.

"Did you meet everyone at the New Conference Hall?"

Perhaps finding it hard to brag about his accomplishment and say he saved them from danger, Masaki made a gesture as if to yield the answer to Mikihiko.

"He got us out of a pretty dangerous situation." Erika, however, snatched the answer away.

Masaki and Mikihiko, as well as Leo, shared a wry grin over that. Masaki had only wanted someone else to answer, so he wasn't unhappy. But it was very much in character for this girl to behave so freely. Insofar as he was able to think that way, Masaki already understood Erika himself.

"Mind telling us about it in the room?" Tatsuya asked, putting a stop to any more standing and talking. It was an unexpected interruption, but Masaki quickly realized the necessity of it, nodding along with Erika and the others.

"Ichijou, are you staying here as well?" Miyuki inquired, probing his convenience in a roundabout manner.

"No, I'm at the K.K. Hotel next door. But I did want to know more about what was happening."

Masaki had parked his bike and then followed Mikihiko's group without going back to his own room because he wanted to know the background behind the earlier attack. His thoughts aligned with Tatsuya's.

"Let's go to our rooms, then," prompted Leo.

"Okay, right after I grab my luggage!"

"Wait a second—"

Erika and Leo headed for the front desk without waiting for an answer, leaving Mikihiko to hurriedly chase after them.

Masaki didn't know Tatsuya was a JDF special officer. Tatsuya had to carefully tiptoe around that part during his explanation—at least, that's what Erika, Leo, and Mikihiko thought.

"We learned that the man who guided the GAA invasion force here during last year's Yokohama Incident is being sheltered in the Kyoto area. I came here on a mission to search for him."

"A mission?! Shiba, you're…?"

"I'm both a student at the National Magic University First Affiliated High School as well as a special officer serving in the Independent Magic Battalion of the JGDF's 101st Brigade."

But hearing Tatsuya explain it all so smoothly made all three of them blink in surprise.

"I…what…?"

The fact was so startling that even someone like Masaki, next in line to lead the Ichijou family, couldn't help but be shocked.

But it didn't allow Masaki to claim he was lying. He swiftly came to the realization it was most likely the truth—by looking at Miyuki, who was waiting beside her brother, and by seeing the unwavering expression on her face.

"Ichijou—I know I don't need to tell you this, but this is secret information."

Masaki nodded, clearly not over the shock yet.

Erika was making a face like she was staring into the distance, thinking things like *So this is how Tatsuya does things...* and *He always drags people into his business whether they like it or not...*

"There's a possibility the operative will cause interference during this year's Thesis Competition, too. I'm having Mikihiko and the others help me with this, because it should help ensure the Thesis Competition's safety, too."

This was the first Erika and Leo had heard of this—how this trip wasn't just to scout things out, but to search for a specific enemy agent, and that they were definitely in danger of suffering major wounds and could have even died from a stray blow.

Still, they both listened to this calmly. At the same time, they thought about whether they'd have turned down this investigative trip if he'd told them beforehand. And almost immediately, they mentally shook their heads no.

The most rattled person at the moment was probably Masaki.

"...You know the name of the one who led the invaders here?"

Still, he was the first one to ask a question. When he did, Mikihiko turned a firm gaze on Tatsuya as well, hoping for an answer. This was information even he still didn't know.

"Gongjin Zhou, he's called. A man who appears to be in his early twenties. But we don't know his real age. Long hair, and from the photograph, extremely handsome. And he apparently uses Qimen Dunjia."

In a surprising turn, Tatsuya unflinchingly gave the name.

"Gongjin Zhou?!" Masaki cried, now even more surprised than Mikihiko was.

"Do you know him, Ichijou?" Tatsuya asked coolly in response—that was exactly why Masaki seemed so surprised.

"Yeah, I do… So it was him. It *was* him!"

Fiery anger lit up in Masaki's eyes. The fire turned into a flame, whirling around.

"What happened?"

It must have been a very important connection. The way he responded made it seem like he'd been badly burned.

"…Last year in Yokohama, part of the invasion forces fled into Chinatown. I went there to get the residents to turn them over."

Tatsuya had gotten a chance to read the report of the Yokohama Incident, but this was news to him. It was the kind of thing the authorities needed to suppress, so the information probably hadn't been put together yet. He decided he'd have to go and view the records of that battle again when he had the chance.

But for now, he needed to listen to what Masaki had to say.

"Against our expectations, the gates to Chinatown opened right away. The young man representing the residents who had arrested the invading soldiers and handed them over to us said his name was…"

Masaki clenched his teeth.

Tatsuya spoke the name in his place. "Gongjin Zhou?"

"Yeah. He gave me his real name, and he grinned…!"

Masaki closed his mouth. Tatsuya could understand what he was feeling now, so he didn't say anything.

"What kind of magic is Qimen Dunjia?"

Erika was the one to change the topic. It seemed like she was putting her own curiosity first, but she was obviously doing it out of consideration for Masaki.

And besides, they did need to share information about the spells their opponent used.

"Not the Qimen Dunjia from Chinese astrology, right?" Miki-hiko asked, just to be sure.

"Right. The true form of Qimen Dunjia, used by ancient magicians from China, is a mental interference-type spell that throws off your sense of direction," Minoru answered.

"Throw off your sense of direction?" Leo wondered. "Like if you're in the water, he can make you confuse down and up to drown you?"

Minoru gave him a look of admiration. This was apparently an application he'd never thought of before.

"You can probably use it like that as well, but its main usage is to ruin pursuers' sense of straight lines, making them go back and forth in winding turns, never letting them catch up even though their target's within sight, dealing mental damage to them—or forcing them to wander for a long time inside a circle made of rock piles."

"...Kudou?"

"You can call me Minoru, Ichijou."

Minoru and Ichijou had introduced themselves right after coming into the room. Minoru had said the same thing to him then, but it seemed like Masaki resisted calling him by his first name right away, even though Minoru was younger.

"All right—Minoru." It seemed he considered it unmanly to insist on refusing. "Aren't you talking about the legend of Zhuge Liang from the *Romance of the Three Kingdoms*?" he asked.

"Yes. Lab Nine didn't only research Japanese ancient magic—they researched Chinese ancient magic, too."

*That makes sense*, Tatsuya thought as he listened. Magician development institutes saw the most activity during the Twenty Years' Global War Outbreak. Ancient spells, like Electron Goldworm, changed to be applicable in a modern magic framework were a real threat at the time, so it would have been unnatural for them to *not* have investigated them.

"The Lab Nine scientists concluded it was highly possible Zhuge Liang learned the immortalist art of Qimen Dunjia."

Erika and Leo offered admiring looks to the mention of an unexpected famous person. Tatsuya had no love for military failures, so he corrected the conversation's course before it could steer away. "Qimen Dunjia isn't just a large-scale spell, is it? Isn't it also a technique useful during individual close-combat? In fact, I'd think that aspect of the spell deserves more caution."

"How so?" wondered Masaki.

Tatsuya refrained from telling him to think about it himself. "Standing still and shooting spells at each other is one thing, but if you're rapidly changing locations during the fight, losing sight of your opponent is fatal."

But he also didn't explain it all the way until the logical conclusion.

"I get it. If he messes with your sense of direction, you won't know which way you were facing."

When it came to Masaki, he didn't need to.

"At the same time, you'll lose track of what direction the opponent is supposed to be based on where you are. Meaning Qimen Dunjia magic can make your enemy lose sight of you."

"Most likely. Miyuki?"

Prompted by her older brother, Miyuki opened her mouth to speak. "Ichijou, during the disturbance, we fought against a user of Qimen Dunjia named Xiangshan Chen at the Magic Association's Kanto branch."

"Is that true?"

"Yes. At the time, I was watching through the floor's surveillance monitors, but I couldn't look at the man as he walked down the hallway and approached. I was looking at the monitors showing left and right of the door, back and forth, but it was like I was only watching the one showing the right."

"How did you break the spell, Shiba?"

Tatsuya privately thought *That's Ichijou for you* at the question. He hadn't asked *if*, but *how*. It wouldn't have been meaningless to ask *if*, but if he had to say which one was more important when discussing actual combat, it was *how*.

"One of our group had special eyes. I had her gauge the timing while I waited for the door to open."

Masaki sunk into thought. Tatsuya stayed silent, waiting for him to speak again.

"...Would that mean Qimen Dunjia has something to do with time? The spell is essentially mental interference that either directs someone's attention in a specific direction at a fixed point or doesn't let them direct it that way. But if you know when the person will reach that junction and decide beforehand right then which direction you pay attention to, you can resist the mind guidance effect... Maybe that's how it is."

"I expected nothing less from you, Ichijou," said Minoru in open admiration after hearing Masaki's deduction. "So the magic interferes with the mind through a combination of time and direction, and not only direction? Now that I think about it, I feel like that makes the most sense."

Minoru turned around to Tatsuya, seeking agreement.

Tatsuya gave him a slight nod.

"Assuming we have the correct interpretation of the spell now, what would you do exactly, Ichijou?"

"Well... I'd predict the opponent's moves without relying on my senses..."

"Then it's something we each need to think about individually."

Pretending to help out Masaki, who was having trouble, Tatsuya put an end to the conversation regarding Qimen Dunjia. He'd heard from Mitsugu Kuroba that the technique was no help if the opponent could see you from up close, so the question of how to neutralize it didn't mean much to him.

"Let's set that aside for now and talk about today. I think the battle you rescued Leo and the others from involved the Traditionalists, a society of ancient magicians harboring Gongjin Zhou. Most likely, they mistook a *shikigami* Mikihiko released for something that was hunting for them specifically, then tried to eliminate what they thought was a search party."

"That isn't all, Tatsuya," Mikihiko interrupted. Not only Tatsuya, but Masaki as well, looked over at him. And of course, so did Miyuki, Minami, and Minoru, who weren't at the scene. "The ones who attacked us were *ninjutsu* users. Probably mages from Mount Kurama or people who deserted from there. But the one at their center was an immortalist from China. Gongjin Zhou isn't being harbored by the Traditionalists. Maybe he was at first, but now I think he's hijacked them."

"Not the Traditionalists, but a part of them," Tatsuya explained.

This time, Mikihiko looked at Tatsuya, face confused. Erika, Leo, and Masaki followed suit.

"We had some developments on our side, too," he went on. "It's a little weak to call a foothold, but we narrowed down the area Gongjin Zhou is likely to be hiding in."

As Mikihiko and the others expressed their surprise, Tatsuya told them about the Traditionalist "conjurer" they'd met on the approach leading up to Kiyomizu-dera.

"To think such a bounded field existed... I suppose it makes sense for those inheriting the traditions of the land of the ancient imperial castle."

As Mikihiko showed his frank interest in the Uji River bounded field...

"If he came out of the Kyoto metropolitan area and went south... that would be south of Fushimi and north of the Uji River. Still, it's too big an area to comb."

"Can we even trust what that old man said?"

...Masaki and Erika brought up reasonable doubts.

"It's a lot easier than searching all of Kyoto without a goal. And we know where he was hiding until last week, right? If we check his earlier hideout, we could figure out if we can trust the guy, right?"

Tatsuya let out a friendly, wry grin at Leo's optimistic viewpoint.

"Even if we find evidence that Gongjin Zhou had been hiding in Arashiyama, that wouldn't prove what the ancient magician at Kiyomizu-dera was saying is true. It's common practice to mix in truths to make the lies more believable."

He turned a more meanspirited grin on Erika and Leo.

Before they could react to it, Tatsuya continued, "That said, I agree with Leo—we should get some evidence he was hiding in Arashiyama. It could be a huge clue if it's true, and if it's a lie, clearing it up quickly would keep confusion to a minimum."

"Shall we go to Arashiyama all together tomorrow then, Brother?" Miyuki asked.

Surprisingly, Tatsuya shook his head. "We'd stand out too much in a big group, and we can't forget to make sure the competition will be safe. Mikihiko, Erika, Leo, would you three do the same thing as today and look around the venue area to see if any suspicious people are hiding or if there's any places criminals or terrorists are likely to hide?"

"…Yeah, sure, Tatsuya."

Mikihiko didn't appear to be in unanimous agreement, but Tatsuya was right—they couldn't afford to neglect the safety of the students participating in the Thesis Competition, especially with him being the disciplinary committee chairman of First High.

"My family should already be making an objection against Mount Kurama over today's attack. I've told several groups in Kyoto that have ties to my family as well. Whether this incident was at Mount Kurama's instructions or was the independent act of a few, it should help figure things out going forward."

"What was the situation anyway?"

Tatsuya, who hadn't heard the details of the attack yet, posed a somewhat belated question.

"Oh, right. We didn't explain it much."

Mikihiko, too, made an *oops* face as though he'd planned to talk about it but forgot.

At times asking for confirmation from Erika and Leo, Mikihiko explained everything from when the *ninjutsu* users attacked them, to how the puppet-controlling, Chinese ancient magician had put them in a pinch, and how Masaki had saved them.

"He had their *skin bitten through* and used their *blood* to make water golems? The more I hear, the more I feel like the immortalist was deceiving those *ninjutsu* users."

Minoru immediately agreed with the doubt Tatsuya expressed. "I think so, too. I'm probably preaching to the choir with Mikihiko, but blood has a particularly important meaning for ancient magicians. Using it to create familiars isn't something they'd have readily agreed to, no matter how much they were trying to keep him happy."

"Then it's easy," put in Masaki. "The Kiyomizu conjurer said the Kurama ancient magicians were the Chinese magician's pawns, but if they weren't overpowered but rather deceived and manipulated instead, we just need to give them the facts: They were tricked. It might not be enough to get them on our side, but we can probably put an end to their hostility."

Tatsuya nodded. "The more chaotic this all gets, the more chances Gongjin Zhou has to flee. I think keeping the confusion to a minimum will let us crush the enemy's plans."

"Then if things evolve into something like last year, we lose—but if we prevent it beforehand, we win, huh?" Masaki, too, agreed with him.

"I can act as part of the Kudou family, alone—but if a large group from the families of the Nine enter Kyoto, that may end up provoking the ancient magician factions as well as the Traditionalists," Minoru hummed, sounding disappointed.

"Indeed," Miyuki offered to comfort him. "They'd also be giving the Traditionalists an excuse, so we should probably avoid that if we can."

"The Yoshida family should be enough to provide support against the Traditionalists. If we do any more than that, some people could get out of control."

With Tatsuya's eyes directed at him, Mikihiko nodded. "Yeah… All right. We'll stick to looking around the competition venue like we did today. I'll also make doubly sure my family knows."

"What should I do?" Masaki asked Tatsuya.

Tatsuya wasn't in a position to command him, so the only thing he could say to the question was "Whatever you want." But he naturally knew if he actually did that, they'd get into a fight.

And Masaki's true intentions were clear from how he was stealing glances at Miyuki.

"If you were to accompany us, Ichijou, it would be very encouraging."

Miyuki preempted her brother and answered thusly, because she figured he was more likely to accept the request if she was the one to ask him to go with them—and not because she thought that hearing it from her would raise his motivation higher. Probably.

"Yes, please leave it to me!"

But either way, with that, their plans for the next day were set.

[ 8 ]

The next day, Sunday, October 21. Today's plan was to continue their two-pronged investigation. However, their level of motivation, especially Mikihiko's, was higher than the previous day now that they knew their true objective.

Tatsuya, Miyuki, Minami, Minoru, and Masaki were going to Arashiyama, while Mikihiko, Erika, and Leo would travel to the Takaragaike-Matsugasaki area, where the Thesis Competition venue was located. The eight planned to leave the hotel early in the morning.

However, an unexpected accident occurred.

"…I'm sorry, Tatsuya," Minoru apologized from his futon in a voice that made it sound like he was about to cry. He'd suddenly come down with a fever this morning and was now in no condition to go out on the survey.

"Don't worry about it. You're not responsible for this."

"I'm just…so frustrated with myself."

Tatsuya's words of comfort only made the other boy scrunch up his face even more bitterly.

"Minoru, don't blame yourself. You've done very well."

The only ones in the room right now were Tatsuya and Minoru. The other members, save one, were waiting in the lobby.

"I'd heard beforehand you're prone to illness. It's not your fault, and I accepted this possibility when I asked you to help us out."

Minoru averted his eyes.

"You've been enough of a help already. Without you there yesterday, we may not have ever discovered that conjurer's restaurant."

"...You mean it?" Minoru asked, his tone timid, still facing away.

"I really do."

Slowly and nervously, Minoru returned his gaze to Tatsuya.

Tatsuya's expression was straightforward as always. One couldn't even charitably call it compassionate. But his face didn't seem fake, like it would have if he had put on a smile for show. If the definition of *sincerity* was honest seriousness, Tatsuya's gaze was sincerity itself.

"You've helped us plenty, and if it comes to it, we'll probably have to get your help again. Don't push yourself—that way, you'll be ready then."

"Am I still...one of you?"

"We won't reach Gongjin Zhou today anyway. That's when we'll need your strength, so take it easy for now."

"...All right."

Minoru smiled weakly. He still looked depressed, but not like he was blaming himself anymore.

"We'll leave Minami here. She might not look it at first glance, but she's a housekeeping expert. And, same as you, she'll be happy if you rely on her. Don't hesitate to bring anything up, no matter how minor."

Minoru gave a slightly abashed look. His face was red from more than just the fever. He was probably embarrassed Tatsuya had seen through to his character—someone happy to be relied on.

"I'll leave your luggage here, so hold the fort while we're gone."

This meant after their investigation was over, they wouldn't be returning to Tokyo right away, but rather, coming back here first.

"You can leave it to me."

Understanding Tatsuya's awkward kindness, Minoru offered a smile.

After leaving the room, Tatsuya spoke to Minami, who had been waiting alone in the hallway.

"Sorry to push this on you."

"No, you're certainly not pushing anything on me. I am well aware that this is my job. I will take care of Lord Minoru."

Nodding to Minami as she bowed, Tatsuya headed for the lobby where Miyuki and his friends were waiting.

Minami watched his back until it disappeared, then knocked on the door to the room where Minoru was resting.

Without waiting for a response, she used the electronic key he gave her to open the door. She did this on purpose so that she wouldn't disturb the resting patient.

She closed the door, then opened the traditional sliding door. Minoru tried to sit up in his futon. Without a sound, Minami rushed over and sat beside him, gently pressing his shoulders back into their former positions.

"Lord Minoru, you needn't mind me. If you did, there would be no point in taking care of you."

She said that in a way that almost criticized Minoru—purposely playing the bad guy so that he wouldn't overexert himself. Minami could never really be the bad guy no matter how hard she tried, of course, but unrelated to that, Minoru properly understood what she really meant.

"All right. I'll be good and sleep."

Minami seemed startled by this.

Knees properly together as she sat at his bedside, not moving an inch, Minami stared at him.

Close to thirty minutes passed like that before Minoru, whose eyes were closed, opened them and flashed her an uncomfortable, dry smile.

"Sakurai, if you stare that much, even a man like me will get embarrassed."

With Minoru's looks, he would have been used to others staring. But it seemed a different story when the person was this close, right in front of him, watching him as he slept.

"I'm so sorry!"

Minami deftly scooted back a few steps, then lowered her head so deeply her forehead seemed in danger of scraping the tatami as she apologized, voice cracking.

Her face, pressed against the tatami, was—though Minoru couldn't see it from where he was—dyed bright red.

Minami, for her part, hadn't intended to be *entranced* by his face. Nobody else was in the room to talk to, and it seemed indiscreet to her to do something like watch a video or read a book next to a sick person, so she'd simply spaced out, mind blank.

But when he spoke up, she wondered if that had really been all it was.

He said she'd been staring at him.

She asked herself—had she really been gazing at his face as he slept, eyes closed?

——And if she had been, then why?

Her already-red face brightened even more.

Even the resting Minoru could see her ears go red, and instead of feeling anguished over her almost groveling pose, he began to worry over her physical condition.

"Umm... Are you okay?"

He started to get up out of bed.

"I'm fine! Please keep resting like you were!"

Rather than using her hands to push him back, Minami, suppressing her tone just before it became a shriek, stood up with her face averted and padded out of the room.

The sliding door shut with a slam. But there was still a little opening.

The outside door didn't sound like it had been opened and closed, though.

Minoru froze for a short while, hand still stretched out toward Minami, who was no longer there.

Originally, Tatsuya's group was supposed to be a five-person act, but Minoru had fallen ill and Minami had stayed behind to take care of him, so they were down to three, same as Mikihiko and the others. Commuters were generally four-seaters, so Masaki had planned to come along on his motorcycle, but now that they were a group of three, he was riding in the same car as them.

Tatsuya and Masaki sat in the front seats, with Miyuki alone in the back. Masaki probably secretly wanted to sit next to Miyuki, and Miyuki would have secretly wanted to sit next to Tatsuya, but both of them decided common sense and manners were more important.

Tatsuya was the one to punch in their destination. From the previous day's meeting, Masaki had thought they'd be going to Arashiyama, so when the commuter parked and Tatsuya moved to get out, he automatically called out after him.

"Tatsuya, weren't we going to Arashiyama?"

"I'm actually getting a look at something that might be a clue before we do," he answered, back still to Masaki, before getting his legs out of the car and turning around. "From here on out, I don't want you to say anything about Zhou."

"...Is it a secret?"

"If possible, I don't want to get a certain someone involved in this."

Masaki stared like he was searching for an answer. Tatsuya thought he'd probably get the wrong idea, but he was the one who set it up that way. He didn't particularly feel the need to make an excuse for it.

After arriving at the meeting place and waiting three minutes, the person he was waiting for showed up.

"I'm sorry I'm late, Tatsuya."

"You're right on time," Tatsuya said to the female university student who climbed out of a commuter and dutifully ran up to him.

"Huh? Miyuki?"

"Good morning, Saegusa. I didn't get to see you last month, so it has been a while, hasn't it?"

Miyuki returned a smile to Mayumi, whose eyes had widened.

"I had no idea you were coming too, Miyuki."

As she said, Tatsuya hadn't told Mayumi he wouldn't be alone.

But Mayumi was too interested in their other companion to complain about it in her usual way.

"Masaki Ichijou, isn't it? This isn't exactly the first time we've met, but I'll introduce myself anyway. I'm Mayumi Saegusa."

In contrast to the uninhibited behavior she displayed in front of Tatsuya, she now feigned friendliness as the daughter of the Saegusa, one of the Ten Master Clans.

"Yes, I remember seeing you. Pleased to meet you," Masaki responded, a little on edge.

As noted, this certainly wasn't the first time Mayumi and Masaki had met. But it had been almost four years since they'd last exchanged words. And this was only the second time they'd actually met face-to-face. They were both celebrities in the world of magicians, so neither had forgotten who the other was, but if they hadn't been, their connection was one that would have been stranger if they'd remembered.

"I'm sorry, Ichijou... Tatsuya, come here for a second."

With a wonderfully feigned smile, she bowed, then left Masaki, linking her right arm with Tatsuya's left—clearly not for any good reason—and dragged him away. After getting a few meters away, she began a whispered interrogation.

"Tatsuya, why didn't you tell me Miyuki would be with you?"

Tatsuya projected surprise. "Because I didn't think it was important enough to mention. Did you think I would leave her behind?"

Mayumi was about to argue, but then resignation appeared on her face. "Right… Miyuki would never let you go by yourself, would she?"

Stopping herself from shaking her head, she suddenly took on a serious look. Her eyes were fixed on a point above Masaki.

"Then why exactly is Ichijou with you?"

"That's just a coincidence. Yoshida and the others were checking the Thesis Competition venue area, and they ran into Ichijou. He came to Kyoto for the same reason. He said he planned to look around to see if any suspicious people were hanging around outside the venue area, too, so we brought him along as a kind of bodyguard."

"Yoshida and the others are here, too…? Oh, that's right—he's the disciplinary committee chairman now, isn't he?"

"I'm impressed you know."

Tatsuya honestly felt amazed that she'd graduated and still kept up to date about those things—he wasn't trying to deflect or anything—but Mayumi gave him a *you-can't-fool-me* look anyway. It showed how much trust Mayumi had in his everyday acts.

"Anyway, does Ichijou know about my business here?"

"I'd never tell him without your permission."

The suspicion in Mayumi's eyes grew even thicker.

Tatsuya knew what that gaze meant, but it wouldn't make him back down. "In any case, may I explain the circumstances to him? I think he'll be a big help," he said, giving her the smile of a con man.

Mayumi heaved a sigh. "Should you really be ordering the son and heir of the Ichijou around like this?"

"I'm not ordering him around. It's not like he's a puppy waiting for instructions," answered Tatsuya in a cheerless voice.

Mayumi let out a chuckle in spite of herself. "All right. I would appreciate it if you could get him to help us."

Perhaps she thought she'd finally won a point. Her mood brightened, she gave Tatsuya permission to explain the circumstances to Masaki.

Led by a detective assigned to be their guide, the four of them entered the police station's evidence vault.

Upon hearing about their search for the criminal who murdered Nakura, Masaki showed a surprisingly forward-looking attitude. He seemed to feel exceeding sympathy at how Mayumi had (in his interpretation) undertaken a private investigation in order to avenge her bodyguard. As someone from one of the main Clans, the sight of someone (in his interpretation) showing such passion toward a subordinate instead of treating them like a tool must have tugged at his heartstrings.

Normally, it wasn't desirable to split your objectives. He who chases two rabbits catches neither, or so went the ancient saying, and the proverb was right a high percentage of the time. But Tatsuya had a hunch:

Gongjin Zhou was the one who murdered Saburou Nakura.

That was what he was thinking. Which was why Masaki getting fired up over a sense of chivalry toward Mayumi didn't conflict with his objective. Thus, there was no inconvenience at all.

As Tatsuya was thinking about it, the detective brought Nakura's effects and placed them on the table. "The clothes Mr. Nakura was wearing. As for the CAD, though…"

"I understand," Mayumi stated. "I'm terribly sorry about that."

Nakura's CAD was in the Saegusa vault per Kouichi's wishes. CADs weren't just packed with the expertise of whatever magic engineer did its tuning; they were also a superb teaching aids from which one could learn through analysis how the magician who owned it used magic. It was normal for magicians not to want to hand theirs over to anyone outside their family.

But Mayumi felt guilty about Kouichi having retrieved Nakura's CAD. If you could understand someone's fighting style to an extent through CAD analysis, you could also infer what sort of spells they used in their latest battle. If you knew that, you could learn things about the crime and also possibly speculate as to what sort of wounds the criminal had. And in that case, you might be able to narrow down the criminal by asking hospitals that had treated patients with the expected wounds. It may have been natural for magicians, but Kouichi's attitude with the police wasn't exactly cooperative—rather, it was very clearly uncooperative.

"I'm sorry, sir. What's this blood?"

The detective shook his head in disappointment at Tatsuya's question. "Unfortunately, all the bloodstains are from the victim."

Doing an exhaustive check on the DNA of the blood stuck to the clothes wasn't easy with modern scientific forensics, but it was possible. Checking if any traces of the criminal remained on the victim's clothes was a basic procedure always followed for homicides.

"It seems as though his abdomen was pierced from behind, his chest skin and his muscles burst out from the inside, and his heart ruptured."

That was why it had been reported as an unnatural death. Of course, the news hadn't delivered information this detailed. Tatsuya had heard about the details from Mayumi.

"Burst from the inside...?" Masaki asked, in a deeply suspicious tone.

"Almost sounds like Burst."

"Shiba, I promise you, the Ichijou family had nothing to do with this!"

The disturbance in his mind easily seen through, Masaki overreacted. Mayumi frowned a little at how loud his voice was in the relatively small room.

Tatsuya wasn't seriously suspecting the Ichijous' involvement, either.

"But no natural phenomenon could have caused an internal chest rupture, and there aren't exactly many people who can use magic to control the bodily fluids inside a regular living person—much less when the target is a magician—enough to cause their body to explode."

He'd said it to get all the information in order.

"But that's…"

——Even so, his tongue had been fairly sharp.

"The Ichijou family's Burst spell isn't that easy to use, right?"

"Of course not! Ah—sorry, I mean…"

"Calm down. I said it *almost* sounds like Burst. I didn't say Burst was actually used, and I certainly don't think any Ichijou family magician was involved in this."

Masaki's face grew a little red, probably because he'd realized how out of sorts he'd been and was embarrassed about it. *Maybe his personality is surprisingly weak to unexpected events*, Tatsuya wondered.

"Magic that manipulates the inside of another person's body is hard," said Mayumi. "But affecting one's own body isn't as difficult. Self-acceleration is a relatively popular spell, for example… Tatsuya, do you think Nakura blew himself up—committed suicide?" she asked nervously.

Tatsuya shook his head. "He may have blown himself up, but it wasn't a suicide."

"Brother, you believe Nakura did this because he knew he had sustained a fatal wound, right?"

Tatsuya nodded at Miyuki, who was waiting at his side, then returned his gaze to Mayumi. "Could what caused his heart to rupture have been some sort of offensive spell?"

"You mean the victim, shot through the stomach from behind and realizing he was fatally wounded, used the spell to try and take the opponent down with him?"

"Saegusa, did Nakura specialize in magic that uses fluids as a weapon?" Tatsuya inquired, ignoring Masaki's question.

"...I'm sorry, but Nakura almost never used magic around me."

Unfortunately, Mayumi couldn't answer the question.

"I see."

No tinge of disappointment laced Tatsuya's voice. But when Mayumi heard the response, she reacted slightly with some haste. "Oh—but I think I heard something when I first met him. Hold on a second."

She folded her arms and thought, groaning a little.

*She's very much...like a manga character.*

As Tatsuya thought of things that could possibly have been rude, Mayumi pounded her palm with her fist. "Right, right, I remember! Nakura said he was good at a spell that could shape water into needles and shoot them at an enemy."

Masaki furrowed his brow. "Needles out of water...? How? And what effects do they have?"

"I don't know how he did it, but if they're needles, he probably used them for piercing," Tatsuya said. "If you use a convergence-type spell, even water needles get the penetration they need to use them at a practical level."

Getting a boring answer in response to the question he'd asked in spite of himself, Masaki almost made a slightly miffed face. But right before he did, he remembered Miyuki was watching. "...Which would mean the victim made his own blood into needles and fired them?"

"A counterattack that was literally in exchange for his life..."

Tatsuya directed Elemental Sight at the traces of Nakura's blood that was stuck to the clothing and recorded the information.

"What are you doing, Shiba?"

"Just thought maybe magical traces were near the abdomen wound."

"I see..."

Fooled by Tatsuya's reasonable-sounding lie, not only Masaki but Mayumi also stared hard in the same way. They weren't directing their physical senses toward the clothes, but their magical ones—but the act of looking at something made it easiest to give your magical senses a direction.

"Hmm... I don't see anything," said Mayumi dejectedly, letting her shoulders sag.

Masaki looked up and heaved a sigh. "Nope. I can feel something like a trace, but it's too blurry, and I can't read any meaningful pattern from it... Shiba, did you find something?"

"I couldn't read any information that would specify the criminal, either. But this wound is likely from an imaginary beast."

"A what?"

"Brother, what do you mean by an imaginary beast?"

Mayumi and Miyuki sought an explanation for the unfamiliar word. Behind them, he saw their detective guide jotting down notes.

Tatsuya tried to make Masaki do the explaining, but Masaki casually looked away. Either he didn't know or he did and didn't feel like going through the effort to clarify for him.

Miyuki was the one asking, so if he had known, he probably would have explained proudly. Tatsuya interpreted that to mean, in all likelihood, it just so happened he didn't know about them, either.

"*Imaginary beast* is a name given to a kind of compound form. Compound forms are techniques that magically bend light and add pressure to adjacent objects, making it look like something formless has an actual form. Imaginary beasts don't twist light to pretend they have a form, though—illusion magic is used to show that form to the enemy. The caster applies anti-object effects to match the constructed form, same as compound forms."

"Compound forms bend physical light, so anyone can see them. Imaginary beasts only appear through mental interference–type magic, so the only ones who can see them are those the caster wants to show them to. Is that right?"

Tatsuya nodded, satisfied at Miyuki's understanding. "Yeah. Very good. To add to that, visual illusions aren't the only thing you can show an opponent. You can use auditory illusions to set up an imaginary beast spell, too."

"Hold on a minute, Tatsuya. From the way you said it, do you mean an imaginary beast isn't really a spell unless someone else perceives it?"

"The biggest difference between them and compound forms is in how the spell's strength grows by making the opponent think something is present."

Mayumi continued her argument, not looking convinced. "Then why would there be an attack from behind? If there was a noise, Nakura would turn around. It doesn't matter if it's a form or a sound— if he could have perceived something was behind him, he would never have gotten stabbed from behind."

"You don't need to make the person perceive where it is."

"What do you mean…?"

"With imaginary beasts, it's actually better not to let the opponent clearly perceive them. Imaginary beasts are just that—imaginary. If the opponent could see them clearly, they'd realize they weren't real. The unease at feeling like something exists, the unstable perception that it's somewhere nearby—imaginary beasts don't exist, but the phenomenon lives because of those traits."

"…I don't really get it."

"Ah, sorry. Was that too roundabout? To put it simply, if you show the opponent a sacrificial pawn, you make them think you'll attack them with magic fields shaped like animals, and then you use that as a stepping-stone to cast a stronger spell. The initial pawn can be a compound form or something else—doesn't matter."

"So being cautious of your enemy's magic makes your enemy stronger…?"

"Being aware of the trick halves the effects. It was the right choice getting to see the physical evidence."

Tatsuya lowered his head slightly in a gesture of appreciation.
Mayumi was at a loss on how to react.

The four of them got into one commuter and headed for Arashiyama. (Mayumi had ended her rental of the one she'd arrived in. It
would now be heading automatically to its next user.)

Tatsuya and Masaki sat in the front seats, with Miyuki and
Mayumi in the back.

No sooner had the commuter drove off than Masaki spoke to
Tatsuya.

"Shiba, about those imaginary beasts…"

Tatsuya and Miyuki didn't mistake whom he was talking to;
Masaki had been asking Tatsuya this whole time about the topic, not
his sister.

"Were the puppet *shiki* we encountered yesterday something
else?"

"I've never heard them called puppet *shiki* before."

Tatsuya was sitting in the front seat on the right, but since the
commuter was moving on its own, there was no need for him to drive.
He could turn to his side without any problem at all.

"They're generally called golems. I think that name should spell
out the difference?"

"Ichijou, Brother, I'm sorry for interrupting."

Miyuki leaned forward slightly from the backseat. Still, she
didn't do anything so lacking in etiquette such as grabbing the back
of the seat or poking her face up there.

"Brother, I essentially only know of golems by name, so would you
be able to explain what kind of things they are in a simple manner?"

For just a moment, Tatsuya gave a dubious look. Golems were
a popular attack method among ancient magicians who were in the
Christian sphere or Jewish. It wasn't possible that Miyuki, who had
been taught with the expectation that she would fight magicians from
foreign countries, didn't know anything but the name.

But after seeing his little sister's eyes dart over to Masaki for a moment, Tatsuya realized her true aim. Part of him thought she was being overly considerate, but he didn't want to waste her efforts, either. For Masaki's sake rather than Miyuki's, Tatsuya began a somewhat detailed lecture about golems.

"Golems are puppets designed to resemble creatures or mythical beasts and are made up of several linked parts. By embedding independent information bodies programmed with movement patterns, you can replicate the motions of the creatures they were designed after by using convergence-type magic to continuously change the relative positions of each of the parts. They're basically magical robots.

"For example, assume you create a giant, humanoid golem out of stone. At a glance, the golem seems to have no joints, like it's just a hunk of stone, and yet, it appears to move as though it were human. In reality, though, it has no parts connected to it to serve as joints. Like with hardening magic, you just station everything in relative locations—essentially, you're just piling up body parts.

"Golems possess physical form—whatever they're composed of. In some cases, they're organic, like if you use wood, and in other cases, they're inorganic, like stone—and in yet other cases, they're amorphous, like water. But compound forms and imaginary beasts are only force fields without physical form. That lack of physicality is an important difference between them and golems.

"As I mentioned earlier, in order to operate a golem, you need to embed independent information bodies programmed with movement patterns. It won't work unless you continuously project that magic program into it. When the magic program loses its effects, the golem ceases to be a golem. And if it's made of something amorphous like water, it will immediately fall apart.

"If it's made out of wood or stone, you frequently use sealing-type magic techniques as a way to affix the magic program to it. But if you're using another amorphous material like water, you'd mix something that could serve as a magical transmitter into the medium and use that as the target for continuously projecting and updating the magic program. In yesterday's case, I would assume the first small golems that appeared were one-time-use, disposable tools, where the magician didn't update the magic program, and then he used the blood stolen from the *ninjutsu* users to serve as the transmitter.

"Before modern magic was established, it was thought that blood had an important magical significance. Ancient magic posits that blood offerings are highly effective, and many spells exist that use it as a medium. From the perspective of modern magic, blood circulates through the whole body, including the brain, and is directly involved in sustaining life. Additionally, the eidos in blood are highly dense psionic information bodies; even a single drop can contain the detailed properties of the user. Thus, as a target for projecting a magic program onto, you could say it's extremely suitable."

"…Then basically, the difference between golems and things like imaginary beasts and compound forms is whether or not they have a physical form, right?"

Perhaps starting to find the lecture boring, Mayumi literally summed up Tatsuya's explanation in a single sentence.

"Based on all that, golems seem easier to deal with since they have a physical form," Masaki followed up.

Tatsuya shook his head a little. "Whether they're compound forms or imaginary beasts, putting in the unnecessary effort of giving it a creature's form is an inefficient way to use magic. If you don't use a magical item at the core, they can be wiped out by magical power focused into a small area—Area Interference—and if you're strengthening the false form with a magical item, all you need to do is destroy that core. Or you can simply destroy the field making up the false form. If the field is applied physically, then you can destroy it physically."

As they were conversing (though Tatsuya was pretty much the only one speaking), the commuter arrived at their destination.

Minami was quietly reading a book next to Minoru.

Aside from a slight fever, Minoru's condition was stable. She had no housekeeping to do in a hotel, nor did she need to fight over food or tea preparations. For the first time in a while, she was taking things easy.

Alone with a young man—or rather, a boy about her age—whom she'd only just met. Plus, he was incredibly gorgeous. Exquisite on the inside, too. And yet, wondered Minami all of a sudden, she was able to relax like this.

It couldn't have been because she was accustomed to Miyuki. She was a woman, and so was Miyuki—though at times, they didn't seem quite the same. Minoru was of the opposite gender. Naturally, she should have felt differently about him.

Of note, when they'd gone to Nara before, and the previous day as well, her heart had been pounding whenever she went near Minoru. She was aware she was nervous. And it certainly wasn't because he was the son of the Kudou family. It was probably because he was a male in her age range. And unlike Tatsuya, he was a *boy*.

His magical talents were wonderful—in fact, they were *incredible*. He might even rival Miyuki, the Yotsubas' finest work.

His extraordinary appearance also went without saying at this point.

And yet, for some reason, she felt close to him. She felt that something about him was the same as her. She knew she was drawn to him, knew she had him on her mind, and because of that, she was tense.

Minami held her warmed cheeks with both hands. Blushing at

fantasies was so embarrassing. She stood up to go wash her face and cool her head.

But she quickly returned to her original position. Not the one where she was reading a book, but the one where she was right at Minoru's pillowside. His breathing had suddenly grown ragged.

His painful exhalations were shallow and short. When she put her hand to his forehead, she felt heat. About to ask the front desk for a doctor in her haste, her hand stopped in midair.

Minoru was part of the Kudou family by birth. Someone who directly inherited the blood of the products of the old Lab Nine. Was it right to have a normal doctor look at him?

She wavered. Minoru's symptoms were not something her own amateur nursing talents could handle. But even so, she couldn't decide whether to call a doctor.

Then, a solution flashed across her mind:

She should just ask Tatsuya.

Flustered, she took out her information terminal and booted up its voice call function.

Tatsuya received the call from Minami right after he'd gotten out of the commuter.

"Minoru isn't well? …I see. You were right not to contact the front desk. I'll give Fujibayashi a call myself… No, it won't be a problem. She actually told me beforehand to contact her if something happened with his health. She'll probably have to go to the hotel, so you keep taking care of him normally… No, don't give him any medicine… Yeah, that's fine. I know you'll have a hard time alone, but I'm counting on you… All right, thanks."

After finishing the call, Miyuki looked up at him from close by with worry.

Warding her off with his eyes, Tatsuya called a number recorded in his terminal.

"Fujibayashi? It's Shiba. Well, Minoru has fallen ill, and Minami, who's looking after him, says his breathing has gotten pretty ragged... He's in room number ___ of the C.R. Hotel... Yes, thank you."

"Was that Kyouko?" asked Mayumi from next to him, also worried.

"Minoru is feeling worse?" his sister inquired, to which Tatsuya nodded without a word.

"Should we go back?" Masaki wondered, his face serious. Though he'd only met Minoru the previous day, he seemed to be honestly worried for him.

"I contacted his family. They should get to the hotel in around an hour."

"Someone's sick? Someone in Kyouko's family?"

Mayumi hadn't met Minoru yet.

"The youngest son of the Kudou family. We met once before, and we had him guide us through Kyoto."

"The Kudous' youngest son—you mean *that* Minoru? If I recall, he was frail..."

It was a little surprising that Mayumi knew about Minoru. But after all, the Saegusa weren't called the most sociable of the Clans for nothing.

Still, she didn't seem to know the specifics about Minoru's constitution, either. Drawing from the information that he was prone to illness, she seemed to have thought of a constitution like Mio Itsuwa's. Mayumi was very close with Mio, so she couldn't help but envision her when she heard "prone to illness."

"He is sickly, but apparently, he isn't feeble. I'm not a doctor, so I don't know the details, but it's more like his magical power is so strong that it's putting too much strain on his body."

"That can happen?"

Mayumi tilted her head, half doubting, but Miyuki suddenly made a face like she'd just remembered something. "In any case, Ms. Fujibayashi will hurry there, so let's move on with our investigation as planned."

Mayumi was acquainted with Fujibayashi as well. Their families had been friends since before Yokohama last year. Naturally, she also knew the link between her and the Kudou family.

Masaki, on the other hand, didn't know anything about Fujibayashi. But he didn't make any comment, perhaps deciding not to probe more than necessary.

Nakura's corpse had been found on the bank of the Katsura River that faced the Moon Crossing Bridge, in Arashiyama Park's Nakanoshima region. It was around where the small sandbars dotted the water, right before the Katsura River veered southward.

The police's inspection of the scene seemed to be over already, and Tatsuya and the others walked there without issue. No bloodstains or anything of the sort were left, of course. It may have been possible to spot traces of it by using Elemental Sight and matching it against the data he'd obtained earlier, but he didn't intend to do something so useless.

"Here?"

"Yes."

Mayumi nodded to Masaki's question. Masaki was being very forward-looking with the search.

"Given the river's flow rate, it doesn't seem like he drifted here from upstream," said Miyuki, looking at Tatsuya. His little sister, it seemed, didn't mesh well with detectives or inspectors.

"Yeah, not much chance of that."

That was his only answer; he didn't say it was because the blood had been scattered in this area.

"Shiba, what do you think the situation was?" Masaki asked.

"Was the victim, Nakura, standing here, and then the criminal came to him? Or did the criminal get here first and let Nakura approach them?"

"I don't know," answered Tatsuya immediately. "We probably won't figure it out just by thinking about it. We don't even know if Nakura and the criminal were meeting here, or if Nakura was one-sidedly attacked."

"True…" Masaki, without showing any needless rebelliousness, agreed with Tatsuya's opinion.

"What should we do now, Brother?" Miyuki asked.

Tatsuya turned his eyes to Mayumi. "I'd like to check the surroundings. Would you mind?"

Mayumi seemed somewhat surprised at the sudden request, but still, she nodded and said, "Yes. I'm the one who asked you to come with me, so if you have any ideas, I'll go along with them."

Rather than following this side of the Katsura River, Tatsuya went over the Moon Crossing Bridge and headed upstream. Still, he wasn't climbing all the way up to the Hozu Gorge, but rather, the hilly area in the southeastern part of Ogurayama in Arashiyama Park's Kameyama area.

Acting on the information he'd gotten from the ancient magician they'd met in the tofu restaurant on the approach leading up to Kiyomizu-dera, Tatsuya was headed for the place where Gongjin Zhou was said to be hiding. He hadn't told this to Mayumi, but she came along without complaint.

It was fairly deep into autumn now, and even Mayumi was in thicker clothes—no sandals were on her feet. But unlike Miyuki, who had gone with a pants-and-sneakers look, Mayumi wore a somewhat long skirt with a wide hem and heeled loafers. One could say she understood what they were doing just because she hadn't come here in high heels, but it still wasn't a good outfit for a short hiking course with lots of ups and downs.

Out of necessity, the four's walking speed became leisurely.

Once they climbed the park hill, there was a sign board saying BAMBOO GROVE ROAD. Tatsuya headed that way without a second thought. His lack of hesitation gave Mayumi a slight feeling that something was wrong.

"Hey, Tatsuya?"

"What is it? Was I going a little too fast?"

Addressed by Mayumi, Tatsuya stopped walking. Masaki and Miyuki stopped with him.

"No, not that."

Now that they mentioned it, Mayumi realized she was breathing fairly hard. It made sense that Tatsuya and Masaki wouldn't be out of breath, but seeing that even Miyuki wasn't struggling made her feel an indescribable unfairness. But she kept a cool face and didn't show it. In times like these, Mayumi was pretty stubborn.

"Do you have a place in mind? This whole time, you never seemed to wonder where we should be going."

Upon her pointing it out, Tatsuya realized his own attitude was unnatural. Indeed, Mayumi was right.

He'd been the one to create that suspicion, so it didn't seem like a good idea to keep the wool over her eyes. But still, he hesitated somewhat at also getting Mayumi involved with this. She might also be a direct descendant of one of the Ten Master Clans, like Minoru, but Minoru was already involved to begin with, and Tatsuya normally never had any contact with Masaki, so he didn't feel bad no matter what happened to him. Mayumi, however, was closer to him, though not all that much. If he got her involved in his own affairs and let her get hurt, he was pretty sure things would get incredibly troublesome for him. He doubted it would happen, but if it was something they had to demand that he take responsibility for, he might end up having to borrow the help of people he did not want to indebt himself to. Tatsuya didn't want to ruin their current impression of him by simply helping her out.

What could he say to fool her?

For just a moment, he wondered about it.

But only for a moment—because he didn't need long.

"Brother!"

Miyuki spread out an Area Interference.

The Demonflame that had flown at him was swallowed in her anti-spell and disappeared. The ancient magic wasn't a physical flame, but a spell made visible by igniting objects it touched. It couldn't break through her Area Interference.

Perhaps the opponent had known that, because wind blades attacked them next. The end result was the same, though. Whether they were vacuum blades or compressed-air blades, the caster had to keep applying magic to them to maintain their state, meaning the attacks would naturally dissipate after encountering a powerful Area Interference.

"Ichijou!"

"On it!"

Tatsuya took charge of the front while Masaki took the rear. Immediately, they formed up around Miyuki and Mayumi, protecting them.

Slender ropes stretched out from the bamboo groves to either side, aiming for Miyuki. The ropes tied together in five colors: blue, red, white, black, and yellow.

Tatsuya grabbed hold of them before they reached his sister. A noise resembling Cast Jamming went into him from the braided ropes.

*Lariats, used by esoteric Buddhist ancient magicians!*

With this technique, instead of spreading psionic noise into the air to prevent magic activation like Cast Jamming, you slung this rope around the opponent and poured the noise into them directly through it, effectively blocking them from casting anything.

Tatsuya didn't dismantle the lariats themselves, only the noise being sent into him. And then, with all his might, he yanked on the ropes with his hands.

Though Tatsuya was powerful, it wasn't as if he boasted super-human strength. Normally, he didn't have the strength to drag two humans out, one with each hand. But they were too baffled at how their spell was broken by something unexpected. Tatsuya was able to drag them out of their hiding places because he'd taken advantage of that opening.

However, Tatsuya, too, had let something slip. Belatedly, he noticed that other figures had vanished. They'd probably put up a bounded field so that they couldn't be touched. Instead of wrapping the field over Tatsuya and the others, they had made a wall barring entry to the path ahead of and behind them, thus warding them off.

But if they didn't have to worry about others watching, that made things convenient for Tatsuya's group, too.

Masaki caused a gust of wind to push back the lariats flung toward him and Mayumi.

The wind itself was the result of magic, so the magic program wasn't affected by the lariats, which blocked magical activation.

Loud noises came from the grove, and bamboo leaves fluttered into the air.

Mayumi had used a spell. Dry Blizzard—the original form of her specialty spell, Magic Bullet Shooter, one which caused hail made of dry ice to start falling.

The carbon dioxide density in the air went from 350 ppm to 400 ppm. From 3 in every 10,000 molecules to 4 in every 10,000. The gases seemed to be overflowing, even though in actuality, it barely contained anything. But with this number, even limited to the tropo-sphere, which extended up to 10,000 meters, it also meant the carbon dioxide alone would lower the pressure dramatically, creating a layer of about 2 meters.

The composition of air was distributed uniformly throughout the atmosphere. If you used magic to skew that distribution, the world—or nature, as you might call it—would attempt to correct it. If you gathered a specific atmospheric constituent—in this case, carbon dioxide—into a certain small area, the density of carbon dioxide in the vicinity would drop. In order to correct this, the world would send carbon dioxide into the area in which its density was lowered. This was accomplished through a chain substitution of gas constituents without producing an air current.

On a micro scale, the carbon dioxide–converging process that was needed to create dry ice with magic would, through the air particles moving faster than the speed of sound, cause a chain reaction of substitutions. However, the truly fascinating thing about this phenomenon was that the magician who caused the event alteration at its origin was not involved in this macro, atmospheric-level change in the air composition. By simply and one-sidedly converging the carbon dioxide needed for the dry ice into an incredibly small area, the *world* would provide the missing materials as it tried to erase the effects of the magic-based event alteration.

In this way, the artificial dry ice hail fell like rain in the bamboo grove. Their speed was far less than the speed of sound, averaging around five hundred to six hundred kph. The bullets, too, were quite a bit lighter compared with lead ones. But the magically hardened pellets were more than fast enough to pierce human skin and flesh.

Six men stumbled out of the bamboo grove. They didn't show any signs of heavy wounds, probably because they'd protected themselves from the dry-ice bullets with magic. Still, blood seeped from several wounds on their arms and legs.

Meanwhile, the two magicians dragged out by Tatsuya quickly fell victim to a cold wave. Miyuki's magic didn't freeze the body; it lowered her target's internal and external body temperature simultaneously, putting the victim into a cold sleep. Miyuki didn't want to kill anyone, so Tatsuya had written in a power limiter on the spell's activation sequence, though it'd been a struggle for him.

Tatsuya swung a flat hand, launching a dismantling spell horizontally along with the motion. He hadn't brought the Silver Horn this time. Instead, he had a bracelet-shaped specialized CAD on each wrist. By putting several targeting assistance antennae in the bracelets and having them work in tandem, he made up for the antennae being relatively short compared with a gun barrel.

For inputting commands, he used the fully thought-controlled CAD hanging at his chest. This was a new, hands-free style he'd done trial-and-error on.

Still, at this range, Tatsuya didn't need a CAD, much less targeting assistance, to accurately land his dismantling spell. His aim was true—bamboo was severed just above the heads of the psionic silhouettes that were shaped like people squatting. It may have been a blow to the sightseeing spot, but he decided to shut his eyes to it.

The ones who couldn't shut their eyes were the Traditionalist magicians who had taken an unknown warning attack. They realized the attack had missed on purpose; faced with that indiscriminate assault, there was no point in remaining hidden.

Either steeling themselves or growing desperate, four people exited the bamboo grove onto the path. With the two they'd taken down first, plus the six in the rear, there were twelve—and one was missing from when Tatsuya had noticed the ambush and done his scan.

"Ichijou."

"I'm on it!"

Tatsuya was well aware of Masaki's abilities. He hadn't been worried to begin with, and as he thought, Masaki didn't seem to have a problem. Tatsuya decided to finish the four in front first.

Before Masaki's eyes, the six magicians formed seals. He knew they were ancient magicians who used esoteric Buddhist magic. And so, in that preparatory motion, there was no hesitation.

And behind him, an activation sequence expanded: Mayumi had moved into a magic-casting stance.

Masaki knew exactly what *she* could do, too.

The eldest daughter of the Saegusa, one of the Ten Master Clans. Former student council president of his rival school, First High, and a genius at long-distance precision-shooting magic.

However.

The Dry Blizzard before—he could tell at a glance that she'd purposely lowered its power. So he didn't intend to force her to fight now.

Because she'd held back, she'd failed to disable the enemies. She'd succeeded at smoking them out, but in Masaki's point of view, that was only because their enemies were idiots.

Or maybe they weren't used to combat. Ancient magicians showing themselves right before modern ones was far from a good idea.

Ancient magic lost out in speed compared with modern magic. This was an undeniable fact. He had heard that ancient magicians of esoteric Buddhism didn't accept it, though, and devotedly worked on developing casting techniques that would rival modern magic in speed. Esoteric Buddhist magic had always featured a high-speed technique called single-character spells, and based on what he'd heard, they were working on developing that concept further.

But even then, it was impossible to outclass modern magic's speed. After all, modern magic was a speed-optimized magic born from a fusion of psychic powers and magic.

That was what Masaki had thought.

However.

*"Kan!"*

Masaki aimed his customary gun-shaped CAD at the same time as the ancient magician said that one word.

A moment later—

even faster than Masaki's magic could cast—

the caster's right hand immediately burst into flame.

"What?!"

"What's that?!"

It didn't look like an illusion. And in fact, it wasn't one. The attackers' clothing, designed to be loose, were the first things that burned. Everything from the right elbow down was the quickest to turn into a black cinder, and the awful smell of burning proteins assailed Masaki's and Mayumi's noses.

"Urgh…!"

Mayumi covered her mouth. The stench, more so than the sight, seemed to have made her feel like vomiting.

Arrested with surprise, Masaki watched the scene, forgetting to pull his trigger.

At least, until swords made of flame came out of the magicians' burning right hands.

The whirling flames coiled like dragons, coalescing into the shape of double-edged swords.

If Mikihiko had been here, he definitely would have called the spell this:

Kurikara Sword.

Two of the men charged forward with swords ready.

Suspicious that all four hadn't come at once, Masaki tossed the red, gun-shaped CAD in his hand into the air, then brought his other wrist up to operate the multipurpose CAD on it, creating a kinetic vector reflection barrier on the men's path.

But that barrier was sliced through by one reckless swing of the ancient magicians' flaming blades.

The Kurikara Sword was a demon-dispelling blade. Swords that cut through "magic." Did that mean, in other words, they were upgraded with the ability to slice through events altered by magic?

"Impossible!" Masaki shouted in spite of himself, feeling the barrier dissipate.

A sideswiping gust of wind attacked the two mages, ruining their balance.

"Ichijou, magic'll be cut through!"

Despite the awkward phrasing, Masaki realized what Mayumi's warning meant. That wind was a natural phenomenon brought about by an event alteration. A phenomenon caused not by the magic itself, but by its effects. Those flame swords couldn't affect that.

Masaki caught the falling red CAD by the grip with his right hand.

Flicking over the activation sequence selector, he put his finger on the trigger.

The six casters, whose right hands were much thinner now—probably burned straight off—raised their flame swords and, this time, all charged toward them at once.

Looking closely, anguish was evident on their faces.

Masaki then realized they weren't using this spell because they wanted to.

*Even these magicians are puppets.*

*Marionettes with their wills controlled by magic, rather than strings.*

Masaki pointed his red CAD at the six flesh-puppets closing in on him.

*Any directly applying magic will be cut down?*

*My Burst is far superior to any of that.*

Six times, Masaki pulled the trigger.

The puppets held their flame swords in front of them, perhaps to defend. But in the end, neither Masaki nor Mayumi would ever know.

The reason being that there was no point to it.

The leg of one of the ancient magicians reduced to living puppets—

The limb burst.

The red blood cells contained within his vaporized blood plasma blossomed out of his torn skin, like flowers scattering into the air.

Masaki had learned a technique for neutralizing opponents without killing them by adjusting the scope of the Burst spell.

Without even a moment in between, the next magician's leg burst.

Burst.

Burst, burst, and burst.

Six crimson flowers bloomed, then fluttered away in the wind.

One leg each brutally exploded, the six mages fell to the ground.

The flames had disappeared from their hands, their spells perhaps broken by the intense pain.

All the blood vessels in their leg ruptured, their muscles and skin torn asunder, their white bones visible within.

Mayumi covered her mouth at the ghastly sight.

She didn't vomit—either because of her pride as a Ten member or as a proper lady.

Masaki, however, his back turned, didn't have a trace of hesitation on his face.

The same phenomenon occurred before Tatsuya, too.

The four casters' right arms began to blaze.

Everything after that was different.

Instantly, a white chill assailed their arms.

The flames resisted the chill, but the chill devoured the heat, covering the burned skin with ice.

Their flames, which could burn demons to a crisp, buckled under this new "demon's" power.

Needless to say, it was Miyuki's magic.

For someone who could freeze the mind itself, freezing a magic program pushing at her from the outside was a simple matter indeed.

Tatsuya pointed a finger at the men's legs.

All four of their thigh areas erupted with blood at once.

The magicians fell over, writhing in intense pain. That pain turned into noise, vibrating the strings controlling them.

The vibrations traveled in the opposite direction.

*There*, thought Tatsuya, throwing a sidelong glance at the bamboo grove.

The disturbance in psycheons had vibrated the psion threads, psions that couldn't escape Tatsuya's "sight."

He aimed the fingers on his right hand into the brush.

A spider descended on him from overhead, which he batted away with his left.

The spider, possessing no physical form, dissipated at the same time he heard the scream from the brush.

"Still feels a little awkward," muttered Tatsuya to himself. He was talking about the combination of CADs he was using: a prototype, bangle-shaped specialized CAD that was called the Silver Torus (not the constellation Taurus, but the geometric figure), which he was testing instead of relying on his usual Silver Horn. At the same time, he was also trying out the fully thought-controlled CAD.

"It looked to me that you used it smoothly and masterfully."

To that, Miyuki offered the opposite opinion.

Neither of them was worried about the six lying in front of them or the owner of the scream they'd heard from the brush. Tatsuya had captured the "existence" of the immortalist who had passed out from the pain, and Miyuki had absolute faith that her brother would never let captured prey out of his grasp.

Tatsuya threw the immortalist he'd dragged from the brush onto the road. The man was fairly advanced in age, appearing to be at least sixty.

Because of the violence with which he was dragged, the man regained consciousness. He stabbed a long needle into a spot near his waist, evidently to block the pain of being shot through the thigh. Likely a sort of acupuncture or moxibustion technique.

That was the only thing the immortalist did; he showed no signs of resistance. He seemed to understand that the moment he tried to use magic, that intense pain would come back. It was difficult to tell whether to judge it sportsmanlike or simply the actions of someone quick to give up.

"Tatsuya, Ichijou, what do you think we should do now?"

Tatsuya and Masaki exchanged glances.

Masaki was the one who broached the topic first. "Normally, we'd want to interrogate this man, but..." he said, casting a sullen look at the old immortalist sitting on the path. He was the only one who was still conscious out of the whole band of attackers. "I doubt he'll answer honestly, and now that we've taken the ancient magicians down, their bounded field should be gone as well."

"Meaning...people will come?"

"Yes. We should be able to claim self-defense for having wounded them...but they were the ones who burned their own arms."

"But interrogation isn't allowed for civilians. If we're careless, it could turn into torture... And then we could be the ones arrested by the police on suspicions of malicious arrest, duress, and assault."

"I feel the same."

"...How about you, Tatsuya?"

"I doubt you two would be arrested, but I agree with the rest. More importantly, wouldn't it be wiser to hand them over to the police like we're supposed to?"

Mayumi, who had been frowning in thought, her lips curled downward, gave a resigned sigh. "I'll have the police come."

"Please, allow me to contact them," Miyuki stated, information terminal already out.

"Thank you, Miyuki."

While Miyuki called the police, Mayumi and Masaki watched on.

They didn't notice Tatsuya staring hard at the esoteric Buddhist magicians lying on the ground.

Nor did they notice how Tatsuya's eyes were gazing slightly above them, unfocused.

Their day search of Arashiyama ended with a police questioning.

Probably because the wounds were so awful. It seemed even the police couldn't just gloss over things, even with the Saegusa and Ichijou names involved.

They also had the poor fortune of ending up with a detective assigned to the incident who was not friendly toward the Ten Master Clans.

Most detectives in charge of magical crimes were magicians, but not all of them were modern ones. In areas where modern magic factions were strong, such as the Tokyo area, police officers were heavily skewed toward that faction. But in places like Kyoto, where ancient magicians held a certain amount of sway, it was either half-and-half or even biased toward the other side.

The detective who questioned Tatsuya and the others was an ancient magician of the onmyoudou tradition. It was certainly better than him being an esoteric Buddhist, but his antipathy toward the Clans undeniably affected the inquiry. Doggedly suspected of excessive self-defense, they ended up mentally exhausted. Neither Mayumi nor Masaki was short-tempered enough to lose their cool, but anyone with a slightly lower boiling point could have caused a disaster.

Additionally, Tatsuya had his hands full making sure Miyuki didn't cause a commotion with the detective for suspecting her brother of unjustifiable self-defense.

Eventually, they were released from the police station, and with a salient decrease in their energy levels, they returned to the hotel. When they got back, Fujibayashi was waiting for Tatsuya in the room. Incidentally, Masaki had said he was going back to Kanazawa and headed for the station on his motorcycle. He would be using a long-distance train he could load his bike onto. As for Mayumi, there was an empty room, so she'd gotten a single-bed room at this hotel.

"You both look a little tired."

That was the first thing Fujibayashi said after a few quick greetings.

"We were held up at the police station."

"What? Did something happen?"

"I'll fill you in on the details later, ma'am. More importantly, how is Minoru doing?" Tatsuya asked, sitting down next to Fujibayashi. Miyuki sat next to him and looked at her as well.

Minoru was asleep. He seemed calm as he did so.

"He took some medicine and went to sleep. He was having a pretty hard time until just a little while ago, though," answered Fujibayashi, her face clouding. Judging by her expression, this was more than simply straining himself a little too much.

"...Listen, Tatsuya. I have a favor to ask."

"What is it?"

With her eyes still slightly averted, it seemed she had a hard time answering him.

Her "favor" only took concrete form after the second hand of the clock had made a full revolution.

"It's about Minoru's body..."

Tatsuya silently awaited her next words.

"He's healthy from a medical perspective, you know. His immune system and nervous system are both perfectly fine. The doctors say they don't know why he's this prone to sickness."

"You aren't asking me for medical advice, correct, Lieutenant?"

"No, I'd talk to Dr. Yamanaka if I needed that."

"Right. Then...?"

"I think—well, it isn't just me. The scientist working for the Fujibayashi family has the same opinion. We think maybe his psionic body is the reason he tends to get sick so much."

The psionic body. One of the many names for the eidos recording information of one's physical body, existing in a layer overlapping with the body. One theory posited they were the truth behind what people had called an "ethereal body" from ages past, but opinions on that were still split.

The psionic body moved in tandem with the physical body. People who had trained to control their body at will could move their body in excess of nerve conduction velocity, without relying on nerve pulses, to control their psionic body. They could also modify their internal organs' functions as well as strengthen them. The psionic body causing changes in the physical body was a concept not at all foreign to magicians like Tatsuya and the others.

"What would you have me do, then?"

The psionic body affected the physical body. That was a popular way of thinking for magicians. It being popular meant there were also many people researching it. The Fujibayashi family scientist was probably one of them. It didn't seem to Tatsuya like she'd have something to ask of him specifically.

"…I want you to *look* at Minoru's psionic body. With your Elemental Sight."

Tatsuya widened his eyes in surprise. Not only him, but Miyuki, sitting quietly next to him, also widened her eyes.

"As far as I'm aware, when it comes to analyzing psionic information bodies…Tatsuya, you're the best. I'm not going to ask you to heal his condition. I was just wondering if you could maybe figure out the cause."

Well, sure, he might be able to do that. It wasn't strange for her to think that way, since she knew his abilities.

"Lieutenant Fujibayashi, do you understand what it means to *show* me something that deeply?"

Tatsuya's eyes could read the information of what something was made of. What comprised it, how it was created. The cause that produced a current effect.

His "eyes" were structural information-reading eyes—ones that could read cause and effect. Showing his "eyes" that level of detail was equivalent to putting the very root of the person called Minoru Kudou on display.

"I do, and I'm asking anyway. I'll take responsibility for this."

"…All right."

Nobody could take that sort of responsibility. Understanding that, Tatsuya nodded.

And Fujibayashi would have understood that, too. She promised to take responsibility for something she actually couldn't fully bear the burden of. Tatsuya didn't know what had her so mentally backed into a corner, but if he was only looking at Minoru's current condition, and not going back into the past, nothing about it was a negative for Tatsuya. Fujibayashi had helped him out quite a few times, too, so he decided that if she really wanted him to do this, he'd grant her wish.

He directed his *eyes* at the sleeping young man. If he was asleep due to medicinal effects, he wouldn't notice the "gaze" directed at him and resist it. And just as Tatsuya suspected, his access to Minoru's psionic body went smoothly.

"Brother?!"

Timewise, it hadn't even taken one second. But when Miyuki's voice dragged him back to reality, a greasy sweat had come onto his brow.

"I'm fine. No need to worry," he said, giving his sister a smile.

Miyuki offered an expression of relief and immediately stood up, before heading to the bathroom at a trot. When she returned, a moist towel was gripped in her hand.

"I can do it myself."

"No, Brother. Allow me to do it."

It wasn't anything to argue about. Tatsuya let Miyuki wipe the sweat from his face.

"…How did it look, Tatsuya?" asked Fujibayashi after Miyuki finished.

In the span of a moment, Tatsuya had a mountain of things he wanted to say to Fujibayashi—no, to the whole Kudou family. By seeing what lay at Minoru's core, he'd learned the secret of his birth.

But he swallowed all of that and answered only what he'd been asked.

"As I expected. When I saw how powerful his magic is after hearing that he was prone to illness but not feeble, I'd wondered whether the psionic pressure was too strong for his body to endure."

"You mean his magical power is too strong, and it's causing abnormalities in his body?"

"The psionic body is a person's psionic vessel. Psionic pressure is the same as physical gas pressure in that it's determined by how many psions are in the vessel and how active they are. In Minoru's case, his psions are incredibly active, much more so than other magicians."

"The psionic pressure is causing his psionic body to break down…?"

"This part is a little hard to explain, but the psionic body is a bundle of countless tiny intersecting pipes, turning and twisting—information in the same form as the physical body. Psions run through those pipes, and I believe their pressure has caused some of his pipes to burst, and that breakdown is feeding back into his physical body."

Fujibayashi was about to let out a cry, but Tatsuya continued before she could.

"I'm not sure if I should call it fortunate, but the broken pipes are made of the same stuff as the psions that caused them to break. If his psions are active, that means the psionic body's recovery is operating properly, too. The cycle of breakdown and repair of the psionic body is being conducted in a short cycle. I believe that may be the cause of Minoru's condition."

"Then they don't stay broken…"

"I think his recovery abilities are actually higher than an average magician's, too."

A look of relief washed over Fujibayashi's face. But soon, the clouds of gloom came back to her pretty features. "But what should we do…?"

"You could suppress the psionic activity directly, but that would mean restraining his abilities as a magician. I doubt either he or his family would want his magical power to decrease. Which means the only way to fix the problem is to strengthen his psionic body."

"How do we do that?"

"I don't know."

Fujibayashi hung her head, hiding her expression. She probably didn't want him to see the conflict on her face.

If one was to consider Minoru's health most important, limiting his magical power was certain to do the trick. But Minoru's magic—being a magician of exceptional quality *was* his identity.

Tatsuya doubted Minoru would be happy if he got a healthy body in exchange for limiting his magical power. But it was doubtlessly more painful for the family than him to watch him live four months of every year in a sickbed.

"…Thanks. It's enough that we know this much now. I'll try asking an expert in the future," said Fujibayashi, still downcast.

Minoru woke up about thirty minutes after that. By then, Fujibayashi had fully recovered, too. Or maybe she was trying hard not to let Minoru see how awful her face looked.

"Minoru, how do you feel?" Tatsuya asked.

"I'm sorry for worrying you."

Minoru deeply lowered his head. Or at least, he tried to. The motion stopped halfway when Tatsuya held up his palm in front of him.

"No need to apologize. If you'd collapsed because you neglected your health, that would be one thing. But this is because of your constitution, right? You're not at fault. I can't agree with apologies when it's not even your responsibility."

Tatsuya's voice was fairly firm. It was less a comforting, consoling tone than a reproving one. Tatsuya had scolded him not to feel overly guilty about things and, by doing so, had encouraged him.

"Sorry… Er, I mean, thank you."

Minoru lowered his eyes. This time, Tatsuya didn't say anything, either.

"Anyway, Tatsuya—" began Fujibayashi, about to say she was ready to hear the police story she'd missed before.

"We're back! Tatsuya, Miyuki? You're early. Oh—Lieutenant Fujibayashi, right?"

"Wait, Lieutenant Fujibayashi's here? Oh. 'Sup. Tatsuya, you got back before us."

"Hello, Tatsuya. Umm, and hello again, Lieutenant Fujibayashi."

Mikihiko and the others, who had been at the Thesis Competition venue, returned then. They all looked surprised that Fujibayashi was here.

"I'm not on military duty right now, so would you mind dropping the *Lieutenant*? Fujibayashi is fine."

Fujibayashi met their surprise with an adult smile. Erika was fine with it, since she was a girl, too, and Leo also had on his normal face. The remaining person showed a normal boyish response. Perhaps it was a good thing Mizuki wasn't here.

Erika sat across from the futon in which Minoru lay. In contrast to Miyuki's elegant sitting, Erika sat in a decorous *seiza* position; it was picturesque, each with a different charm.

"Minoru, how are you doing?"

"I'm, er, I'm fine now. I'm sorry for worrying you."

Erika was certainly a beauty, but objectively speaking, Minoru's features were better-looking. Getting flustered at her friendly smile regardless was a very age-appropriate, cute thing to do. Part of that may have been his situation, in which no girls his age around him would interact with him the way Erika did—friendly to put it in good terms, and overly familiar to put it in bad.

"Oh, okay."

Erika, too, knew it wasn't the time or the place to tease Minoru for his inexperienced reaction.

Tatsuya reseated himself to face the center of the room. Miyuki, too, followed suit, edging closer to him. Fujibayashi moved to Minoru's side, and in exchange, Minami moved to Miyuki's. Erika moved straight across from Tatsuya, and then Leo and Mikihiko sat down as well. Now they were all sitting in a circle.

"Let's trade information on what happened today," Tatsuya prompted.

"I'll start." Mikihiko nodded. "Though, there's almost nothing to discuss. We didn't find any places where suspicious people might be hiding. No response from my *shikigami*, either. And a lot of police magicians were out on patrol, maybe because of what happened yesterday. With all of them around, I don't know if even foreign secret agencies could cause anything like last year."

"I guess it's thanks to you that the Thesis Competition will be safe, since you risked your lives yesterday."

"Risked our lives… Well, I guess you could put it that way."

Mikihiko looked unsatisfied, and next to him, Erika and Leo were arguing—"Yeah, it's your job to risk your life, huh?" and "What was that?!"—but nobody paid any attention to them.

"Anyway, we did get somewhere with preparing for the Thesis Competition, but nowhere with searching for foreign operatives."

"Just the guys we captured yesterday should be enough. The police seem to be on the case with their hideout, so we can leave that up to the authorities. And searching for operatives is supposed to be the police's job anyway."

"Brother, saying that won't get us anywhere."

With Miyuki putting in her two cents, Tatsuya took a turn at being the reporter. "We were attacked at the foot of Ogurayama."

"The foot of Mount Ogura," Minoru murmured. "The Kameyama region of Arashiyama Park?"

Responding with a nod, Tatsuya continued his explanation. "There were thirteen attackers in all. Twelve esoteric Buddhist magicians and one defected immortalist. We handed them all over to the police."

"I expected that from Tatsuya, Miyuki, and the heir to the Ichijou family. You could throw ten times that at them and they wouldn't care."

"They weren't easy opponents."

Grinning dryly at Erika's words, Tatsuya suddenly remembered the doubts he'd had earlier.

"Mikihiko, the attackers were using fire to make these double-edged swords with snakes or dragons coiled around them. Do you know what kind of spell that was?"

Mikihiko, suddenly questioned, wasn't able to respond right away, but even so, he produced an answer within ten seconds. "…That must have been the spell Kurikara Sword."

"The one Acala is said to possess?"

"Yes. The spell models itself on Acala's demon-slaying sword and borrows its power. The symbolic power is the destruction of demons. Applied in modern magic terms, it would be a type of anti-magic spell that destroys magic programs, which have been overwritten by eidos by coming in contact with a target in the process of casting magic."

"Huh… Pretty cool that ancient magic has a spell like that."

Mikihiko frowned at the words Erika let slip. It had felt like the remark of a modern magician looking down on ancient magic. But Erika frequently said insensitive things without trying to be mean. He changed his mind, figuring it was a little too late to go fault-finding with her.

"But I'm surprised you ran into magicians skilled enough to used advanced magic like that. Because of how it works, the Kurikara Sword disables the caster's own magic as well, so it's incredibly hard to maintain."

"What if they tried to use it anyway?"

"They wouldn't be able to. The spell's casting point is the caster's hand—the Kurikara Sword disables any magic its flames touch. It's not enough to just avoid touching the blade. You need to maintain a little distance between the materialized flame sword and the hand. Any magician without that technical skill would never be able to use it… Of course, if another magician had used a spell to force them to use it, then it's a different story."

"If they were forced to use it, what would happen to them?"

"It would set their hand on fire."

"What?!" cried out Erika, leaning back. Miyuki frowned in distaste.

"It may be given form with magic, but the Kurikara Sword's flames are the real thing, materialized. If someone made you hold on to something like that for a while, of course it would set your hand on fire. I hear rumors of terrible spells that burn a person's arm in order to construct the sword with it, but that's not a *demon-slaying* sword. It would be more like a demon's *people-slaying* sword."

Tatsuya and Miyuki furtively exchanged glances. With their eye contact, they decided not to go into the details.

"I see. They must have been pretty experienced, then."

"You guys are amazing for beating them unharmed."

"Miyuki and Ichijou deserve the credit. Anyway, I wanted to talk about what we do now."

"Huh? Aren't we checking out of the hotel and going back to Tokyo today?"

As Erika said, their plans were originally to check out in the evening, though it was irregular, and return to Tokyo.

"You should all go back to Tokyo as planned. I'm going to be staying another night. Tomorrow, I'll go to the police again and ask about the guys they arrested today."

"Brother, in that case, allow me to—"

"Miyuki." Tatsuya cut off his sister halfway through. "You're the student council president. You shouldn't be taking two straight days off school at a time like this."

Tatsuya was more important than school for Miyuki, but she was powerless to resist the strongly worded order.

"...All right."

"Then I'll come, too! I've got plenty of connections in the police."

"Erika... Skipping school isn't very admirable."

"Skipping school?! How rude!"

With Erika turning away from him, Tatsuya turned to Mikihiko. "And the disciplinary committee chairman being absent two days in a row wouldn't be good, either."

"What, so *you're* fine?"

"My position demands I do a little bit more investigating on something."

Mikihiko and Leo both knew Tatsuya's *position*. Erika had caught on to even more of the details than them. With that said, they had no choice but to back down.

After seeing Miyuki and the others off at the station, Tatsuya went back to the hotel. It took a lot of work to get Miyuki on the train, but he managed to return her to Tokyo. He'd been prepared to change his plan when she'd clasped his right hand in hers and said "Please, Brother, be careful..." with tears in her eyes, but that hadn't been necessary.

With Minoru's condition stable, Fujibayashi ended up bringing the young man home. Minoru seemed to want to go with him on the following day's search, but he already had too many school absences. Firmly admonished by his older sister Fujibayashi, he agreed to go home.

Fortunately, the hotel had an empty room. Moving from a Japanese-style room, which was too big for one person, to a western-style single, Tatsuya was now sitting in the lounge face-to-face with Mayumi.

"I suppose I can't tell you that you should be going to school, huh?"

"Not at all. Something came up that I need to look into a little more closely."

"Something...for your other job?"

There were others in the lounge. They couldn't put up a sound-proof field in a place like this. Mayumi chose to disguise her words in another way.

"Yes, so you don't need to worry about anything."

"Honestly, I appreciate you saying that. I felt like I was more than a minor nuisance today."

Tatsuya shook his head, then changed the topic. "About tomorrow, would you mind staying here for me?"

"Here... You mean at the hotel?!"

Tatsuya nodded, and Mayumi's mood visibly worsened. "Am I that much of a hindrance? I mean, maybe I didn't help very much today, but—"

"That's not it," Tatsuya reassured with a smile and a shake of his head. "I consider your abilities to be quite high," he asserted, peering directly into her eyes.

Mayumi's cheeks flushed, and she looked away. "Then why are you leaving me here?"

"It isn't because it'll be dangerous."

Mayumi had probably figured he'd tell her it was too dangerous. She looked back at Tatsuya with an expression of surprise.

"At the rate we're going, we'll never see an end to this. Tomorrow, I'm going to be somewhat more forceful with how I approach things. I don't want civilians to have to see it. Especially not a lady like you."

Mayumi once again averted her eyes. "I...I'll be fine. I may not look like it, but I'm used to roughhousing."

She certainly did make it through the Yokohama battlefield, and she'd fought against Ganghu Lu, the Man-Eating Tiger, as well. She might have been fine with roughhousing, but her tongue had grown rather dubious.

"Even so. I'm the one who doesn't want to be seen," he said, resignation mixed into his voice.

Eyes still averted, Mayumi began to play with her fingers restlessly. "If that's how it is, then, well, I suppose there's no helping it."

As she ended the sentence, face fully away from his, her body suddenly gave a start, as though she'd just realized something.

"...Whoa, whoa."

Mayumi returned her gaze to Tatsuya. Her eyes were narrowed in suspicion.

"I almost fell for the same old trick again."

Tatsuya put up his hands and shook his head, feigning ignorance, while the woman stared at him thinly. "I wasn't trying to pull one over on you. I'm serious—I wouldn't want a civilian to see this."

"You can't fool your senior that easy."

Mayumi was still staring hard at him. Internally, Tatsuya was nonplussed. He couldn't recall ever having deceived Mayumi or trapping her. She seemed to have some kind of odd idea in her mind.

Not wanting a civilian, especially a woman, to see was undeniably the truth. But there was nothing to be gained by having a staring contest like this.

"...All right," Tatsuya finally sighed. "But in exchange, promise not to pass out—no matter what—all right?"

So warned, Mayumi preened. "I'll be fine. Despite my appearance, I am an adult, you know."

*An unreliable one*, thought Tatsuya, but he would never say that out loud, of course.


"Oh, good, you made it back."

*"I was so anxious because you weren't with me, Brother."*

"It's okay. I was watching the whole time. I never let you out of my vision."

*"You're right. I'm sorry."*

"Nothing to apologize for. In fact, now I'm the one who feels sorry. I'll definitely come home tomorrow, so make sure to lock up before going to bed tonight."

*"Come, Brother. How young do you think I am?"*

"You're my little sister no matter how old you get."

*"...I believe those words are for a parent to say to their daughter."*

"But you wouldn't want *our* father saying it, would you?"

*"I suppose not... As you command, I will be sure to lock up extra carefully and then go to sleep. Good night, Brother."*

"It's a little early, but good night, Miyuki."

Right after the call from Miyuki ended, there was a knock at the door of Tatsuya's room.

Moving right up to the door, he turned on the monitor placed there. On it was a dressed-up Mayumi.

"What's going on? It's late," asked Tatsuya as he opened the door. It was still only eight PM, but a young woman shouldn't be visiting the room of a man who wasn't her boyfriend by herself at this hour.

That's what Tatsuya thought, at least. Mayumi seemed to have other ideas.

"Tatsuya, you haven't had dinner yet, right? Want to go eat?"

She was right—he hadn't. But he'd planned to have simple fare in a cheap restaurant nearby. He hadn't intended to use the hotel's high-class restaurant...

"At the restaurant here, you mean?"

"Yes—the French place in the basement. When I asked the front desk earlier, they said there were openings, so I got ahead of myself and made a reservation."

It seemed already decided that he'd be escorting her.

He had to take caution to make sure his expression didn't sour.

"All right. I'll get changed, so could you wait in the lobby?"

"Oh, you're fine like that."

"No, I could never go in this."

Mayumi's outfit was a black, A-line dress with a matching black lace gown on top—both chic and pretty. Her shoes and accessories complemented the outfit, too, so he couldn't possibly sit with her in his normal clothes.

Tatsuya flashed a pained grin and shut the door.

"Wow! Tatsuya, that looks really good on you!"

"Not as much as yours does, Saegusa."

Tatsuya's words weren't modesty, but his actual feelings. His outfit was nothing but a suit and a necktie, enough to meet the bare minimum dress code; he'd brought it here in case of emergency.

"Let's get seated, then."

The restaurant wasn't as formal as Tatsuya had anticipated. There were no waiters, only a waitress to show them to their table.

"After you."

Tatsuya went behind Mayumi and pulled her chair out.

"Oh, well, thank you." She tossed a smile over her shoulder and sat.

After settling in across from her, Tatsuya waited for Mayumi to pick up her menu before opening his own. It was the kind printed on paper, unusual in this day and age.

"What'll you have, Tatsuya?"

"Let's see. I'll probably have the main course."

"I see. The à la carte sounds fun, but maybe a regular meal is safer at a place we've never been to."

With that sort of exchange, both of them ordered the main course in the end.

Nothing noteworthy happened while they were eating. They didn't know who might be listening, so they couldn't exactly talk about the incidents they'd been dealing with. Halfway through the meal, Mayumi *had* muttered about how inconvenient it was not to be able to use a soundproof field, but that was the only time Tatsuya warned her with his eyes.

He'd learn something in these two days. The people of Kyoto

were hostile toward magicians. He'd thought they'd be friendly or, at the very least, neutral, since the Magic Association's main location was here, but the reality was quite the opposite.

*Has there been some trouble between the Association and the local residents?*

The situation was bad enough to make him consider the possibility. That was why he adjusted his CAD slightly higher up his wrist to completely hide it in his sleeve. He decided it was best to avoid saying or doing anything that might give him away.

Additionally, Mayumi wasn't wearing one at all. Whether it was so she didn't provoke those nearby or simply because it didn't match her outfit, though, he wasn't sure.

The real trouble came after they finished their dessert, while they were enjoying their postmeal coffee. Specifically when Mayumi suggested going to the bar.

"…I know you don't need me to tell you this, but I'm still in high school."

"Oh, come on. Not a single person thinks of you as a high school student anymore. You don't even look like one with the uniform on."

Mayumi's remark was an innocent one—but that innocence was what delivered such a boring shock to Tatsuya.

The shock must have worked, because Tatsuya ended up being dragged in front of the bar against his will.

Just before they went in, Mayumi turned around and brought her mouth close to Tatsuya's ear. "No calling me Saegusa here. Call me Mayumi, okay?"

"…Why?"

Tatsuya's response came a moment later. He'd uncharacteristically allowed Mayumi to catch him off balance.

"Well, being too formal just makes it sound like we're in school, doesn't it? I already call you Tatsuya anyway."

What in the world was she up to?

"If they think we're students, it'll be trouble."

After adding on a seemingly forced reason, Mayumi looped her arm around Tatsuya's and dragged him into the bar.

It was a cozy place, with only one counter. The only other guests were a couple near the back. The bartender only gave them a glance as they entered, then continued stirring cocktails.

Tatsuya had Mayumi sit on the opposite end of the counter, then sat beside her.

"An Alexander, please. Tatsuya, what do you want?"

"One Summer Delight."

The well-tanned bartender turned his eyes to stare at Tatsuya. But he nodded without saying anything, grabbing a measuring cup.

Looking more closely, the bartender was less tan than leathery—his skin was firm, like his body had been well-trained in the sun. His movements, too, were sharp, and he gave the impression of someone who had undergone very specific combat training in the past. Tatsuya couldn't help but wonder what the man used to do.

"Why something nonalcoholic?"

But Mayumi seemed more interested in Tatsuya's order itself. A Summer Delight was made of lime juice, syrup, and carbonated water. As she said, it was a nonalcoholic cocktail.

"Please, I beg mercy, my lady."

"Huh?"

"As your humble bodyguard, I mustn't dull my movements should something happen."

"Huh? What?"

Mayumi probably wanted to enjoy pretending to be lovers. But it went against Tatsuya's creed to let someone else pilot his ship.

The bartender, rumbling a shaker hard, poured the slightly brown, cream-colored liquid into a footed glass, then placed it in front of Mayumi.

The one he addressed was not Mayumi, but Tatsuya.

"Are you serving as her bodyguard, sir? If I may, you look quite strong despite your youth."

"I'm still in training."

"How modest of you."

The bartender took out a new shaker, then poured lime juice and red grenadine syrup into it, adding in a little bit of sugar syrup.

He shook it more lightly than last time. After adding the contents to the carbonated water in the glass, he placed the completed drink in front of Tatsuya.

"If I may be so rude, sir…" prefaced the bartender, moving his face closer to Tatsuya. The couple sitting on the other end of the bar were off in their own little world and didn't seem to be listening to them.

"Would you happen to be a magician?"

Tatsuya didn't let surprise show on his face. "If you knew that, would that make you a magician as well?"

The couple in the back got out of their seats. The bartender gave a polite bow and saw them off.

As he cleaned up after them, he continued the interrupted conversation.

"It was a long time ago, sir. I lost my magician's abilities during a training accident."

"Is that so? I'm terribly sorry."

The bartender looked up and shook his head at Tatsuya's apology. "Like I said, sir, it was a long time ago. And I was the one who started this conversation."

And then Mayumi broke in with a peeved voice. "Can I get another, please?"

"My lady," Tatsuya quipped again, "I believe you may be rushing things—"

"I'm fine. And I don't need any sass from my abstinent nondrinker Tatsuya."

She didn't seem to appreciate how the conversation had turned. Or maybe she didn't like their newfound roles he'd created.

"I'm terribly sorry."

The bartender apologized, interpreting it as his own fault, then went back to washing, a wry grin on his face.

But Tatsuya wasn't about to halt their conversation just yet.

"There is something I would like to know, if that's all right."

The bartender gave him a look asking if it was okay to leave *her* hanging, but Tatsuya didn't feel any need to improve Mayumi's mood.

"Did something happen between the Magic Association and the people of Kyoto?"

"Why that question, sir?"

"It may be my imagination, but to me, it seems the people here don't have a very good impression of magicians."

"Ah, so you noticed that the people from Kyoto aren't so friendly to our type."

The bartender wiped his hands with a towel. With his hands now dry, he started polishing the glasses. Tatsuya saw it, thinking maybe his dedication to not using machines was to more properly play the role of the bartender, a measure to maintain the look and feel of a bar.

"There wasn't any particularly major trouble. It was more of a series of minor differences. All things that people who came from somewhere else tend to do. With the people doing it happening to be magicians, though, the people here have reacted more extremely."

As Tatsuya made a face like that was hard to swallow, the bartender offered a plate with a piece of chocolate on it. "For the young lady."

"Thank you."

Tatsuya took the plate and put it in front of Mayumi. She took the piece and put it in her mouth, then turned her cheek almost audibly at him.

He and the bartender exchanged pained grins.

The bartender, still smiling with his eyes, continued to talk. "I believe it was because Kyoto was chosen to host the Magic Association's main headquarters. Kyoto residents may feel as though magicians have taken over the city."

"Taken over? Any magicians living here are residents of Kyoto, too."

"Ever since I lost my magic, I've come to understand how terrifying the existence of a magician is to someone who can't use magic. If magic is used on someone who has no magical ability, there's nothing they can do. More than that—they'll be hurt or have precious things lost, before they even know what's happened. And in the worst case, they could be killed. And I know what you're about to say."

The bartender stopped Tatsuya, who was about to speak.

"Nobody can do anything against a gun, either. But think about it the other way—gun ownership can be regulated, but magic ownership can't. For nonmagician locals, magicians are strangers from somewhere else who carry invisible guns and full stocks of ammunition they can never be separated from. Kyoto isn't special in that regard. It's something that can happen anywhere."

Mayumi's gait upon exiting the bar was fairly dubious.

*I told her three was too many.*

Tatsuya was complaining to himself, but it made no difference now. He hadn't known that cocktail had over 20 percent alcohol, either.

"Here's your room, Saegusa. Please get a grip."

"Urm... Thanks, so much, Tatsuya."

Mayumi looked like she was about to fall over and go to sleep on the spot. They got to her room fine, though, so that would have been mission accomplished for Tatsuya.

"Krrr..."

Seeing Mayumi about to slide down into a seated position in front of her door, though, even he couldn't just up and leave now.

"Saegusa, where's your key?"

"Right here!"

Mayumi waved her card key around. And then, for some reason, she went to slip it inside her cleavage. Tatsuya quickly snatched it away before she could.

*…What was she trying to get me to do anyway?*

Feeling a slight shudder, Tatsuya unlocked the door and went inside.

Fortunately, the common development of underwear being scattered all over the room didn't come to pass.

"Saegusa, if you want to sleep, then get into bed."

"Okay!"

Tatsuya had learned something: Mayumi was the type to revert to childish tendencies when drunk. He had a feeling there were a lot of that type around him. It was better than complaining drunks and crying ones, but it still required some work.

Stepping toward her bed, he hastily supported Mayumi right before she fell.

He brought her over to the bedside.

"Here's your bed, Saegusa. You should take off your clothes first. Your dress will get all wrinkled."

Mayumi held up both hands in front of Tatsuya.

"…What is it?"

"Take them off!"

He'd seen that one coming, and now his head was starting to hurt in earnest.

Monday, October 22. Tatsuya had once again come to Sagano, Arashiyama. This was the spot where he'd been attacked by ancient magicians the previous day.

Mayumi, saying she didn't feel well, was resting in the hotel—suffering from a hangover, needless to say. Tatsuya considered that the only plus to come from last night's events.

No sign of any police. At least, none doing any investigations into the incident the previous day. The Ten Master Clans–hating detective didn't seem to care to do a real investigation into it. Or maybe some other emergency cropped up. Either way, police oversight had been one of the things Tatsuya was concerned about, so this was a good thing.

Standing at the scene, he recalled the information he'd read the previous day. He'd gotten his data from a source who was in a cold sleep, wounded, and unconscious at the time—which kept any obstructing psionic wave emission to a minimum. From that man, he'd discerned the location of the group to which that ancient magician had belonged to—their hideout.

If he headed straight through the bamboo grove, he'd stand out more than necessary. He headed down the path instead, comparing the data in his memory to the map he called up on his information terminal.

He found his destination pretty easily.

It was an average house, albeit a large one. Actually, with how large it was, maybe it couldn't be called average.

At a glance, the building looked like a town center, the likes of which still remained in certain areas.

Tatsuya scanned the building with Elemental Sight in such a way as to not reveal himself. They didn't seem to have any particular traps set up to prevent intrusion. Without hesitation, Tatsuya slipped through the gate.

Even after getting onto the grounds, he didn't particularly sense any magic. But he'd verified after looking from the outside that it wasn't just an empty shell.

He placed a hand on the sliding door. Naturally, it was locked. A double lock, requiring both an electronic key and a physical one. Unfortunately, Tatsuya couldn't open either. He didn't have any magic that convenient. Instead, he decided to open the door with the magic he had on hand.

The door's lock broke into pieces.

Just like when he'd gone through the gate, he opened the door without any hesitation and went inside. Immediately, wheel-shaped weapons flew at him. Circular blades, each with eight radial spokes. It was an esoteric Buddhist spell tool called a magic wheel, though they seemed to be using it like a projectile weapon.

After Tatsuya avoided the deadly wheel, it stopped in midair before crashing through the door, then veered back along its initial trajectory. The one coming from another direction also turned and went back in the same way. Looking closely, thin psionic threads extended from them.

*Yo-yos?*

Their motions were the spitting image of the classic toys—which would make dealing with them easy, too. As he dodged the magic wheels again, which now numbered four, he dismantled the psionic threads.

The chakrams continued on through the door and outside.

He sensed confusion from near the wall. After dismantling the four threads, Tatsuya made a jump toward the caster, who was hidden with optical camouflage.

He could tell the transparent figure, shimmering like a mirage, had readied something like a dagger, with a blade on either side of the grip. This, too, was an esoteric Buddhist spell tool called a *dokkosho*. And the fact that it was reformed as a weapon was the same as the yo-yo-like magic wheels before.

Tatsuya detected a magic program for launching lightning attacks that was projected onto either end of the *dokkosho*. However, the eidos overwrite wasn't complete. Ignoring the precast magic, Tatsuya used flash casting to cast an oscillation spell one meter from the palm of his hand, then rammed it into the figure's chest.

Due to the virtual wave motion caused by the oscillating waves onto the solid body, the same sort also used in Active Air Mine, the body tissue one millimeter below the skin vibrated uncontrollably, starting from the point that his palm had touched. The vibrations traveled through the man's bodily fluids and spread to his upper body, and then he crumpled. With his optical camouflage dispelled, he was wearing the same outfit as the previous day's attackers.

As an invisible person—invisible through optical camouflage, rather than his body structure itself being invisible—approached from behind, Tatsuya crouched and swept his leg around in a wide arc reminiscent of Chinese martial arts. It wasn't to cause the opponent to trip brilliantly over his leg, but to trap the man's outstepped foot with his own.

The invisible man wobbled. And within that shimmering mirage, the man's back was visible.

A palm strike loaded with an oscillation spell. The second person fell to the floor.

"I know where you are even if you're invisible. Why not stop this futile effort and show yourselves?"

Men of varying ages began to appear from the mirages in answer to Tatsuya's provocation. They numbered ten. Fortunately, none were women. Tatsuya wasn't the type to hold back just because someone was female, but it was more difficult for him.

"Why aren't Marici's methods working…?!"

*Because your magic shows a lack of experience*, was what Tatsuya wanted to say. If Yakumo, for instance, had used the same technique, even Tatsuya wouldn't have had an easy time pinning him down.

"Bind him and eradicate him!"

One of the men barked the order. He didn't appear to be the oldest, but Tatsuya definitely felt the strongest magical power from him. He set his target to that man.

Tatsuya purposefully proceeded to the middle of the floor. The room was boarded, like a place for kendo, with no furniture to get in the way. *So it wasn't a town center, but a dojo*, he thought, even though it wasn't the time for that.

Surrounding Tatsuya, the ten magicians moved around him in even intervals.

A regular decagon. Two regular pentagons with one shifted three-hundred-sixty degrees—or two alternating pentagrams.

Five magicians, leaving one in between each pair, threw lariats at the same time.

Not toward Tatsuya, but toward their comrades diagonally in front of him.

Those who threw the lariats grabbed the end of other lariats thrown by the others.

A pentagram constructed with five-colored lariats.

Tatsuya was looking at it from above.

The pentagram was likely a technique for pressuring someone in the middle from five directions and strangling them.

But Tatsuya wasn't obligated to stand idly right in the middle of the enemies until the circle's completion. As soon as the lariats were thrown, he'd jumped straight up.

Kicking off the air before he reached the ceiling, he headed for one of the pentagram's vertices.

A flying kick, one seldom used in matches. But it was also a surprisingly practical skill to catch the opponent off guard.

He'd created a foothold with magic, then sprung off it to accelerate his kick; it slammed into one caster's face with the force of all his body weight plus that speed.

The pentagram fell apart. But that wouldn't be the only thing in their hand.

Before he fell, Tatsuya landed on the floor, flinging a knee out at the magician next to him.

A spell triggered only when creating a foothold. Such a magical fighting technique was only possible with flash-cast speed.

The esoteric Buddhist magicians gathered here were not physically weak by any means. They were still first-rate brawlers who attached importance to the more rigorous asceticisms. But it only mattered if they could fight normally. Tatsuya's acrobatic movements were something they virtually couldn't keep up with.

The enemy ancient magicians were only able to respond to his surprise attack when they'd been culled to five.

Right before the sixth, or the eighth if including the first two, received Tatsuya's attack, the caster behind him loosed an electric attack toward Tatsuya.

If it had been modern magic, he would have directly produced an electric current in the target.

But one of the traits of ancient magic was that electric attacks were launched from a single point—the caster, or a spot in the air—at the target.

In terms of electric attack magic, the difference didn't normally cause a problem. The speed at which the electricity traveled toward the target was one hundred thousand kilometers per second. It arrived at the target instantly. It wasn't possible to be aware of the electric attack first, then dodge it.

Right before the electric attack spell had gone off, Tatsuya had stopped his attack and jumped far to the side.

The caster trying to land the attack lost sight of where Tatsuya was. However, it was too late for him to stop his spell.

The lightning bolt fired from his *dokkosho* spell tool caused friendly fire.

Confronted by the reality of the situation, the others hesitated to use magic at all.

The opening this provided was more than enough time for Tatsuya.

Granted speed equal to self-acceleration magic by using reflective force fields as footholds, Tatsuya knocked out every last one of the ancient magicians.

The ancient magician acting as this base's leader awoke to intense pain shooting through his body.

His thoughts were scrambled. He would have stayed unconscious, except the pain was too intense to *allow* him to.

"Come to? If you understand what I'm saying, nod. I'll lighten the pain a bit."

The only thing that made it into the man's mind was that this pain would lessen, so he exerted himself to bob his head up and down.

As promised, the pain lightened a little.

His vision, blurred by the agony, cleared up just a little bit.

It was a young man.

The man had a biker helmet hiding his face, and he was straddling him.

The leader tried to form a seal and use an art.

That instant, a mind-bleaching pain assailed him.

"None of that, now. Just answer my questions."

The leader strained to nod, indicating he'd obey the voice.

The terrible pain grew slightly lighter.

This time, only a little of his thoughts returned—his vision remained blurred.

"Gongjin Zhou was here, right? A Chinese Taoist who fled from Yokohama Chinatown."

Without even considering the idea of lying, the leader nodded earnestly.

"And that man was here until Friday the twelfth. Is that right?"

The twelfth, the twelfth... The leader thought as hard as he could, but his head wasn't working right. And then, remembering that Gongjin Zhou had indeed departed here on Friday, he nodded several times.

"Where did he say he was going?"

A newly horrific pain washed over the leader. Strangely, however, his thoughts alone cleared.

His eyes were hazy, and he couldn't move his limbs, not even his fingers. And yet, his mouth moved freely.

"Said he was...going to Uji. Said there's a good hiding place near the Futagozuka Burial Mound...didn't say any more...don't know if...lying or telling the truth."

"Your subordinates were being used as puppets by a Chinese immortalist. Did you permit that?"

"I am...not their master...not in a position...to order them..."

"But you're their leader, right?"

"They're comrades...we are equal...we don't give or take orders..."

"I see. Thank you."

A moment later, the most tremendous pain of all shot through the man. His mind shut off, a circuit breaker tripped within it.

Tatsuya sent Fujibayashi a message, telling her this location and that he'd knocked out the Traditionalist magicians. He figured it would be redundant to add in a request at the end that she come take the ancient magicians into custody. He didn't have to actually write that out for Fujibayashi to arrange for their pickup.

He weighed the validity of the information he'd gotten out of this base's leader. It was hard to believe their group had no clear command structure. Group combat coordinated only through the sharing of a common purpose didn't seem possible.

But the part about where Gongjin Zhou was hiding did match the information he'd gotten from the conjurer at Kiyomizu-dera. He couldn't discard the possibility that the former esoteric Buddhist monks here were in league with the conjurer to provide him false information, but if he went so far as to doubt that, he'd need to doubt countless other things. One needed to know where the cutoff point was.

He decided that after he got home, he'd report to Hayama that it was highly possible Gongjin Zhou was hiding out in the vicinity of the Futagozuka Burial Mound in Uji.

With that settled, Tatsuya returned to the hotel only to be welcomed back by Mayumi, who was offended but was also averting her eyes in embarrassment. She told him off for some time, and while her mouth produced statements regarding his coldheartedness and his reneging on promises, her cheeks were flushed, and her eyes never met his.

He had an idea as to why she seemed so embarrassed.

Last night, Tatsuya had received the unreasonable demand from a young woman (meaning Mayumi) that he take off the clothes she was wearing. Finally fed up with everything, he had quickly stripped her dress off, tossed her underwear-clad being into bed, and left the room without looking back.

Even though it had been an ordeal and a half, he was still grateful she had thrown herself upon him, rather than a guy who would've taken advantage of the situation.

"Er, by the way…"

Having rallied off so many firm complaints before now, Mayumi suddenly began to trip over her own tongue.

"Well, there was just, I guess, something I wanted to ask you."

*How nice it would be to say "I refuse" or "I have the right to remain silent,"* Tatsuya thought blackly. He'd realized from her attitude what she was about to ask.

"I…"

And then, despite knowing they were in a room alone together, she looked around as though nervous she'd be overheard, and brought her lips closer to Tatsuya's face.

"…Why was I sleeping in my underwear?"

He very much wanted to retort *because you told me to take your clothes off,* but he couldn't possibly say that, either. "Maybe you got undressed by yourself? You were fairly drunk, but I would think you still had enough sense not to get in bed while wearing your dress."

Backing off from Mayumi's lips, which were centimeters away from contact, Tatsuya delivered his answer with an air of nonchalance.

"Would someone drunk still be able to think about that?"

"I wouldn't know. If you don't even know yourself, then there isn't any way I would."

"...You know, Tatsuya," Mayumi hummed, directing her eyes, red with embarrassment, at him for the first time since he'd returned, "I'm not exactly a heavyweight, but I am the type who remembers what happened just fine."

Tatsuya wanted to flee the scene. Unfortunately, though, he knew that escape was impermissible in this situation. It'd just make him look guilty.

"...I don't think you had to be that rough with me."

He had indeed thrown her into her bed roughly.

*But is* that *the part that needs to be criticized?* he wondered, suspicious. But if he were to ask if that was more important than her being exposed in her underwear, he would have been stepping on the tail of a king cobra.

Mayumi was watching him, still looking embarrassed.

With the incredibly awkward air having settled in like it owned the place, the last thing waiting for Tatsuya was the mentally laborious mission of seeing her back to the station closest to where she lived.

The instant Tatsuya put a hand on the gate door to his own house, the front door opened.

"Welcome home, Brother."

Greeting him as he arrived back home was, as always, Miyuki.

"Thanks. Sorry about all that."

The traces of irrepressible worry and an air of relief were visible on her face. She knew logically there were none who could harm him, but her feelings of anxiety were separate from that.

Miyuki shook her head at his apology. "No, don't be. Just seeing you safe and healthy again is enough for me."

* * *

Right after entering the house, he was forced to relax in the living room. Minami had snatched away his travel bag with his clothes in it, and Miyuki had escorted him to the sofa.

It was pointless to resist at times like these. He wasn't being served, but rather, being forced to accept service. He obediently let the two of them do as they wished.

Miyuki sat next to him, watching happily as he drank from his coffee cup. But when he put the cup on the table, she suddenly became restless. She would look at Tatsuya, then away, and then back again.

"It's fine. The job I was asked to do is going smoothly. In fact, at this stage, you could say I've fulfilled enough of my responsibilities to our aunt."

Thinking Miyuki probably wanted to know of today's results, Tatsuya preempted her and said things were going well.

"No—I wasn't doubting you, Brother..."

But it seemed what Miyuki wanted to ask was something else.

"Go ahead. What did you want to ask?"

When Tatsuya tried to draw her out, Miyuki, wavering even more, eventually shook off her hesitation and asked, "Brother, what was the cause behind Minoru's constitution?"

Taking an unforeseen surprise attack, Tatsuya was unable to immediately answer.

"It's what I mentioned yesterday—his magic power is too strong, and his body can't withstand it."

Miyuki's face clouded, and she knitted her brow in worry. "That's his current state, though, isn't it? Didn't you see the cause of that, Brother?"

"...Why would you think I did?"

"You seemed to be acting extremely unusual at the time. What in the world could have been worrying you so?"

Without meaning to, Tatsuya found himself speechless. And that was the same as confessing there *was* something else.

"Brother, please. Let me hear what it is that worries you. Allow me to share in your concerns."

Miyuki was looking up at him, eyes absolutely earnest. He could tell she wanted nothing more than to lighten the burden on his heart.

"You're better off not knowing."

And that made Tatsuya even less willing to talk about the secret he'd learned with her. ——Incidentally, though, Tatsuya didn't feel much of a taboo against any invasions of Minoru's privacy or that of the Kudou family's.

"Please, Brother. You don't need to suffer alone!"

But with her holding back tears and pleading with him, he eventually couldn't hide it anymore.

"All right. It's fairly shocking, so I want you to prepare yourself to hear it."

Miyuki gasped. Seeing his younger sister's posture straighten, Tatsuya abruptly got right to the point.

"Minoru and Fujibayashi are half siblings, with the same father."

As she comprehended the meaning, she covered her mouth with her hands.

"How can that be?! I mean, Minoru's father… His younger sister is Fujibayashi's mother…"

"Minoru is engineered. Probably born from artificial insemination. It was not an act of incest, strictly speaking, but he is still a child born from a brother and sister."

Miyuki's face tightened in shock. She needed a fair bit of time before she could produce words again.

"Then… Minoru's    constitution    is    a    harmful    effect    of inbreeding…?"

Tatsuya shook his head. But that wasn't an expression of certain denial.

"We can't say for sure. The issue is the imbalance in his psionic body, and physically, he's healthy. It may have been some bug that cropped up during the engineering process."

He paused there and sighed.

"But we can't reject the possibility that his condition is caused by genes that are too alike. Even the magician-development institutes avoided using genes from parents and children and from siblings. We still understand very little about the ways genetics affect the psionic body and the mind."

The blood drained from Miyuki's face.

She was as shocked as if this all had been *about her*.

[9]

October 27, Saturday. With the Thesis Competition occurring the next day, First High's representatives and support team, including security, set off for Kyoto that afternoon. First High's presentation would be sixth, starting at 1:40 PM, so if they'd chosen to depart the morning of, they would certainly still make it. But on years when the competition was held in Kyoto, First High traditionally stayed over the night before.

In a large bus and a truck carrying the presentation's experimental apparatus, they headed for an exclusive terminal. They first traveled to a certain station on the outskirts of Kyoto in a car-train (a high-speed train capable of holding both vehicles and passengers with luggage), then went from there to a hotel in Kyoto.

The C.R. Hotel in which First High always stayed tended to be too posh for high school students, but traditions once ingrained were difficult to change. None of the students ever complained they wanted a lower-grade hotel, either, so things had remained the same for a long time.

"We're heeere!"

The first one who got off the bus was Kanon, who had been enjoying the bus trip with Isori. Her hopes of doing so for last year's Nines had been dashed, and she was certainly making up for it this time. She should have gotten her revenge at this year's competition; maybe she was the sort of person who became obsessed with something if it had failed to go her way even once.

The last one to alight was Izumi. Miyuki, as student council president, was actually supposed to be the one making sure everyone got off the bus with all their property intact, but Izumi had volunteered for the job, insisting it was too far below Miyuki's station.

In exchange, Miyuki handled their hotel check-in. Tatsuya and Honoka split the job of passing out the room keys.

And so, the students of First High scattered to their assigned rooms.

The rooms they were staying in were twins, cheaper than the Japanese-style ones. Tatsuya's roommate ended up being Mikihiko. Noncoincidentally, of course—they'd meant for that.

"Mikihiko, can you handle things now?"

"Sure thing. I'm disappointed I can't come along, though."

"I couldn't ask that much of you. And there's the information disclosure problem. More importantly…"

"What's up, Tatsuya?" he wondered, as Tatsuya began to struggle with his words.

"…Nothing. I want you to take care of everyone from school. I doubt anything will happen, but it's best to be vigilant."

"Yeah, I get that."

What Tatsuya had almost done was point out that Mizuki was here, too. The art club had been heavily involved in creating the experimental apparatus this year, and they'd been prioritized as members of their support team, with her among them. He'd been wondering if Mikihiko was thinking about her.

But in the end, he hadn't said any of that, deciding it was none of his business. He figured it wasn't the kind of thing an outsider should meddle with.

"I might be out pretty late. I'll tell you if it seems like I won't be back."

"All right. Be careful."

Hiding his holster and his favored handgun-shaped CAD, the Silver Horn, tucked inside his blouson, Tatsuya raised a hand in response and left the room.

The first place Tatsuya headed was a smaller, less conspicuous hotel than the C.R. Hotel, where the First High students were staying. It was one which the Kuroba family frequently used for work.

"Hello, Tatsuya."

"We've been expecting you."

In the lobby, Fumiya and Ayako, respectively, had been waiting for him.

"Sorry for having you come all this way."

"Don't be," Fumiya encouraged. "We were the ones who brought this matter to you in the first place."

"Well, let's not stand around talking. Why don't you have a seat, Tatsuya?" Ayako added. She led him to the sofa, and after having him settle in and taking her own seat across the table from him, Fumiya brought drinks.

Tatsuya was about to ask if it was okay to drink beverages here, before spotting a 3H wiping down another table. Actually, that type of machine was a business model called a Humanoid Servant or, more frequently, a Servanoid. Deciding it wouldn't pose any issues, Tatsuya eagerly accepted the drink.

Ayako deployed a soundproof field. No alarms went off at the unlawful usage of magic. It seemed this hotel wasn't simply a place the Kuroba family frequented, as he'd heard, but one which had been modified to perfectly serve the Kurobas'—the Yotsubas' needs.

"And that's that. Tatsuya, everything has been arranged at your request."

"We've gotten the same kind of model of motorcycle as the kind you usually use. It's parked in the parking lot."

"And as for clothing, we've arranged knife-proof and bulletproof articles, if you would care to change."

"There are boots, gloves, and helmets all ready to be used for combat as well."

"You've certainly spared no expense…"

Tatsuya nearly broke out into a laugh at their efforts, which far exceeded his expectations. Of course, he realized they were doing so out of earnest concern for him, so he didn't actually laugh.

"Thanks. I'll make use of all of them."

Fumiya and Ayako offered sincerely happy-looking smiles at his words.

"Then I'll show you to your room."

Ayako put down her half-finished cup of tea and stood up. Fumiya rose without finishing his drink, too, so Tatsuya followed suit.

The outfit they'd brought for him fit to his body so well that it was a little creepy. He was extremely curious as to where they'd gotten his sizes from, but somehow, he got the feeling he was better off not asking that question, so he didn't.

"How much have we narrowed it down?"

Tatsuya was asking about Gongjin Zhou's hiding place, needless to say.

He'd given the information he'd gotten on Monday to the Kuroba family through Hayama. They'd been using it to search for the man this past week.

"We've almost pinpointed him."

"I see—fine work as always from the Kuroba," Tatsuya said. "And?"

Fumiya hesitated slightly. "Well, it's hard to believe, but…"

"There is almost no doubt that he is being sheltered at the JGDF's Uji Resupply Base Number Two," Ayako answered in his place, since he was indeed having trouble saying it.

Tatsuya didn't say *but that's ridiculous.* "I see. Makes sense he was hard to find, then," he noted, moving to the communication console.

"Fumiya."

"Yes, sir!"

Addressed by an almost chillingly stoic voice, Fumiya gave back his reply more formally than he needed to.

Tatsuya's voice was proof that his emotions had reached a limit. As someone unable to experience emotions any stronger than a certain amount, the moment his anger reached that threshold, he would express only emotionless intent to others.

The JDF unit's traitorous act went beyond what he could tolerate. Ever since Miyuki had been shot by a rebel soldier in Okinawa, he had almost zero tolerance for betrayal.

*A blade of ice glitters when unsheathed*, went the saying. The expression referred to how a well-sharpened and polished Japanese katana glowed in a cold, eerie manner. And it tended to fit Tatsuya when he lost himself to anger.

"Can I communicate with the outside?"

"Just a moment."

Fumiya reached out from his side and input a security code on the keyboard.

At his prompt, Tatsuya sat down in front of the console.

Tatsuya entered a complicated code. After waiting about five seconds, a female officer appeared on the monitor.

*"Tatsuya, what's going on?"*

The code Tatsuya had input was the emergency call code assigned to Fujibayashi from the Independent Magic Battalion.

"Lieutenant, I am currently in Kyoto."

*"I see…"*

With just that, understanding came over her face.

"Have you found him?"

Fujibayashi gave a resigned sigh at his question, which he'd purposely omitted words from.

*"We have a good idea where Gongjin Zhou is hiding."*

Tatsuya hadn't only told Hayama about the intel he'd gotten from Kiyomizu-dera and the Traditionalists in Arashiyama—he'd told her, too. Even for the JDF, Gongjin Zhou was a very dangerous criminal who had brought a foreign military force here. They didn't need Tatsuya to ask them to look for him. And Tatsuya had intended to take advantage of that.

"Where is he?"

Fujibayashi offered a bitter look at his curt question.

*"…Military police are planning to mobilize. Please don't intervene, Specialist Ooguro."*

"You can't apply special officer regulations to this. *Ms.* Fujibayashi, where is Gongjin Zhou? Please answer me as a relative of the Kudou family, which promised me their cooperation."

*"…Inside the JGDF Uji Resupply Base Number Two. Tatsuya, please, just leave the rest of this to the JDF. Even if it is you, if they find out you illegally entered the base, we'll all be in a lot of trouble."*

"Understood. Good-bye."

*"Tatsuya?!"*

Without clarifying what he "understood," Tatsuya ended the call. Not only that, he used the console to lock down the circuit.

Turning around, he nodded to his cousins, who were watching their conversation wide-eyed from behind him. "I have confirmation now. What's the plan?"

Gathering himself, Fumiya answered, "We begin the operation at sunset and infiltrate the base."

"What's our entry route?"

"We'll be marching in through several gates and *not* doing anything like jumping over fences," Ayako stated.

"Of course, we'll station people outside the gates, too, in case the target flees the complex."

"Would have liked more people…" Muttering, Tatsuya stood up. "Fumiya, Ayako, I'm going to grab a little more combat power. He might not have time to meet us on-site, but when the time comes, I'll charge in, too."

"All right. Communications won't work from now on."

"Be careful, Tatsuya."

"I want both of you to keep your wits about you, got it?"

"Yes."

"Of course."

Nodding at their replies, Tatsuya headed for the parking lot, where the motorcycle they'd gotten was waiting.

He knew instantly which bike was his. With his key pointing an arrow toward it, there was no way to mistake it.

The western sky was already getting red. There wasn't much time left until the operation began. Still riding the bike, he used voice input to operate the wireless interface of the information terminal built into his helmet to call Masaki Ichijou's phone number.

*"Shiba? What's going on?"*

It seemed Masaki found it surprising to get a call from him. If Tatsuya had gotten a sudden call from Masaki, he might have had the same reaction. And Tatsuya knew this going in, so he decided to be direct.

"Ichijou, we've narrowed down where Gongjin Zhou is hiding."

*"Really?!"*

"Really. Where are you right now?"

*"Near Kamigamo Shrine."*

*He's here, like I thought.* He'd heard Third High planned to go to the Thesis Competition and go home the same day, but with Masaki having come the week before to scout things out, Tatsuya figured he'd have to arrive the day before the competition.

"I'll be waiting at the Uji Futagozuka Park's southwest entrance until five PM."

*"Five?! Got it. I'll get there in time."*

Masaki was probably about to say there wasn't enough time. But he seemed to immediately comprehend what Tatsuya meant by specifying a time. He rudely hung up the call, doubtless because he'd sprung into action right away.

As an enemy, he'd be a nuisance, but he was a reliable ally. Tatsuya appreciated people who were quick to understand things.

*I should hurry, too.*

It would be pathetic if he was late after calling Masaki outside like that, so he brought his motorcycle onto the highway.

In one room of the JGDF Uji Resupply Base Number Two, Gongjin Zhou, whom Tatsuya and the others were searching for, had finished his preparations to depart.

"Mr. Zhou, are you leaving already?"

An officer in his thirties, standing next to the door with his back straight, addressed Zhou in a reluctant voice.

"Captain Hatae, it pains me to part as well, but it seems they've sniffed this place out."

"Really? That's unfortunate. We would never let any so-called magician upstarts saying they're from the Ten Master Clans lay a finger on you as long as you're in this base."

Captain Hatae was both a GAA appeasement advocate and a soldier with a tendency to admire Chinese ancient magicians and adhere to the idea that modern magicians were upstarts without even a century of history behind them. He had bought into Gongjin Zhou's insistence that he hadn't been involved in the Yokohama Incident—or tricked into doing so, rather, and now sheltered Zhou out of a sense of justice, seeing the Kuroba's pursuit as the personal vendetta of modern magicians.

"There is nothing to be done about it. General Kudou is there, after all."

Zhou smiled thinly. The smile suited his chiseled features well.

Captain Hatae bit his lip. Gongjin Zhou was right—if HQ instructed him to abide by an investigation order, Hatae, who was only a company commander, couldn't dispute it. And former general Retsu Kudou naturally held enough sway to quash any resistance he may have had to an investigation based in official procedure.

"I had wanted to learn many more things about the hermit arts…"

"I am still no more than a fledgling Taoist myself. I lack the experience to see even a path to corpse liberation, much less to the winged emergence. It would be presumptuous of me to pretend to expound the arts to another person…"

With his usual excuse, Zhou gently refused Hatae's request.

Captain Hatae changed the subject, not seeming visibly offended. "When will you depart?"

"I believe I shall take my leave this evening."

"As the investigation is scheduled to begin early tomorrow morning, that would probably be wisest, but…"

"I am grateful simply that you found information on this surprise inspection with no written notice," said Zhou, lowering his head.

Hatae offered an even more apologetic expression. "However, the gate is locked at night."

"I can manage that, at least, on my own." Zhou smiled confidently; his face reminded Hatae of what magic the man specialized in.

"Yes, you can, can't you? At least allow me to prepare a car for you. It will be a personal belonging, not a military vehicle, but I doubt you will be followed in it."

All public vehicles, not just military ones, had tracking devices to prevent theft. There were ways to fool the devices, but using a privately owned vehicle would be more certain.

"I truly thank you for doing so much for me," offered Zhou, bowing his head politely.

As Tatsuya was leaning against the motorcycle borrowed from Fumiya, he spotted a red motorcycle coming his way after fifteen minutes of waiting.

*He really likes red, huh?*

He said that to himself offhandedly. Third High's school color was red, so maybe it was an expression of love for his school. It couldn't have been deliberately to match his nickname.

"Sorry to make you wait."

Getting off the bike and taking off his helmet, Masaki spoke up to Tatsuya in that way.

"No, it's still ten minutes before the time I said. More than enough time for the mission."

It was currently 4:50 PM. The sun would set at 5:10, so they still had plenty of time.

"How are we doing this?"

At least, enough time to explain the mission's details to Masaki.

"That's where Gongjin Zhou is thought to be hiding," Tatsuya said, pointing southward.

In that direction was a JDF base.

Masaki couldn't immediately fathom what Tatsuya's gesture meant. But after a few seconds, he realized what he meant by "that," and his eyes widened.

"Wait, inside a JDF base?!"

"The JGDF Uji Resupply Base Number Two. It's highly likely Zhou is hiding out in there."

"…Are you certain?"

"It's a possibility. We'll be going in to see if it's true."

"We're going inside the base?!"

Masaki's face had gone past *Is this guy serious?* to *Is this guy insane?*

But for Tatsuya, trespassing into restricted JDF areas and crossing blades with JDF forces were both things he'd experienced before. He had no reason to balk at either of them at this point.

"A certain group of magicians are mobilizing in secret to capture him."

"Separate from the military police, you mean?"

"Yeah. It's not an official operation."

Masaki correctly realized that implied it was an illegal operation.

"They'll be sneaking into the base through several gates soon."

"From the gates? …Oh—exotype magic users, then?"

Tatsuya nodded at Masaki's question.

Masaki then had a guess as to who this "certain group of magicians mobilizing in secret" was.

A band of magicians specializing in exotype magic that would go against the JDF. Masaki could only think of one possibility. "Shiba, are you—"

"I'm separate from them." But before the question could take form, Tatsuya cleanly cut it down. "It's almost time. I'll jump the fence and infiltrate the base. What will you do, Ichijou?"

Masaki couldn't answer immediately. Trespassing on JDF property was clearly an illegal act. He hadn't yet reached Tatsuya's level where he could put his law-abiding spirit to rest whenever the situation called for it.

His parents would probably tell him to prioritize his duty to Ten Master Clans over his morals as a citizen. His father, especially, might have done more than give him a push on the back: He might have kicked him in the ass if he saw him dithering like this.

The issue was his position as a Third High student. With the Thesis Competition so close at hand, if he got into a scuffle with the police, and not for a petty crime but for a serious offense on top of that, they'd probably have to withdraw from the competition. The shock that would deal to Third High's students, whether they were seniors, juniors, or freshmen, was certain to be a major one. And he would agonize over wasting all his friends' efforts.

*...But I'm part of a Clan.*

The time Masaki actually spent hesitating was only a few seconds.

"...I'll come. This wouldn't have happened if that man hadn't tricked me last year. I can't turn away."

Tatsuya threw a glance at the information terminal set up on his motorcycle handlebars. "The operation starts in five minutes. Let's go, Ichijou."

"Right."

At the same time, the two of them put on their helmets, got on their motorcycles, and sped off.

Meanwhile, on the east side of the Uji Bridge, right next to the Byoudou-in—a temple famous for its Phoenix Hall's exquisitely beautiful atmosphere—a car was parked.

"Thank you. I'll call you when I'm done, so could you just wait somewhere nearby?"

The one who said that to the driver and then exited the car was a young man, beautiful enough to make you doubt your eyes.

A passerby who just happened to be there at the time gazed at him as though possessed. Given the time of day, with the sun just moments from setting, Minoru radiated a nearly divine aura.

A man in late middle age walked up to him from behind. He wasn't exactly large in frame, but it was obvious his body was thoroughly trained, and one could tell without explanation he was the young man's bodyguard.

"Lord Minoru, shall you be waiting here?"

"That's right."

His tone of voice was one accustomed to using people, clearly different from the one he'd directed toward Tatsuya and the others.

"If Zhou successfully escapes the encirclement, he will need to flee here. Should that happen, I'll need to slow him down."

"But if he needs to cross the Uji River, there's a bridge in Ooshima as well."

The bodyguard expressed his doubts cautiously. He wasn't nitpicking his master's viewpoint—he was just afraid their work would be in vain. If the suspect fled along a different route, it would be a waste of effort for Minoru, who had forced himself outside like this despite the fact that he was still recovering.

"Yes, but that's only a highway. If he goes onto the highway for a time, his escape options will be limited. To make the best use of Qimen Dunjia, he needs the freedom to move in any direction. He won't use the highway."

"Isn't it also possible he'll flee east…?"

"Mount Takemine is to the east. Considering his escape route thus far, he favors populated areas to mountainous ones. Probably because that's the kind of technique Qimen Dunjia is."

"However—"

"Enough already." As his bodyguard tried to offer even further worries, Minoru aggressively cut him off. "Are you saying my deductions are wrong?"

The bodyguard fell silent. But not out of reserve toward his master's family. The air drifting from Minoru's body was so cool, so clear that it had knitted his mouth shut.

"It's time. Begin the operation."

"Yes, right away, young one."

Answering that way was a man who was still wearing sunglasses despite the sun having set, after which a light smacking sound came from the back of his head.

"You moron, it's *young lady*! He's dressed up in—"

"Be quiet!" Fumiya, who had become "Yami," cut off the argument between the men in sunglasses. "This is no time for banter! Begin the operation!"

"Yes, sir."

The men in sunglasses all dropped to one knee in a bow, then blended into the twilight sky like a mirage.

"Geez... These are supposed to be the best illusion users the Kuroba have...?"

After Fumiya pressed on one of his temples and moaned to himself, Ayako, disguised as "Yoru," approached from behind and offered words of consolation. "Yami, you'll just have to ignore it when you give them commands. Personality issues are totally separate from competence. You wouldn't want an incompetent subordinate whose heart is in the right place—you'd want one who could get the job done even if they have a bad personality, right?"

"Well, yeah, but..."

"Anyway, Yami, it's started."

A loud alarm went off inside the base. Their men would never have fudged things up like that. They had a lot of character blemishes, but their abilities were good enough that Fumiya had to acknowledge them.

"I wonder if that's Tatsuya."

"Yes, he's probably busy playing decoy for us. Perhaps he plans to drive our prey from the north to the south."

"Why would he do something that dangerous?"

"Because he's confident. Confident he can make it through any situation, no matter how perilous it becomes. That's why he always voluntarily takes on the most dangerous missions."

"...Yeah."

"What would really be inexcusable is if we were to let his efforts go to waste. We must make sure we pin down Gongjin Zhou."

"I know."

Behind Fumiya waited a small passenger vehicle that was painted indigo. It wasn't their normal car, of course. It was a special-order robotic car—a chassis as solid as a tank, and an engine that rivaled racing machines.

The alarms went off in JGDF Uji Resupply Base Number Two. Not only that, but more than a few gunshots could be heard.

"What's happening?!" Captain Hatae yelled from outside the room.

The face of the subordinate waiting outside paled. "Intruders in the base! Two insurgents! Both appear to be magicians!"

"*What?!*"

Hatae's shock was certainly no exaggeration. Even just one magician was a powerful combat force. You couldn't draw broad conclusions since each individual magician's abilities differed greatly, but it was said that the average combat strength of a magician belonging to the military rivaled an entire company of normal soldiers. A more powerful one could be a combat force on the scale of a battalion.

And there were *two*. Furthermore, not ones who were secretly trying to sneak into the base, but ones who were storming in through the front door—they couldn't possibly be below average.

"Give me a sitrep!"

"The insurgents are destroying resupply material as they make their way here. We're responding, but they won't stop!"

Gongjin Zhou, who hadn't even looked up at the emergency alarm as he was packing his things, clicked his bag shut and quietly stood up. "This will do."

"Huh? Mr. Zhou, what are you...?"

"This is a good opportunity. You all, eliminate the intruders. Using this base's full capabilities against them."

As soon as Zhou said that, a shudder ran through Hatae and his subordinate as though they'd been electrically shocked.

That wasn't a disturbance localized to this room. The same thing happened to every soul in the company Hatae commanded.

"Captain, I will take you up on your offer and borrow your car. The key?"

With stilted motions, Hatae held the key for the car.

"Now, what are you doing? You must take care of the intruders. Any blackguards who would trespass on a base must be thoroughly wiped out, so that not even a fragment of their corpse remains, or the military will lose its prestige."

"Yes. This is a challenge to the JDF's honor. How dare they look down on us. Wipe them out."

"Yes, sir."

His tone, in contrast to his words, was dispassionate.

And on the necks of Hatae and his subordinate as they turned on their heels and left the room was a marking resembling a spider bite.

The two who had intruded on the base were still wearing full-face motorcycle helmets, but just in case, Tatsuya searched out all the surveillance cameras and dismantled them.

Of course, the out-of-sight surveillance cameras were not the only things he was dismantling.

"What *is* that spell?!"

"No time for that."

Tatsuya coldly spurned the question. Since they were being careful not to use names, their conversation continued to get more unfriendly.

"I've never heard of a spell like that!"

Maybe it couldn't be helped that Masaki shouted that. This was the first time he was seeing Tatsuya's dismantling.

Wherever Tatsuya pointed his CAD, weapons of all kinds fell to pieces and scattered to the floor. The guns broke into their component parts. Vehicles first lost their wheels, then their doors, and then all the plugs would come out of the inside, eventually reducing even the engine to its constituent pieces.

"You're taking too long with the fuel."

"This isn't easy, you know!"

Masaki was doing his best to not ignite the leaked fuel. First, he vaporized the hydrogen storage liquid by using convergence magic to decompose the hydrogen gas. Then he shaped it into a sphere, making the hydrogen gas itself into a hydrogen balloon, then jetting that up into the air, which didn't contain the heat of fire. The difficulty of the spell itself aside, its processes were far more complicated than the dismantling Tatsuya was doing.

"I'm sure making things blow up isn't the only thing you're good at."

"I know that!"

Masaki was following Tatsuya's instructions even while complaining because he'd decided this technique was, for him, going to be useful in the future as well. Using magic to vaporize only fuel, then using convergence magic to separate it from the resulting heat and venting it up into the air... With this method, he could disable armored weapons without accidentally killing anyone. It was a much more versatile attack spell than Burst for certain.

As they were wrecking any weapons they came across, the gunfire coming at them suddenly grew more severe. The bullets also changed from disabling rubber bullets to live ammunition.

Masaki instantly put up an anti-matter barrier. Tatsuya secretly used an area-mounted dismantling spell to make up for the parts he couldn't completely cover. They split left and right, jumping behind cover.

"They shot at us!"

"Live bullets. Looks like they're being manipulated, too. Same as those ancient magicians."

Understanding dawned on Masaki's face.

The crazed magicians who had come at them with self-immolation attacks, one step away from blowing themselves up, at Arashiyama: They had been controlled by a Chinese immortalist hidden in the brush.

With a roar, a tank appeared from behind the building. And not only the one, either—there were four, in combat formation.

"Now they're bringing out *tanks*?!"

"What a farce. It's like they *want* infighting."

They were smaller varieties, classified for use in urban combat, but it was a massive excess of force for two pedestrians. Still, depending on how you thought about it, you could say it wasn't enough for two magicians.

And in this case, it was the latter.

"We're going straight through. Don't blow them up."

"You're asking…ugh, fine!"

Masaki was about to say *You're asking the impossible*, but when the turrets wheeled around to point at them, he seemed to realize complaining wouldn't work.

The caterpillar treads, along with the wheels inside, popped off at the same time. The cannons fell, and the turrets went out of alignment. The armor plating broke apart all at once.

It happened at the same time for all four tanks.

The fuel leaked out of their engines.

Before it could ignite, it vaporized and ascended into the sky, dissipating and mixing into the atmosphere.

"Nice work."

"Compliments from you don't mean much."

Tatsuya offered a mean-spirited grin at Masaki's sullen attitude. "Want me to tell Miyuki to compliment you instead?"

"D-don't be an asshole! This isn't the time for that!" It frightened Masaki to an amusing degree. "Anyway, let's get going! We can't let Zhou esc—*there he is!*"

"What?"

Tatsuya directed his "vision" toward where Masaki was looking.

He didn't ask if he was certain. Masaki had confronted Gongjin Zhou face-to-face before; he'd never mistake someone he'd met in such a unique, impression-leaving situation.

Gongjin Zhou was riding a gunmetal sedan headed for the south gate. Just as planned—driven out of the base in such a way that he wouldn't raise flags in any of the monitoring equipment stationed all over the base.

*What is this…?*

Tatsuya detected something he remembered, an anomaly, within Zhou's eidos. Not something originating with his—but something that had wormed its way *into* him.

*A bee sting… I won't let your death be in vain.*

Tatsuya swore a convenient vow to a dead person, a stranger he'd only met once.

"Gongjin Zhou is approaching this south gate," Fumiya stated.

"Maybe he sensed our family building up at the other gates. As expected of a magician who broke through a Kuroba net and escaped," Ayako responded dryly.

"I would hope he did."

Fumiya sat in the rear seat of the robotic car. Ayako slipped in next to him.

At the same time, the gunmetal sedan Gongjin Zhou was in burst out of the south gate.

"Follow him!"

"Yes, young ma—or rather, young lady."

"Doesn't matter! Get moving!"

Though they were called robotic cars, they needed an emergency driver to operate them outside the public transportation system. After yelling at the leader of the sunglasses-wearing men, chosen to be that driver, Fumiya made him pursue Gongjin Zhou's car.

*I don't have a good feeling about this...*

As the car traveled south, Gongjin Zhou felt as though something was slowly squeezing him—something he'd never felt before.

Looking only at the results, he'd escaped the enemy's grasp by a hairbreadth once more. He was nonplussed by the persistence of the Kuroba—or rather, the Yotsuba—but he was used to the constant pursuit, despite the changes in difficulty from day to day. For the last decade, he'd been leading a stable life in Chinatown, but for three decades before that, he was always on the run, having to hide out every day.

*Whoops... I'm still only twenty-four now.*

That's what it said on his identification. He'd purchased it from a shop in Chinatown, but that was four years ago as well, and he remembered the documents submitted at the time said his age was twenty.

*Ages, just like names, are no more than labels for us.*

Perhaps because his thoughts were elsewhere, Gongjin Zhou didn't notice the figure standing on the road blocking the car's progress until the car's collision prevention system kicked in.

Zhou was about to beep the horn, but then uncharacteristically, he paled.

He'd just seen the boy's face.

Beautiful, fair, otherworldly features.

Zhou himself boasted an elegant handsomeness, but this young man was far beyond that.

But this wasn't the first time he'd ever seen this pretty boy.

He knew who it was: One of the very few magicians he had it in his mind to be highly cautious around.

"Minoru Kudou! Why are you here?!"

He'd learned of the young man's true abilities when he'd sent his pawns after him in Nara. Zhou disengaged the collision prevention system and tried to drive forward anyway.

Minoru's right hand came up toward the car.

Sparks flew inside the hood.

Just before the engine exploded, Zhou leaped out of the car.

He felt a terrible chill in his spine. He'd never experienced one like it up against Mitsugu Kuroba or Saburou Nakura.

Minoru Kudou hadn't shown a moment's hesitation in blowing up the car. He also didn't have a moment's hesitation getting pedestrians and cars driving in the other direction mixed up in it.

Pedestrians were certainly around. And other cars were definitely passing through. This young man hadn't spared even a thought for any of them right from the start——

That callousness clashed with his unrealistic beauty, making him look not like a man, but like a demon.

Zhou removed a command-tile from his inside pocket and aimed it at Minoru. Instead of a composite form, he called out an imaginary beast right from the start. His gut told him the way to deal with this young man was to only use his best, most lethal attacks.

A black unicorn burst out of the command-tile, charging toward Minoru at a blinding speed.

Humans couldn't react to that speed. Minoru couldn't avoid the charge, and the black beast's horn pierced Minoru's body—and passed straight through.

"Parade, is it?!"

Zhou knew this spell—it was the Kudou family's secret technique. It overwrote not just one's figure, form, and position, but also the positional information stored in one's eidos—the ultimate camouflage spell.

He changed his escape plans. He couldn't break Parade. That single attack had made him understand that.

Minoru reached his right hand toward Zhou.

A flash of electricity appeared one meter to the right of him, on the road, then disappeared.

Minoru tilted his head. The gesture had none of the fleshy movement of a human—it was more like an angel. His expression, too—smiling with an utter lack of compassion—was also just like an angel's.

Electric flashes burst up from either side of Zhou.

Minoru wasn't missing. Zhou's Qimen Dunjia was throwing off his aim.

However, Zhou was the one feeling dread. He thought he'd veered Minoru's sense of direction by 90 degrees. But in actuality, Minoru's eyes were still on him, and his aim wasn't off by any more than 30 degrees.

He summoned every shadow beast he could from his command-tile.

At the same time, he took out a black handkerchief and spread it out in front of him.

The shadow beasts all passed right through Minoru.

The black handkerchief fell to the road.

Minoru glanced downstream along the Uji River, then flashed an innocent smile.

*His eyes could see eidos*, and he hadn't lost sight of Zhou's shadow—not his figure, but his eidos' *shadow*—as he fled.

Gongjin Zhou had fled down the Uji River at a speed of forty to fifty kilometers per hour. It was a Taoist technique famous for appearing in *Water Margin* called Divine Movement.

It was taking him back toward the base, but on the way there was a highway bridge. He'd go underneath it and cross to the other bank.

But suddenly, a girl appeared in his way. She hadn't jumped out from the roadside—she'd abruptly appeared out of thin air.

"Quasi-Teleportation?!"

One of the parasites he'd led here had known the same spell. But it hadn't allowed that person to appear out of the blue, without any forewarning like this.

The bob-cut girl, the hem of her jumper dress fluttering, thrust out with knuckle-dusters.

Her fists weren't in range.

Nevertheless, Zhou felt such terrible pain in his right leg that he could no longer stand.

He immediately unfurled a white handkerchief.

The handkerchief rolled out, big enough to completely cover him.

In its shadow, Zhou stabbed himself in a pressure point with a needle to cut off the feeling in his right leg. The intense pain continued, but he shut it out of his mind, telling himself it was no more than an illusion.

Then he took his last command-tile, which he'd brought as a backup, out of his pocket.

When the cloth blocking his vision fell away, the bob-cut girl was no longer in front of him.

Instead, standing there was a young man with cool features aiming a red handgun CAD at him.

"Masaki Ichijou…!"

"It's been a while, Gongjin Zhou. You sure made a fool out of me back then."

Zhou tried to jump into the Uji River.

But the water's surface exploded, blocking him, spraying water everywhere.

"Entering the water when faced with the Ichijou family's Burst is the same as charging into a pile of bombs."

The voice came from behind him. He turned around.

"Tatsuya Shiba…"

Zhou used everything he had on Qimen Dunjia. And then he'd tried to slip past Tatsuya.

But Tatsuya's flattened hand met him on the way. Zhou knew it had the sharpness of a magical sword that could cleave steel, so he was forced to backstep using the leg he had no feeling in.

Tatsuya and Masaki once again had him in a pincer.

"Why won't my Qimen Dunjia technique work?"

Even at this stage, Zhou was wearing a smile.

Was it a bluff, or was he truly relaxed? Masaki couldn't decide what his true feelings were.

Tatsuya didn't *care* what his true feelings were, however. "Qimen Dunjia is brilliant. I'd heard it lost its effects at point-blank range, but… Your technique definitely worked. I couldn't tell you were trying to pass by me."

"…Then I don't understand. Do you mean to say your attack was a fluke?"

Tatsuya's lips twisted.

His smile wasn't as handsome as Zhou's, but the essence of it was the same as his.

An empty smile, devoid of emotion.

"I didn't know where you were. But I did know exactly how the blood of Saburou Nakura inside you was moving."

Zhou's eyes widened.

Masaki got the feeling he'd just seen, for the first time, a raw emotion from this age-unknown Taoist.

"Saburou Nakura's blood… From back then?"

"Did he stab you with a needle made of blood or something? Still, two weeks in, the foreign body inside you should have disappeared. He must have put a lot of willpower into it."

"Willpower, is it? I'd thought modern magic theory had discarded factors like that."

"No matter how you try to explain something away, if something exists, it exists. If it doesn't, it doesn't."

"No, there are things that exist but do not—things that are null and yet still exist."

Tatsuya aimed his silver CAD at Gongjin Zhou. "Save your lecturing for your jail cell, please. Though, we may not give you much time for it."

"Then I will be killed regardless?"

"I'm not your executioner."

"Meaning there's no point in begging for my life."

Tatsuya didn't give any further answers. "As long as Saburou Nakura's blood remains, you cannot escape me."

That was Tatsuya's ultimatum.

"This is it, then…" Gongjin Zhou heaved a sigh.

A moment later, he jumped at Masaki.

The Divine Movement technique didn't use leg strength to run. Even without feeling in his leg, as long as it was still attached, he could trigger the spell.

Masaki wouldn't have known how it worked.

But his reaction was the by-the-book kind for cases like this. It would be dishonest to say it worked out for him out of sheer coincidence.

The moment Zhou jumped, Masaki had pulled his red CAD's trigger.

With almost zero delay, magic activated: Burst.

Not to vaporize all the blood in his body, but an improved version that vaporized blood locally.

Both of Gongjin Zhou's calves burst from within.

His Divine Movement was broken, and he fell onto the road.

"Yes, this *is* it."

His CAD still at the ready, Masaki urged him to surrender.

Zhou immediately got up. Maybe his dignity couldn't suffer lying there in such an unsightly way.

"It does look like it's over."

Slowly, he stood up, even though he shouldn't have been able to use anything from the knee down.

With almost ghostly movements—

"But none of you are capable of capturing me."

—Zhou smirked.

A smile like a mask.

"I will never perish. Even should I die, I shall continue to exist!"

"Ichijou, back off!"

Tatsuya shouted and leaped backward.

Ichijou put distance between him and Zhou in the same way.

A moment later,

all the blood spurted out of Zhou's body,

and the red blood turned into a red flame.

"Ha-ha-ha-ha-ha-ha-ha-ha-ha…"

Within the scorching flames: loud, lingering laughter,

continuing until the fires disappeared.

When they did, not even bones were left.

"Is Gongjin Zhou really dead?" Masaki muttered, but only after twilight had shifted to night and the stars had begun to glimmer.

"He hasn't escaped. Those flames definitely snuffed out his life."

Tatsuya wasn't looking at Masaki's face. His eyes were directed up at the Uji River.

"Oh." Masaki looked off vaguely in the same direction, nodding. He didn't ask for the reason why he knew that.

"Is the Yokohama Incident cleanup finally over now?"

"Yeah."

"Good… Things were looking shaky."

"What things?"

Tatsuya turned around to Masaki. Even he didn't understand what he'd just said.

Masaki, too, looked toward Tatsuya. "Never thought he'd hijack the JDF and bring out tanks. We were on the verge of seeing infighting."

"The magical shoot-out was almost a spectacle, and it happened right in the city. They already have one foot in that door."

Masaki laughed at Tatsuya's annoyingly serious answer. "In that case, they'll have to fix things up quickly and quell the unrest before it spreads, and then we'll all live happily ever after."

"I guess you could say that."

Tatsuya, too, laughed out loud.

Their laughing voices melted into the forlorn autumn wind and vanished.

When Tatsuya went back to the hotel to return the motorcycle, Fumiya and Ayako were already there.

"Well done, Tatsuya," said Ayako.

"Same goes to the two of you," he complimented. "That was some great teamwork, as usual. We stopped him thanks to you."

The two of them looked away bashfully. Without looking into his eyes—doubtless in part to hide her embarrassment—Ayako asked, "By the way, Tatsuya, how did you know where that man was? We were chasing him in the car, and we still lost sight of him."

"Suffice it to say, a certain magician's vengefulness chased that man even after death."

"Ah?" She made a look like she didn't know what he meant. Fumiya stopped looking down and tilted his head, too.

"I still don't know how it happened that way. Once I know more, I'll tell you."

Tatsuya entered a double room, where the rooms were separated with a sliding door. It was the room where the clothes had been waiting for him when he'd first arrived.

He left the door open as he was getting changed and spoke to Fumiya. "Fumiya, could you report to Hayama that the mission's complete? There's a few others I need to follow up with."

"Yes, it's nothing. You can leave it to me."

Now finished changing, Tatsuya came out. "Thanks," he said in place of a good-bye, leaving the hotel behind him.

[10]

The next day, Sunday, October 28.

It was finally the day of the 2096 Thesis Competition.

Tatsuya, not part of the nine schools' combined security team, but participating only as a support member for First High, was able to move about with relative freedom.

When Miyuki was temporarily released from judging during the lunch break, she accompanied him to meet Mayumi, who had come to the venue.

"I see… Nakura's murderer took his own life?"

"He did it as a result of us cornering him, so I hesitate to call it suicide, but yes."

Tatsuya had told Mayumi that they'd resolved the Nakura murder case.

"It's better this way. After all, it means you took revenge for him," she said, smiling at him like a weight had been lifted from her shoulders. "Thank you, Tatsuya. I'll cancel your debt from the other night."

"Saegusa, that's—"

"See you. Keep the place secure, would you? And do your best with judging, Miyuki."

Without waiting for Tatsuya to respond, Mayumi stood from her seat and vanished into the crowd of people in the lobby.

"Brother…"

Left in the tea room were Tatsuya, still holding in his hands the bomb she threw at him, and Miyuki, watching him with a false smile.

"What does she mean by *the other night*?"

"Well, that's… Um."

"That's what? If you have no objections, then please, tell me. Or…"

Miyuki placed a palm on Tatsuya's hand.

"…is there something objectionable about it?"

Miyuki's hand was soft, and a little chilly. And it had Tatsuya bound in place.

"…This shows that a responsive alloy plate is not a necessary condition to cast sealing-type magic. Seals only guide the flow of psions, and as we've just shown, using a seal pattern to project it yields the same effects. Hence, we can conclude that at its essence, sealing-type magic is not dependent on physical seals."

First High's presentation, with Isori as the leader, ended. Boisterous applause went up from the crowd.

"This is the biggest applause yet," offered Miyuki, released from judging duty because it was First High's presentation, to Tatsuya, who was in the seat next to her.

"The actual presentation was revolutionary, too. I expected nothing less of Isori."

Tatsuya gave his own seal of approval to the contents. At this time, they both felt like it was good enough to win the competition.

"I must return to the judging seats now, Brother."

"Second High is next, right? …Hm. What?"

"Oh? Isn't that Minoru?"

A stir rippled through the building. Most of it was probably surprise at Minoru's beauty when he got onstage to set up. Tatsuya and Miyuki, of course, were surprised for a different reason.

Then, a message came from the program director.

*"We have an announcement for all attendees. There will be a substitute in Second High's presenter. Because the original presenter has fallen ill, the representative has been changed."*

"…Miyuki, you'd better get to the judges' table."

"Yes, I should. I will see you soon, Brother."

More than half the spectators would get out of their seats during the time between presentations. A portion of them, the school cheering section, would switch out as well. But in this prep time, not a single audience member rose.

As the uniquely odd atmosphere continued, Second High's presentation started.

*"Second High's presentation will now begin. The title is, 'A Hypothesis Regarding Notable Concepts in Mental Interference-Type Magic's Principles and Activation Sequences.'"*

The stir in the venue grew louder. The principles of something still almost fully unexplained—mental interference magic. Any thesis dealing with it was sure to be something ambitious and revolutionary for magic studies.

"…As you can see from these observation results, at the same time as a person perceives something, psionic information bodies are newly formed. And these information bodies break down at the same time the person ceases to perceive it. The point to note here about these psionic information bodies, which are formed through one's perception, is that when the perceiver actively eliminates the object of perception—for example, via instant incineration—this breakdown begins in advance of the actual destruction.

"…Many of the observational results you've seen match the hypothesis that psions are particles that give form to will and thought. They show that a person's passive perception does not create psionic information bodies; instead, their active mental processes are creating them.

"…For a person's will, or in other terms, their mind, to apply some sort of effect to this physical dimension, we believe they must convert will into psionic information bodies. If we adopt this hypothesis, we can interpret perception-type psychic powers, beginning with telepathy, as also being magic that uses psionic information bodies.

"…We believe that the psionic information bodies formed through will—mental activity—possess the characteristics you've all just seen. Of course, this can't explain all of their characteristics, but if we can define the displayed factors as an activation sequence, the formularization of mental interference-type magic is sure to accelerate by leaps and bounds. At the same time, this would lead to the development of anti-magic that can nullify mental interference-type magic. And it would be a good opportunity to dispel the superstitious fears surrounding mental interference-type magic.

"As such, mental interference-type magic doesn't have any essential differences from the four families and eight types. The mind, too, as long as it is connected to the physical world, will produce psionic information bodies. These are psions showing the form of the will. Thus, if we create a magic program that alters these psionic information bodies, we will be able to alter real intentions in relation to this world, at least—the conscious mind. This magic alters a person's perception and, consequently, alters their active will.

"…If we assume a person's mind is not split into a conscious mind and an unconscious mind and is instead a single entity where one part is conscious and the other unconscious, then by observing and analyzing the psionic information bodies produced by the will's formation, we should be able to expand all mental interference-type magic into a true form of technology."

Minoru wrapped up the presentation with that.

For a moment, there was silence.

And then the venue erupted into thunderous applause.

\* \* \*

The 2096 All-High Magic Thesis Competition. The crown of victory rested upon the head of Second High, which had appointed Minoru Kudou, a freshman, as its main presenter.

It was the moment a new star had been born in all the National Magic University-Affiliated High Schools, from First through Ninth.

Meanwhile, even at the Yotsuba main mansion, an even more serious presentation than the Thesis Competition's, though smaller in scale, was occurring.

"As you've heard, in this incident, Tatsuya Shiba was not forced onto this mission, but he loyally carried it out anyway, achieving the results our client wanted. He is a useful element of the Yotsuba, and I don't believe his loyalty to his work presents any issues."

As everyone looked on with sour faces, Maya slowly opened her mouth to speak. "This mission was a test for Tatsuya. The results are as Hayama reported. Do you not all feel the same way?"

"We've no choice but to acknowledge him," said the head of the Shiiba family, opening his heavily shut mouth.

"His abilities are certainly worthy," said the head of the Mashiba family in agreement.

"This time, he passes. This time," said the head of the Shibata family—*Shibata* written with different characters than in Mizuki's surname—without trying to hide his displeasure.

"Should we not discard this odd preoccupation with him?" suggested the head of the Mugura family.

"Agreed. Thinking back, weren't we too expectant at the beginning? Perhaps we must strive for objectivity now," nodded the head of the Tsukuba family.

"I think it's too soon to pass final judgment," objected the head of the Shizuka family carefully. "If we're to speak of objective evaluation, it is also objectively true that Tatsuya Shiba only possesses biased talent."

Everyone's eyes moved to the head of the Kuroba family, Mitsugu Kuroba, who had been keeping his silence.

"What are your thoughts, Lord Kuroba?" the Shibata head prompted.

"I failed in this mission. I don't feel as though I have the right to offer my opinion on this matter."

A heavy silence fell over the room.

Then, a ladylike voice that didn't seem to mind the oppressive air put an end to the debate.

"In that case, let's reserve our conclusion until the New Year Reception."

And that voice did so by asserting they'd reach final judgment at the beginning of next year.

The family heads gathered here couldn't raise any objection against the head of the Yotsuba clan.

*(To be continued in the* Yotsuba Succession Arc*)*

# AFTERWORD

How did you enjoy *The Irregular at Magic High School*, Volume 15, *Ancient City Insurrection Arc, Part II*? The subtitle may have been more accurate as *Ancient City Insurrection Attempt Arc*, but subtitles can easily be spoilers, and more importantly, *Attempt Arc* isn't a very good name, so I hope you will find it in your heart to understand.

The Yotsuba branch families have appeared at last. They were just side characters in this episode, but it's a matter of deep importance to me that they finally showed up. Well, sure, they'll be side characters in the future, too, but they're an irreplaceable cast of characters that will play a major role during a big turning point in *The Irregular at Magic High School*, so I've been having them wait in the wings for a very long time. The episode in which they appear for real will be one of the climaxes of the story.

The branch families' actual appearances were all written in from the very beginning, but I only decided on their last names fairly recently. I racked my brains over them, finding a lot of things didn't quite work for me. Shiiba, Mashiba, Shibata, Kuroba, Mugura, Tsukuba, Shizuka. Among them, I think *Shiiba*, *Mashiba*, and *Shibata* are easy to understand. They're all variations on the Yotsuba/Shiba shift.

Some may have already realized this about *Kuroba*, but it comes from "clover," as in a four-leaf clover.

*Mugura* comes from a plant called a *Yotsuba-mugura* in Japanese, or "four-leafed creeper."

*Tsukuba* originates in *Tsukubane-sou*, or "shuttlecock-grass." It's a perennial herb in the lily order that has four leaves.

*Shizuka* I got from a plant called *Hitori-shizuka*, or "single-man's quiet." This is another perennial herb with four leaves.

While looking all sorts of things up to choose the last names, I learned that it's a struggle to make names follow a regular pattern.

One last thing, and this is a bit of a fictional inside story. In the story, it's said that Zhuge Liang had mastered the art of Qimen Dunjia (purely a background setting for this series), but the essence of the Qimen Dunjia used in the Yokohama Disturbance Arc and this Ancient City Insurrection Arc is something I created based on my own personal interpretation of the one that appears in the *Romance of the Three Kingdoms* (Eiji Yoshikawa's version, to be precise). In other words, it's not that Zhuge Liang knew Qimen Dunjia, but that I defined the arts Zhuge Liang used as being Qimen Dunjia—that would be the correct order of things. That's not to say Eiji Yoshikawa's *Romance of the Three Kingdoms* doesn't depict anything like that with Zhuge Liang, but the essence of Qimen Dunjia in this story is an original creation.

I'd like to sincerely thank again everyone who has stuck with me this far. And if it's all right with you, I want to ask for your support on Volume 16, the *Yotsuba Succession Arc*, as well.

*Tsutomu Sato*

# Volume 16
# Set to release in summer 2020!

Here's the official Twitter!     HTTP://TWITTER.COM/DENGEKI_MAHOUKA

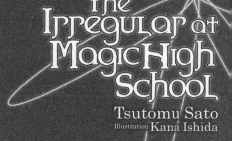

# The Irregular at Magic High School

**Tsutomu Sato**
Illustration **Kana Ishida**

December, AD 2096.

Miyuki receives an invitation to a New Year's gathering at the Yotsuba main residence where influential figures convene.

Unlike past years, it comes with instructions that she must be in attendance on New Year's Day.

Upon seeing this, Miyuki feels that the time has finally come.

The nomination of the Yotsuba family's next head.

——If she's chosen as the successor, her brother won't have to put up with life as a pariah.

——But such a position surely comes with an appropriate fiancé.

Miyuki's mind scatters in a thousand directions.

Once school closes for its winter break, Tatsuya, Miyuki, and Minami head for the main household.

After foiling an unknown interloper's attempt to interfere, they finally arrive at the Yotsuba mansion.

And are welcomed by the beguiling smile of the matriarch of the family, Maya Yotsuba.

Only one day remains in the year 2096.

And that night, Maya utters a shocking "lie" to Tatsuya: that Miyuki isn't his sister.

But what is Maya truly after…?

Could rapid developments be coming for this brother-sister relationship?!
The Yotsuba Succession Arc!

---

**Now presenting your favorite magic school series in manga form!**

**See how the other half of the Shiba household lives!** *The Honor Student at Magic High School*, **Vols. 1–10 on sale now!**

Art by Yu Mori
Original Story by Tsutomu Sato
Character Design by Kana Ishida

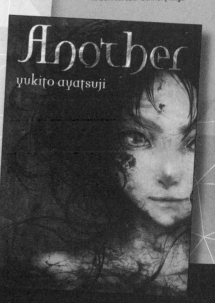